Each Other's Arms

NATALIE FREEDMAN

PHOENIX VOICES PUBLISHING

Copyright © 2024 by Natalie Freedman Second Edition

All rights reserved.

No part of this publication may be reproduced, stored or transmitted in any form or by any means, electronic, mechanical, photocopying, recording, scanning, or otherwise without written permission from the publisher. It is illegal to copy this book, post it to a website, or distribute it by any other means without permission.

This novel is entirely a work of fiction. The names, characters and incidents portrayed in it are the work of the author's imagination. Any resemblance to actual persons, living or dead, events or localities is entirely coincidental.

Natalie Freedman asserts the moral right to be identified as the author of this work.

Natalie Freedman has no responsibility for the persistence or accuracy of URLs for external or third-party Internet Websites referred to in this publication and does not guarantee that any content on such Websites is, or will remain, accurate or appropriate.

Designations used by companies to distinguish their products are often claimed as trademarks. All brand names and product names used in this book and on its cover are trade names, service marks, trademarks and registered trademarks of their respective owners. The publishers and the book are not associated with any product or vendor mentioned in this book. None of the companies referenced within the book have endorsed the book.

Contents

Acknowledgement	1
1. Part One	2
2. Part Two	14
3. Part Three	98
4. Part Four	111
5. Part Five	114
6. Part Six	178
Study Guide For Book Club and You	275
About the Author	277
Also by Natalie Freedman	278

Acknowledgement

THANK YOU

To all the Phoenix Voices administrators for all your help.

And to those most dear:

The Lopez family; Victor, Tami, Robert, Vanna, Sara and Haylee

The Rheinstein family; Paz, Aliah and Zack

The Freedman/Grossman family; Cara, Evan. Jordan and Alexa and James Doyle

The Freedman/de los Rios family; Carlos, Marni and Ben

The Leake family; Kevin, Annie, Dovid, Elisheva. Hadassah and Akiva

The Wexler family; Edythe, Royce, Patricia, Wyatt, Jameson and Winter

The Harnik family; Teri and Patti

Sunny Chaim; 22 pounds of Whippet/Bishon love

The unforgettable Philip Luis Clar, James Freedman and Ted Gibson

Part One

THOUGHTS ABOUT ALEX

After Jeanette's funeral, I thought about Alex's kiss while I was talking and while I was doing the dishes.

What did it mean? Why had I allowed it, participated in it? Why, in the moment of his unexpected grief, had Alex reached for me, as naturally as a sunflower reaches towards the sun? Remembering past comfort? "She's not you," he'd replied to my question about Anita.

I was so happy to be pregnant after trying for so long. My older children were happy, too. And Anita was also pregnant. Or so I'd thought, But when Alex had come to pick up the girls, I'd asked him when she was due. "She's not expecting," he'd answered. "She just needs to lose some baby fat from when she had Saul. Saul is only six months old."

I couldn't help but think about my first pregnancy, about what a mensch Alex had been. At lunchtime, at school, I took a walk down the leafy streets for exercise. And I relived our senior year at college. Every minute. Even that horrendous argument.

THE GLORY OF LOVE

This was a story that I was not going to share with my friends, The Romance Club, the three modern nuns and their cook who loved to hear stories about Alex and me. It was too spicy.

So I typed it up and stored it in my locked desk.

Alex answered our phone. "It's your Aunt Viv. She wants to know if you want to go to Ciro's with them tonight, to the 7 pm show."

"Louis Armstrong?"

"No, it's Jimmy Durante. She says he's very funny."

"Okay, let's go. I don't particularly like him but we'll have fun."

The show turned out to be just wonderful and all four of us laughed a lot.

"It's still early," said Uncle Ted. "Do you want to drive along the Pacific Coast Highway and we can stop at a viewing point and Alex can show us some stars?"

"You can have a view of Mars tonight," said Alex.

So we drove along with the ocean to our left. My uncle glanced back to the backseat. "Nice cuddling, you two. Viv, get over here. We can cuddle, too."

Viv smiled and inched close to Ted. "Okay, you two. Sing with us. " Viv and Ted didn't exactly sing on key but there was enthusiasm in the car. We all sang: *You've got to give a little, take a little*

And let your poor heart break a little.
That's the glory of, that's the glory of love.
You've got to laugh a little, cry a little
Before the clouds roll by a little
That's the glory of, that's the glory of love.

Then we sat on a bench, and Alex guided us in scanning the night sky.

"What a fun evening," we agreed when we got home.

"Alex, why are you in the refrigerator? I was hoping we could, um……"

"What were you hoping, um? You can say it. We're married three years, soon we'll be parents. You can tell me what you want."

"I want you to make love to me. I know I have raging hormones and we made love before we left but I'm very hot again. I'm sorry."

"Listen, 'I'm hot for you' are the words every guy longs to hear. I just want a little something to eat. Oh, good. Yesterday's lasagna. I'll heat up a piece. How long will it take?"

"Ten minutes."

"Okay. Sit here. Don't you want to eat something? Just water? All right, I'll entertain you. You remember that asshole Doug from JPL? Well, I told you that Wanda is pregnant again, right? So Friday he wanted to give me two slutty girly magazines. I said, 'What do I want with these?'

"So he says with his usual low class assholeness,' So you can jerk off while she's pregnant. I already used these.' Well, it seems that when Wanda is pregnant, she doesn't want to be touched. 'It makes her puke,' says Doug in his classy way."

"So then I smile and say, 'Well, Valerie's not like that. She was always into sex but now that she's pregnant, she's insatiable. Two, three times a day.'"

"'You're making that up,' says Doug. 'Both my mother and her mother told me that women do not want to be bothered when they're pregnant. How come Valerie is like that?'"

"'She's Romanian,' I told him. "You really are something else, Vibila. Remember, the girl who wouldn't open her mouth!"

"Ha ha. Swagger, swagger. Feel pride. You know it's all you, Alex. You make me so crazy in bed."

"But when I met you, you were so prissy. 'Kiss my cheek. Kiss my lips. No tongue in my mouth!' Remember I told you, one day you'll tear your pants off, you'll be so eager!"

"And your point is that now I've become that eager?"

"Look at me, darling. Whenever you're hot, just ask. I can and I will take care of you. Do you think this lasagna is done now? Another two minutes? All right, I'm still entertaining you," he sang:

As long as there's the two of us We've got the world and all its charms. And when the world is through with us, We've got each other's arms.

We have to win a little, lose a little And sometimes have the blues a little.

That's the story of, that's the glory of love.

Alex ate the slice of lasagna in six bites, drank some water and guided me into bed.

"What a dilemma. My wife can't get enough!"

I DON'T CARE

This was also a story that I would NOT share with the nuns. It really was too personal and maybe showed Alex in a poor light. But it was true.

Now I was in the fourth month of my pregnancy. It was a Saturday and Alex's birthday. We went to the Sea Lion restaurant in Malibu with both sides of the family and had a fabulous sea bass dinner. Then we walked on the beach and my turquoise dress fluttered in the breeze.

"Valerie," said my Uncle Ted. "You won't believe it! A customer brought in a genuine Van Gogh painting for me to frame. Also a real Velasquez! He's coming to pick them up tomorrow so if you want to see them, I can take you now. It's not everyday you can get up close to a real Van Gogh."

"Do you want to go to the art store?" I asked Alex.

"No."

"Do you mind if I go? I'll just take a look. It won't take long."

"Do whatever you want," said Alex. That should have been my warning right there. Alex took his mother home and my uncle took my mother and me to see the famous paintings. Magnificent! Real! Then he drove my mother home and then me.

When I entered the apartment, Alex was sitting in a chair, clearly angry. "You left me alone to go with your uncle on my birthday," he said.

Then I realized that Alex had been with his mother all the way home from Malibu and she'd undoubtedly said terrible things about me, stirring him up.

"Your mother said I was wrong to go see the paintings, didn't she?"

"Yes, and she was right!"

"Look, Alex. I made you strawberry pancakes for breakfast. Then I hiked with you in Griffith Park. Then we made love in the shower. Then we took a nap and then we made love in the bed. I bought you a nice present. Then we had a wonderful sea bass dinner at The Sea Lion. Then we walked on the beach, holding hands. I thought we had celebrated your birthday quite thoroughly."

"You chose your uncle and some old paintings over me!"

"That sounds exactly like your mother."

"Leave my mother out of this. This was your decision."

"Why don't you just spank me then?"

"I can't spank you when you're pregnant. And you enjoy it too much anyway."

"Good night, Alex. I love you and I wish you a happy birthday but this is ridiculous." I went to bed and he stayed up, reading.

In the morning, he was doing his karate exercises. I tried for cheer. "Good morning, sweetheart."

"I'm still very angry with you. You left me on my birthday."

"Alex, this is childish. I didn't leave you until 9 pm and I was home by 10:30."

"Now you're calling me names. I am not being childish." Alex was advancing on me in his karate gi and he looked ominous. I was in our small entry hall next to a little table holding a silver bowl with three lemons in it. Impulsively, I threw a lemon at him, hitting him in the chest. He was two feet away and I threw another lemon, hitting him on the face and then I threw the silver bowl which also hit his face.

"I told you not to throw things at me!" he grabbed me and pushed me to the wall where I hit my shoulder against our tall oak chest.

"You push your wife who is carrying your child!" I screamed, more from the shock of it than pain. But my shoulder did hurt and tears blinded my eyes. I blinked my eyes and saw Alex wiping blood from his cheek with the belt of his gi.

"LISTEN TO ME!" he shouted.

I saw my purse on the entry hall table, grabbed it and opened the front door, dashing down the steps.

"VALERIE!" yelled Alex but I knew he'd have to put some pants on.

I ran down my street and as luck would have it, a bus was waiting on the corner. I got in and rode the twenty blocks to my mother's stop. I walked to her apartment and saw Alex waiting outside his car. He could drive faster than the bus.

Still the angry face. He had a band-aid where I'd cut him with the silver bowl. But this man, whom I loved, had pushed me, pregnant, into the wall. My shoulder ached. My dog, Lucky, heard or sensed me outside the apartment and barked a welcome and my mother appeared at the door.

"Both of you, come inside. I'll make breakfast. We'll talk."

"I DON'T HAVE ANYTHING TO SAY TO HIM," I yelled.

"WELL, I HAVE A LOT TO SAY TO YOU!" he snarled.

"Please," said my mother. "It's a shonda (disgrace) for the neighbors."

I ran up the stairs and my mother put a soothing hand on Alex's shoulder. "You know, Alex, why don't you let her calm down this morning? Maybe go for a hike with your friends? Come back this afternoon. I'm sure you both can work it out by then."

Without another word, Alex got back into his car and drove away.

I walked into the apartment. "Do you know what happened?" I said to my mother. "Do you know what he did?"

"No, and I don't want to know. You don't tell me when you make rapturous love and I don't want to hear about when you quarrel. I'm not going to interfere. Let's eat breakfast."

"He pushed me into a chest!"

"You know, I had a feeling that we shouldn't have gone to see those paintings."

My mother fussed around, bringing me iced tea, bagels and cream cheese, then a bowl of fruit. She had me put my feet up and put on the television. I was so exhausted in every way that I fell asleep. My mother put a quilt over me.

I woke up hearing the insistent ringing of the doorbell. My mother went downstairs and let Alex in. I ran into the bathroom and locked the door.

"Valerie, come out!" More forcefully, "Valerie, I want to talk to you!" Then, "Answer me!"

"I don't care!" I said.

"If you don't want to talk, let's go home and forget this whole business. You have to come home. You have work tomorrow."

"I don't care."

"Valerie, you're being extremely unreasonable."

"I don't care."

"Alex, I don't know what happened and I don't want to know," said my mother." But you did hurt her shoulder. It's bruised. I had to give her an ice pack."

"I had no intention to hurt her. I was just trying to keep her from throwing things at me. Like she did here." I was sure he was pointing to his poor little cheek.

"Let her stay overnight. It'll all blow over. She loves you and you love her. Every couple has these little spats."

"I'm going now, Valerie," yelled Alex. "Last chance to come home."

"I DON'T CARE!"

I heard the front door slam.

"You're going to work from here?" said my mother. "Wear this robe and I'll wash your clothes for tomorrow." I called the counselor who drove me to work and gave him my Mom's address. The next day I went to work and tried to concentrate on the inevitable camp problems. I came home to my mother's and we ate dinner. Alex arrived and I went to the bathroom again.

"When are you coming home, Valerie?"

"I don't know."

"What's your plan? Are you going to raise the child by yourself?"

"A lot you care about the child. You throw your wife into a chest and you can injure the baby."

"It was an accident. I didn't mean to hurt you. And you started throwing first, as I recall."

"Leave me alone, Alex. Just leave me alone. Why don't you go over to your mother so she can say more bad things about me?"

"I don't understand her," said Alex to my mother, "She's never like this."

"I think part of it is being pregnant. She was afraid that you might have hurt the baby."

"She hit me first."

"I know, I know," said my mother soothingly. "Let's give it one more day. Maybe the two of you should go see a marriage counselor,"

"I'm leaving, Valerie. 'I don't care!'" he said in a squeaky mock Valerie voice.

He left and I came out of the bathroom.

"Valerie, if you don't want to be married you don't have to be. You can always come home and I'll help you with the baby as much as I can. But I don't think that's what you really want. What do you really want?"

"I don't care," I said.

"For a writer and a debater, you're very nonverbal."

"Well, you won't let me tell you what happened."

"If you tell me, and then I call him up and scream at him, and then you kiss and make up, then I'll be the interfering one. Just like his mother."

"His mother is a big part of the problem. You were right. You do marry his family."

We watched TV, went to bed and I went to work again.

As the counselor dropped me off at my Mom's, I saw Alex leaning against his car. He did look very handsome in his light gray summer suit and his turquoise tie, the tie I liked so much.

"Hello, Valerie," he said quietly.

My Mother came down the stairs, holding Lucky on his leash. She handed the leash to Alex. "Help me out. Walk him. Both of you. Walk him at least ten blocks."

We walked silently. Then Alex tentatively put his arm around me. I shook it off.

"Don't touch me. We're just walking together for the dog."

"I'm sorry. I would never do anything to hurt you or the baby."

"But you did."

"Valerie, I said I was sorry. I was trying to get you to stop throwing things at my face. I'm sorry. How many times do I have to say it?"

I considered. I looked at his face, looking handsome and sincere. And it came to me that I did care. "I'm sorry, too. Is your cheek okay?"

"Yes, is your shoulder okay?"

"Yes." We stopped in the middle of the street and kissed until Lucky yanked on his leash.

"This has been a bunch of foolishness on both our parts," he said.

"I know."

"Have you eaten? Let me take you out to dinner."

"All right."

"And then you'll come home?"

"Yes."

"Are you only coming home because you can't wear that outfit any more days?"

"No."

"Why are you coming home?"

"Because our love is stronger than hurting each other."

My Mother was thrilled that her dog ploy had worked. She kissed us both. "Kiss and make up so I can see it," she said. So we did.

"I'm going to take Valerie out to The Tam O' Shanter Inn. Won't you join us?"

"No, no. You two have a lot to talk about. And my dinner's all ready."

"How about we take you there next week?"

"Sounds good," said Mother.

At The Tam O' Shanter Inn, we always ordered their chopped steak, baked potato and minted peas. "So what have we learned from this?" Alex asked me.

"I've learned that your birthday doesn't end until midnight. And I have to attend to you for twenty four hours."

"Very funny. Did you also learn not to throw things at me? This isn't the first time."

"It's defense. You are much stronger than I am. I can't give you karate punches. And what, sweetheart, have you learned from this?"

Alex took my hand in his across the table. "I've learned that

I still can't function without you. For Monday and today, I was miserable at work and I kept making math mistakes. And when I came home, nothing was cooking and no sweet hello. And the bed was big and lonely."

I smiled my biggest smile. I was thrilled with his answer. "I guess we still love each other very much and we love our marriage, too," I said.

"I guess you're right."

As we walked to our car, a balloon seller stood on the corner, surrounded by children. Alex bought a purple balloon. "Let's put both sides of our argument figuratively into this balloon," he said.

"And then what?"

"And then we let it go. Hold on to the string with me. Release it!" The purple balloon sailed into the sky, higher and higher, smaller and smaller. "This argument is officially over and we don't mention it again," said Alex. "Now I want to take you home and make love to you until you say stop because you're so sore."

"I won't care," I said, kissing him.

THINGS DON'T STAY THE SAME

Again, a personal story just for me.

A few days after Alex's birthday, he had a Staff Meeting/Dinner at work and so I met my mother for dinner near her house——my treat.

"Thank you for being so wonderful and understanding during our argument," I told her.

"So I take it you made up in the most significant way," said my mother with a smile.

"Yes, we're still in love. The entire thing was really stupid."

"But you know what, Valerie? Your relationship has changed. When you were in high school and that first year of college, you were so in awe of Alex. You seemed to be willing to go to almost any lengths to keep this young man in love with you. He ignited something in you that no one else had and he was like your addiction. You would do anything for him. At least that's the way I saw it."

"What are you saying? He's so wonderful."

"He is wonderful. A very worthy young man. But you don't even realize what's happened. In the almost three years that you've been married, you've turned things around. You are now the powerful person in your relationship."

"That's ridiculous, Mom."

"No, it isn't. He dominates you in the little things. But you control his emotions. He loves you and he needs you."

"He did tell me on Tuesday night that he needed me to function."

"See! Things don't stay the same."

"So what does it mean?"

"It means that you hold his heart in your hands, so be careful with it. At the same time, I'm glad to see that you're not such a pushover anymore. 'Yes, Alex, No, Alex, How high, Alex?' You're going to be a mother and I'm glad you found the strength to assert yourself. When you came to my house you were saying to him, 'You can only push me this far, Alex. And no more."

"I still love him like crazy, Mom."

"Of course you do," said my Mother. "But you have more confidence now. And that's a good thing. My little girl is growing up. Don't ever forget that he doesn't want to be in his house without you."

"Thank you, Mom."

We walked to my Mom's apartment where Alex would pick me up. I realized that she was telling me, 'Love him, but don't take any shit.'

Part Two

THE FALL SEMESTER OF THE SENIOR YEAR

SEPTEMBER, showing photos to the nuns.

"Here we are, on vacation in Santa Barbara. My obstetrician said that since I was entering my sixth month of pregnancy, it would be a good idea to limit riding in our bumpy Jeep as much as possible. Alex mentioned at the Chinese restaurant that he'd like to take me on a short vacation before our senior years began but there was a problem with the car. Immediately, Aunt Viv spoke up.

"'Alex, take my car for this weekend. It's my pleasure.'"

"Aunt Viv really liked Alex and was nicer to him than she was to almost anyone. He was very polite to her and held her chair out for her at the restaurant. Recently, in the bathroom, she'd said to me, 'Not only is he very cute but he's so knowledgeable about sex. He's the one who told Uncle Ted about the Ben Wa balls.' And she'd smiled happily. I'd felt too embarrassed to say anything. This was my aunt, for goodness sake!

"So Alex and I borrowed her car and had the best time, going up the coast to Solvang, Hearst's Castle and Santa Barbara. I was wearing a shift dress and only had a little bump. I wanted to look nice for Alex and had a makeup lady at the beauty parlor apply makeup for me before we left at 11 am."

"'Take it off,' said Alex. 'You have such a darling face. You don't need to wear makeup. But I'll admit it, when you've had your hair done and it's all curly down your back, I do love that style.'"

"You're not upset that I've gained weight?"

"'Of course not. You're beautiful and radiant. And so into sex! Don't forget," he sang: *You're the same on top Just different on the bottom.*'"

"When school started, Alex seemed a little more relaxed. "They wouldn't ask anyone to leave Caltech in his senior year, would they?" I asked."

"'It's been known to happen,' said Alex. 'Last year, one guy. But not like the 32 guys who had to leave from our freshman year.'"

"So do you feel more secure? You're sleeping through the night."

"'Yes, a little. Thanks to you.'"

"And all the studying you do every night."

"I was embarking on three new programs. I had signed up at the Paul Popenoe Clinic on Sunset Blvd. for a pre natal exercise class. I went three afternoons a week and it covered breastfeeding tips and basic baby care.

"From 9 to 10:30 am every morning I had a job teaching social studies and reading at a private school. I said nothing about my pregnancy and neither did they. I didn't really show yet in my shift dresses.

"And I enrolled in an eight unit class at UCLA called Exceptional Children.

"I would study about some possibilities for my baby due to the rubella. It was an amazing class, co-sponsored by the Education and Psychology Departments. Each student was permitted to adapt the class to his or her interests. From a long list of disabilities that could affect children, each of us chose three. We then did extensive research about our three subjects and prepared three term papers. We also spent ten mornings in a nursery school which specialized in preschoolers who had that disability. We observed and played with the children. I was going to be prepared IF my baby was born impaired, the one chance in four possibility."

"I spent two weeks at the John Tracy School for children who were deaf. Then I spent two weeks at a preschool for children who were blind."

OCTOBER

"The last rotation was at the Ena Dubnoff School. Most of the children were in wheelchairs and had other physical disabilities. The teachers were marvelous, filled with patience and caring. My baby could have these symptoms. I felt I could learn techniques. The teachers massaged the arms and legs of the young children and showed me how to do it. But after the third morning, I ran into the street and sat on a bench, crying and crying. It was devastating to see these children in their wheelchairs, struggling in so many ways. Some of them could not talk and most were not toilet trained, even at six or seven years old. I cried for nearly an hour, "A teacher came out to check on me. 'This is not a good placement for you,' she said. 'You're too close to this situation.'

She knew that my baby could have cerebral palsy. So my professor gave me an alternate assignment. I was also taking a class in American poetry at UCLA and I spilled out my emotions, writing sad poetry.

FINDING HER FATHER

"And then something odd came about. My mother's father had deserted the family when she was a baby. She had never known him. As a result, with not enough money to support the family and my mom's mother being ill, my Uncle Ted and his older sister, Mattie, had to be placed in orphanages. There was no welfare then or aid to dependent families. My mother was too young to be placed in the orphanage and my grand-mother raised her until, after many years, she was able to bring the two older children home also.

"Now, at dinner, my mother said, wistfully, 'I wish I could meet my father, just once.'

"How could you find out his whereabouts?" I asked."

"'My cousin called me from New York last week, just to say hello, and she said that my father has been living in Los Angeles for some time.'"

"Could you call her and get more information?"

"My mother soon found out that her father was working as a carpenter for Paramount Studios on Melrose Avenue. This was really amazing because the Paul Popenoe Clinic, where I was taking prenatal classes, was directly across the street from Paramount Studios.

"I resolved that I would find my mother's father for her."

"It was easy for me because I usually ate a late lunch after doing the prenatal exercises at the Clinic. I'll just eat at the Paramount Studios Commissary, I thought."

"So I started eating there twice a week. After three weeks, I spotted him. He was a man who seemed to be in his late sixties. My Uncle Ted was in his late forties and this man looked like an older version of my uncle. They both had a mustache. My uncle was balding and this man was bald. He was the same height as my uncle. As I scrutinized, I saw my uncle's features. They were both handsome men.

"He carried a tool box with black initials on it, I couldn't see what the initials were. The next time I went to the Commissary, the counterman saw me looking at him. 'That old geezer comes in every day at 2:30 when his shift is over. Every day he orders the same thing, coffee and pie.'"

"I leaned over and then I saw the initials. J.G. Immediately, I went over to him. "Are you Jacob Goldblatt?"

"He gave me a look of total alarm. In a flash he'd thrown dollars on the counter, picked up his toolbox and fled out the door.

"'Are you some kind of collection lady?' asked the counterman, grinning.

"I called my mother when I got home. "I found your father. He may not want to meet us. But we can go to the Commissary at Paramount Studios at 2:30 and see him."

"'Let me call Ted and see what he says.'"

"Shortly after, my mother called back. 'Uncle Ted says to forget all about it. He says if he meets our father, he'll want to kill him. He was three when this man abandoned the family and he never contacted his children to see how they were doing, let alone his wife. And all the grief he put our mother through and our grandmother also. So Valerie, forget about it.'"

"I will."

"I got off the phone and told Alex, who was eating dinner. 'It probably wasn't just his mother and his grandmother who had to suffer,' he said. 'He and his older sister had to spend many years living in an orphanage because of the selfishness of this man.'"

"Alex, I just wanted to give my mother her wish."

"Alex rose from the table and gave me a big hug. 'I know, darling. You wanted to be a uniter of families. You wanted to be a problem solver. You wanted to be a smart detective and you wanted a happy ending. Sit on the couch, Nookums. I'm going to run this as a movie for you.' He gave me his infectious grin, about to enjoy this."

"'The earnest young pregnant lady says, 'Jacob Goldblatt?' The older man is shocked. 'How would you know my former name?' 'I am Shaina's daughter' she says. 'And this bump is your great grandchild.' 'My granddaughter!' he says. 'How I have longed to meet you!' Now the entire Commissary bursts into applause at this touching scene."

"Oh, Alex."

"'I'm not done. He's afraid to touch you and so he just tenderly touches your shoulder. 'My granddaughter!' Fade out on both your faces.'"

"Oh, Alex."

"'Wait, I forgot something. He speaks. 'I am an old man now. I have a nice house in Hollywood. I want your mother to have it.'"

"Oh. Alex."

"'Unfortunately, darling, life is not a Hollywood movie. And one other thing. What about that blabbermouth cousin who told your mom his occupation? Don't you think she told him, 'Your son Ted and daughter Shaina are also living in Los Angeles.' So if that man wanted to connect with you…….'"

"Too logical, Alex."

"So did you ever connect with your grandfather? "asked Sister Mary Louise. She and Sister Agnes had walked over to play with the baby.

"No. My Uncle Ted said 'Drop it,' so I let it go and didn't go to the Paramount Commissary again."

"But Alex was sweet, trying to comfort you by making you laugh," said Sister Agnes.

"Yes, Alex was sweet," I said, flooded by memories and trying not to cry. "The next thing that happened terrified me."

CARL SANDBURG

The three nuns and Mrs. O'Dell were listening closely.

"It was late October. Alex was still overwhelmed with the work at Caltech. He had to write a five page English paper. He had a long list of choices. 'I have more homework this year than ever. How will I get to this?' he said."

"I had a paper due in my Poetry class but it had to be on Carl Sandburg. This was one of Alex's choices. So I spent considerable time writing the paper. I typed a separate paper for Alex with his name on it. My paper was due first and I received an A.

"Then Alex turned in his Carl Sandburg paper. A week later, my professor, Dr. Elizabeth Crawford, called me into her office. 'I wanted to discuss your Carl Sandburg paper. It was interesting. I enjoyed reading it. And I also enjoyed reading your husband's Carl Sandburg paper!' She was very grave and serious and I felt a huge panic. We'd been discovered! Could they kick Alex out of Caltech because of this? Could they kick me out of UCLA? Would neither of us graduate in June? Dr. Crawford's face was stern as she peered at me through her black framed glasses."

"Then she smiled and put me out of my misery. 'My husband is Dr. Kopeck and he teaches English and Humanities at Caltech.'"

"Oh, no."

"What a horrible, scary coincidence," said Sister Agnes. "You can't make these things up."

"Dr .Crawford went on. 'Actually, the joke is on us, Valerie. My husband is writing a textbook and he had deadlines so he asked me to grade these senior English papers. And that's how I got the pleasure of reading about Carl Sandburg a second time. And word for word from your paper.'"

"'What are the odds of that happening, you two married students and we married professors? And Ed and I have different last names.' Now she laughed. 'We were both being good wives, trying to help our husbands!'"

"Will Alex's paper be okay?"

"'Oh, I gave him an A. Ed says he's a serious, congenial fellow, a senior, and I see that you're pregnant. One more paper is due for both of you and you have to have him do his by himself. Agreed?'"

"Definitely, Dr. Crawford. In class you mentioned that you have two small children. Would you give me some advice as a working mom?"

"This gracious woman smiled again. 'One——-always have a back up plan. Two——have a back up plan for your back up plan. Three——arrange to take your kids to the dentist and the doctor yourself. The kids want you to be there, not the Nanny.'"

"Thank you, Dr. Crawford."

"'You're welcome. And the next English paper he writes himself. It won't hurt him.'"

YOU'RE LATE AGAIN!

"Was he grateful to you that you wrote his English papers?" asked Sister Mary Louise.

"Well, yes. But in my 7th month, I made him very angry. I went out to lunch with my creative writing teacher, Brenda, who had a young baby. We got to talking and I arrived home an hour later than I'd told Alex. He was not only very worried but had punched a hole in the bedroom wall.

"Another hole?" I said. "Now you've punched a hole in both of the places we've lived."

"He shook his head, still upset."

"Is EXASPERATED and FURIOUS going to come?"

"'And spank you? I can't do that while you're pregnant. While you're pregnant you get angry words and scolding.'"

"Angry words and scolding last too long. I'd rather have EXASPERATED and FURIOUS."

CAMELOT 1970

"This happened almost two years ago," I told the nuns. "My fourth daughter was born and of course she was adorable, Neal's grandfather had died shortly after Jeanette. He was a wonderful gentleman. When I had Neal tell him that I was a Litvak, a Jew whose family comes from Eastern Europe or Russia, he was delighted. I knew that he also was a Litvak. He wrote me the following letter.

"'Dear Litwak Valerie, Yes Litwaks are good people, almost always honest. I am glad you married my Neal and wish you happiness in your marriage. Your new Zaidie.(Grandpa)

"There was another letter".' Dear Marisa and Talia, I am your new Zaidie. I am sure that you are very good girls. Be sure to listen to your dear Mama and Papa. Love, Zaidie Emanuel.

"If the baby was a boy, we would call him Emanuel. So we named our baby girl Emory and called her Emmie.

"When Emmie was two and a half months, Alex was back from Israel. I opened the door when he came to pick up the girls.'

"'Hi. How is the baby doing?'"

"She's fine. Eats every three hours which is good and sleeps six hours at night."

"'Well, you're getting there.'"

"What?"

"'You're getting there. Like an emerging matzoh ball.'"

"You've got a lot of nerve! The baby is only ten weeks old."

Alex shrugged. 'You're too pretty to let yourself go.'"

"What a lot of chutzpah you have!" I stormed out of the living room. "How dare he!" I muttered to myself. I had lost several pounds since the birth and I was nursing which helped. I had gone back to my normal weight after Shoshana's birth five years earlier. Just before Emmie was born, Neal had commented that I was "ginormous, ha ha" at a holiday party, to Erica and Steve. Erica glared at him. 'She's a beautiful pregnant woman,' she'd told him and I had told him privately that my weight was no joke at 39 weeks. 'Sorry,' he'd said. No comments since from Neal and now a crack from Alex."

"The next day I took the baby with me and joined Weight Watchers.

Alex went to Israel for his two month stint and then he was in my living room again."

"'Well, Valerie, much better,' he said."

"You have no right to comment about my weight."

"'How much have you lost?'"

"I was about to say, None of your business, but found myself saying, 'Sixteen pounds. I have another seven to go. Talia is across the street at Mo's house and Marisa is showering. They'll be ready soon.'"

"'That's good. Remember in 1961 when we saw "Camelot?"

"And both of us loved it.'"

"I remember."

"'And King Arthur says, ' Guinivere is such a special wife.'"

"Again, I didn't know what to say." So I sang:

"Oh, what do the simple folk do. When they are feeling so blue?"

"Alex grinned. *"They sing,"* he said."

"'They sing?'"

"I surmise."

"'Okay, what do they sing?'"

Alex stopped grinning and now looked intense. His nice baritone:

"'If ever I would leave you, it wouldn't be in summer. Seeing you in summer, I never would go.'"

"But you did leave me. In March, '63 and then you left me in November."

"'I regret that now. And then you didn't come with me to Israel.'"

"We've been over and over this. Why are you bringing it up now? And why care about my weight?"

"'Because I know how lovely you can be. And that's what I want, when I get you back.'"

"How can you talk like this? You're married to Anita and I'm married to Neal."

"'Does he make you happy?'"

"Most of the time."

"'When does he not?'"

"Really, Alex. My weight and then my personal life."

"'I told you at the funeral that neither one of us wants us to be over.'"

"Talia walked in then and next came Marisa, braiding her wet hair."

"'What are you doing, Mom? Daddy?' Talia asked."

"'They're singing,' said Marisa."

"'What are they singing?'"

"'Sappy songs.'"

"Alex still had his intense look. Then he got up and hugged both girls. He sang:

"We know that there is not
A more congenial spot
For happy ever aftering
Then here in Camelot."

"'Kiss Mom goodbye.'"

"He sang as he walked to his car with his girls."

"It wouldn't be in autumn..."

THE NEXT DAY

A story that I didn't share with the nuns.

The phone rang. Without a greeting, Alex said, 'Are you alone?'

"Yes."

"Do you remember in our first year after a dinner at the Temple, you started to cry about Jocelyn Lerner? And I said that I wished my father were still alive so he could give me advice on how to handle you?"

"I remember."

"Well, now I know how. From *Camelot*." Alex sang:

"How to handle a woman?

Mark me well, I will tell you, sir.
The way to handle a woman
Is to love her, simply love her
Merely love her—-love her—-love her."
"And I intend to." Click.

I shook my head, smiling. That determined man. It was a pursuit, round two.

DON'T BE UPSET

"I was in my seventh month with Marisa and Alex and I were having a Shabbat dinner by ourselves in our apartment. I had made his favorite dessert, chocolate mousse, and we were finishing it when the phone rang. It was my mother and she was crying. "You're being evicted from your apartment?" I said. "What happened?"

"I turned to Alex. "She can only stay there one more month because the landlord wants her apartment for his son. And we've rented there for eight years."

"Alex took the phone. "Don't be upset. It's all going to work out. Tomorrow morning I'll come over and take you to find a new apartment. Valerie will be busy with her Seminar Group who are meeting here. And I think we should look in the Fairfax area. It's much nicer and you'll be near Uncle Ted. And when it comes time to move, Ted and I will move you and Sebastian and Nathan will help. You just buy them some pizza and beer. See you at 9 am,"

"See, you are the kindest, most wonderful man! You were planning on mountain climbing."

"I'll go on Sunday. Your mother is very sweet and she gave that trait to you. How is she going to find an apartment if she doesn't drive or have a car? This is what a son in law does. And what you're going to do is give me more mousse. It's really good."

"Alex helped my mother find an apartment that was sunnier and only $15 more a month. It had better access to shopping on Fairfax Avenue since my mother carried her shopping bags. When it came time to move, Alex rented a truck and six men, including Geoffrey, moved her things on a Sunday afternoon. After, instead of pizza, my uncle took everyone out to Lawry's for prime rib."

"He's more of a son than a son in law." said my mother.

"'And did she like Neal as a son in law also?' asked Sister Agnes."

"No, she never liked Neal. One time he scolded Marisa too harshly and she told him off. He responded by telling her she was fat. He later apologized but she had no use for him after that. She was always polite but she didn't laugh at his jokes, barely entered into conversation with him."

BARTA FROM AMSTERDAM

The nuns always told me that they wanted to hear my stories of survival in the Holocaust. 1970

"Peter is an 8th grader in my Holocaust class. After class he told me that his Mom was coming into the class to meet with me. 'It's about my Oma, my grandmother. She just arrived from Israel for my Bar Mitzvah next week.'"

"Margolit, his mother, greeted me. 'It's about my mother, Barta. I read the book you edited about Holocaust survivors. Maybe you would like to interview her for a sequel to your book. She was a real hero and her cleverness saved me and my sisters and brother.'"

"I would love to meet her."

"'Come for lunch tomorrow. I'll make Indonesian food. My mother was an English teacher in Amsterdam before the war so she speaks English.'"

"I brought her flowers to welcome her to Phoenix and sat down with Barta and Margolit to a very spicy and delicious chicken curry. Margolit was a pretty blond woman in her early forties and Barta was a sweet looking and plump woman around sixty five,(I thought.)"

"'As Margolit told you, I was an English teacher at the Montessori school in Amsterdam. Both my husband Friedrich and I were born in Amsterdam. We married after college and thought it would be nice to have our children close together so they would be friends. Friedrich had bought an umbrella factory and when the Nazis took over Holland in 1941, we were of course frightened. At that time, Ilse was seven, Willemina was six, Margolit was five and Jacob was four. They were adorable children, we thought.'"

"'After three months had passed, I was fired from the Montessori school because the Nazis said that they would close the school if they employed any Jews. My Dutch Directors had tears in their eyes as they told me and gave me a large box of food to bring home. The next week they expelled all the Jewish children, about a third of the school, again by order of the Nazis. The Nazis had proclaimed that they were looking for Jewish people who had arrived in Holland from Germany but that no Dutch Jews would be harmed. Of course we didn't believe them because they had already proven themselves to be liars.'

"'Didn't Father try to have us leave Holland then?'"

"'Yes, he did. He tried to get us visas for America, for England and for Spain but every country refused. He decided to sell his umbrella factory to gather some money for our escape. Days later, Nazis came into his factory and took it over. Jews were no longer allowed to own businesses.'"

"'Is that when Father buried the umbrellas?'"

"'A few days before, Friedrich and our gardener dug a deep hole in the garden and buried our two guns and about forty umbrellas there. 'When all this craziness is over, we can sell them,' said Friedrich."

"'One of Friedrich's employees, a young man named Hans, took over the umbrella factory, paying weekly money to two

Dutch collaborators. Hans proved to be a fine young man, He said that he was part of the Dutch underground. Friedrich had paid for an operation for Hans' two year old a few years before and Hans never forgot that his little girl recovered."'

"'Jews were only allowed to shop between 3 pm and 5 pm, And a few months later we were forced to wear yellow stars of David on our clothes."'

"'Hans warned my husband that he should go into hiding but Friedrich said that he couldn't desert his family, and leave them to fend for themselves without him. He began to try to make arrangements for all of us to hide. The next day, two Nazis and two collaborating Dutch police came to take Friedrich away. They gave him ten minutes to pack a suitcase. 'Use all your cleverness to save the children, Barta' he told me. 'All four of them must survive!' Then he kissed us all and was put into a truck. Days later, Hans told me he'd been taken to Westerbork. It was a transit camp in northeastern Holland and the Jews taken there were then taken to Auschwitz and Sobibor."'

"'After Friedrich was taken away, Hans warned me not to leave the house. Jews of all ages were being picked up from the streets and taken to concentration camps. Hans came once a week late at night. I gave him plates and bowls and serving dishes from my collections of Delft and Meissen. I was sad to see these lovely items leave my home but Hans sold them and brought us food. Meanwhile, Jewish friends and neighbors were being taken away by the Nazis. I knew that I had to think of a way to save us and quickly. The Nazis were so powerful. What were they afraid of? I wrestled with this question for days and then it came to me. The Nazis were afraid of serious illness, of epidemics. Hans verified this for me. 'Go to see the Minister of Health,' he advised me. 'He is also a member of the Dutch resistance, He'll help you.' So the next afternoon, I went to see the Minister of Health."'

"'Is there a disease where my children would be contagious and need to be quarantined?' I asked him."'

"'Madam, diptheria is such a disease. If one of your children were to get it, it would present itself as a very raw and red throat. If you called me tomorrow, I would send one of my public health nurses to examine your child. If it is diphtheria, she will need to place your house under quarantine for six weeks. Signs would be placed on your door and windows of extreme contagion and no one could go in or out. This is so contagious that it might be that after six weeks, another one of your children might contract it. Do you understand what I am telling you, Madam?'"

"'I told him that I did and thanked him.'"

"'And then I was the first one to get diptheria,' said Margolit. 'Mother put mustard on a spoon and rubbed my throat until I cried. She cried too but said she had to save us. The next day, the public health nurse came to the house. She barely looked at my throat and put up the red signs on the outside of the house. We were locked in the house and Mother taught us. After six weeks, we did the same thing with Ilse and the public health nurse came again. This time she brought a package with her. It had five small Droste chocolate bars in it and also her old Red Cross nurse's uniform. 'It may be helpful for you if you need to go out,' she said to Mother."

"Barta took up the story. 'After Ilse, we treated Willemina's throat and this procedure had bought us a little more than four months of safety. 'I know that you want to repeat this with Jacob,' said the public health nurse. 'But it's not safe. We have had two Nazi officials make inquiries.'"

"'Of course I had hoped that the Nazis would forget about us. Hans found out from a member in the Resistance, one who actually worked at the Nazi headquarters as a secretary, that we were about to be arrested and taken to Auschwitz. 'We have to arrange hiding places for you tonight,' said Hans. But when he came in the middle of the night, the Resistance was only able to find a hiding place for Jacob and one for Margolit. My heart was wrenched as they took my little ones away, And why? For the crime of being Jewish. Margolit was being very brave although her lips were quivering. Jacob did not make a sound but tears fell from his eyes. 'Where are we going, Mother?' he asked me. 'Somewhere safe,' was all I could answer." Jacob was only six and Margolit was seven.'"

"Dr. Ron Mandell was Margolit's husband. He came into the family room with the rest of the relatives whom he had taken for a sightseeing trip to Frontier Village. It was a town where actors dressed in clothes of the 1890's and visitors could ride stagecoaches, print old fashioned newspapers and dip candles. There was a saloon with singers and barbequed foods. Another cantina had Mexican food. Margolit introduced me to Ilse and Willemina and their husbands and their combined four children. Then Jacob, a handsome, balding man, shook my hand. 'Not married yet,' he said to me. 'But soon.' They were all from Israel and had come for the joyous Bar Mitzvah."

"'This is Morah Valerie, Peter's Holocaust teacher,' said Margolit. 'Mother and I are telling her our story.'"

"'I'm at the part where Hans took you and Margolit away,' said Barta.'"

"'It was nice to meet you,'" said Ilse, "'But I don't care to relive any of that.'"

"Nor do I," said Willemina."

"How about a swim in the pool? said Dr.Mandell. They all smiled pleasantly and left the room."

"Jacob sat down at the table and poured himself some soda. I can tell you about my experience," he said. "Hans took me to the northeastern part of The Netherlands, the farm country. He left me with an older farm couple and I was beyond fortunate. They were nice, kind people and pretended that I was their grandson. They showed me how to milk cows and make butter and gouda cheese. And for Christmas that year, they gave me a puppy as a present and showed me how to care for it. They told me not to tell any of the neighboring farmers that I was Jewish as the Nazis could kill them for sheltering a Jew. They took me to church every Sunday. I missed you terribly, Mother, but it could have been much worse. Like Margolit."

"My fate was very different from Jacob's," said Margolit. "Jacob stayed with this farm couple the entire two years. I lived in twenty seven different homes. Sometimes I only stayed a day or so and then it wasn't safe and they had to move me. Some families were nice to me and some not so much. Often one of the couples would argue about me. The mother would want me gone because it could endanger the rest of their family. Or the father would want me to leave. I would hear them arguing about me in the night and it made me feel awful, like I was worthless garbage to throw away. I never knew when they were going to move me. The longest I ever stayed was four months. I tried to help with the cleaning and the farm work, to make myself useful. In two years, no one bought me new clothes or said loving words to me. But I knew I was lucky because stories about Auschwitz and many other concentration camps began to be circulated, stories so horrible that they might not be true."

"Do you remember the Sunday that we saw each other in church?" asked Jacob.

"That's my sister," I whispered to Oma.

"Don't greet her," said Oma. "It could bring danger to both of you. So we just smiled at each other and the next Sunday, she was gone.'"

"So tell her what happened to you and our sisters, Mother," said Margolit.

"'The morning after Jacob and Margolit left, Willemina woke up with a high fever, aching all over. And I had just used up my last aspirin. There was a children's clinic three blocks away and I knew I had to take a chance and take her. With gratitude, I put on the Red Cross nurse's outfit that the public health nurse had given me. I dressed Willemina in an old coat that had no Jewish star on it. And I told Ilse that if we both were picked up by the Nazis, she would have to hide in the house until Tuesday night when Hans would come. The three of us were so scared that we couldn't look at each other.'"

"'I set out, holding Willemina's hand, and tried to have a casual expression on my face. Two women, shopping, bid me a courteous good morning. Finally, we arrived at the clinic, waited our turn and were able to buy a small bottle of aspirin. After a few days, Willemina got better. But there was no civilization to the way we were living. We were frightened every day and the older children truly understood that fear.'"

"'When Hans came that Tuesday, he said,' We got word that you will be picked up in the morning. The Nazi Commander called you 'that diphtheria family'. No Jew must be left in that neighborhood, he said. Pack some food and warm clothes so we can leave.'"

"'Hans took us to the country where we slept in a barn. There were many mice and bugs in the hay. Willemina started to cry and Hans told her very sternly not to make noise. We were hiding with about thirty other people. In the morning, Hans returned. He had found a place for Willemina. It was not ideal, he said. She would be working in a small hotel, making beds, washing sheets and dishes. 'When will I go to school?' asked Willemina. Hans by this time had no patience left for Willemina.' You're not going to school,' he said curtly.' At least you will not be attacked.' I begged him to take Ilse also but he only had room for one girl.'"

"'And as it turned out, he was wrong, Willemina was attacked. They gave her a small attic room and the owner of the hotel came to her bed many nights. My poor little girl begged for him to get off her. He put his hand over her mouth. She was only nine and then ten years old.'"

"'Meanwhile, thanks to God, I didn't know about this. I thought she was safe. Ilse and I and the other thirty people stayed on in the barn for another several days. One afternoon, we heard a large truck rumbling up the hill and we were caught by Nazis. They roughly loaded us all into the trucks and took us to Westerbork"'

"'The food was meager and terrible and the living conditions were primitive. Yet, some people endeavored to make things more bearable for the children. One woman was an art teacher and she made charcoal sticks and showed the children how to draw faces and trees. Another man had been a famous comedian and he wrote funny little skits for the children to act in. This actually brought a smile to Ilse's face sometimes. One of the jokes was that life could never get worse. "' "'And then we were all put on trains, destination: Auschwitz. The food was more scanty and the living conditions worse. It was a place we all believed to be hell. There was a particularly sadistic German guard and she had a pushed in face with a crooked nose. She especially hated pretty girls like Ilse. We worked in the clothing rooms, sewing and mending clothes for long hours. When a garment was mended nicely, it was put into a pile to be sent back to Germany. The guard hit us with a baton if she thought we were working too slowly"'

"'Then one morning, she counted off about sixty young girls like Ilse and had them march off with a guard. 'Where are you taking them?' I screamed. The second time I yelled, she answered me. 'Taking these Jew bitches to be fixed,' she said. In the afternoon, the girls were brought back in beds. 'Where is Sarah?' shouted her mother. 'Sarah didn't make it,' said Gilda, the guard. Looking at our puzzled faces, she snarled, 'The line of Jewish babies ends here. No more Jewish babies. The Third Reich has solved the problem of Jewish babies. All your girls have been sterilized. Like dogs.'"

"'Ilse and the other girls were bleeding and moaning with pain. One of the other mothers was a doctor and she told us what to do, how to make bandages out of old clothes and keep the wounds clean. 'First we keep them alive and then we mend their sanity.' Ilse was eleven and twelve during those years, as the oldest daughter, she had played with our babies the most.

"I probably won't live,' she said, 'but if I do I will never be a mother.' 'Yes, you will,' I told her. '"

"'Our agony went on for five more months. Late at night, one of the German doctors came to the bed I shared with Ilse and gave me medications for her and many of the other girls to take. 'I make amends the best way I can,' he told me. 'You are a good man,' I told him and I believe that the medications helped her to recover. Then we woke up one morning and the guards were running away. It was May 8th,1945 and Germany had lost the war. Most of the nightmare was over. It was Victory in Europe Day. Ilse and I were sent to a hospital for four weeks where they gradually fed us nourishing food. Ilse and I both gained about twenty pounds. At first, I was too weak to walk more than a few steps but gradually my strength came back. I couldn't wait to go to pick up my three children. Sadly, I learned that Friedrich had died in .Auschwitz'"

"Did you know Anne Frank and her family?" I asked."

"'Yes, I did know Anne. She was a student at the Montessori school. I remember a high spirited girl, often giggling with her friends. My own children were younger than her.'"

"Before the German invasion in 1940, were there many Jews living in Holland?"

"'Around 140,000 Jews. Around 106,000 Jews were sent to Nazi death camps where more than 100,000 of them were murdered. An estimated 22,000 Jews went into hiding like my three children. About half of them survived.'"

"Only around 11,000?"

"'Yes. You see how lucky my children were.'"

"Then what happened?"

"'Ilse and I traveled back to Amsterdam and went into our house. Nothing was there! All the furniture, except for one large cupboard, was gone. There was not a pot or a plate in the house. Neighbors told me that many people had been taking things. A few neighbors lent us some essential items. At night, Ilse and I dug up the umbrellas and guns from the garden and were able to sell them in the next few days. At first, I went to pick up Jacob because Hans had told me where his farm was. Jacob was thrilled and I was able to thank the lovely couple who had taken such good care of him. Jacob begged to be allowed to take his dog, Chou Chou, and Oma and Opa agreed and I agreed. I had brought them some difficult to find foods. They told me to stay at their farm while I searched for Willemina and Margolit. I had visited Hans and brought presents for his family. But he didn't know where Willemina and Margolit were. The small hotel had closed."'

"'After about a week, I found Margolit, living in a room of a church. How thrilled we were to be reunited! But we couldn't find Willemina and after a week, we returned home. I bought a few dishes and pots and bought the children urgently needed clothes. And then I went to the Tulip Market and bought two large bouquets and brought them to the Minister of Health and his nurse. I thanked them for the knowledge of how to save our lives. I thanked Hans by legally turning over the umbrella factory to him and he agreed to give us a monthly allowance. We had to hang on until September when the Montessori school would open and I could go back to teaching and the children could go to school. Every other day, I went to the offices of the Jewish Agency to see if I could find news about Willemina.'"

"Then, two days after we all returned to school, the Jewish Agency located Willemina! She was in a hospital in the country. She had stomach ailments. I soon brought her home and she slowly got better with a good diet. In 1948, Israel became a country and a year after that, we all moved there. We moved to a Children's Village where Jacob was able to continue working with farm animals, which he loves. In two months, we'll all be together again for Jacob's wedding to Nadia, a lovely Russian girl from the Children's Village.'"

"'After we moved to the Children's Village,' said Jacob, 'I wrote a letter to the Yad Vashem to tell them about the Shupp family and how they risked their lives to save mine. Israel chose to honor them and we sent them tickets to come for a two week visit. At a beautiful ceremony, Oma and Opa were given the Medal of the Righteous Among the Nations. Their names were engraved on the honor wall in the Garden of the Righteous in Jerusalem. They were made honorary citizens of Israel.' Jacob was beaming."'

"What a wonderful thing to happen to this couple," I said."

'It was,' said Barta. 'Because of their kindness and firm Christian faith, my son is alive. One last little story to tell you, how Ilse became a mother.'"

"I'd love to hear it."

"'The children grew up in the Children's Village and Jacob and I still live there in small apartments. Ilse finished high school and did her military service and then decided to become a nurse. She was always a caregiver. In 1955, a religious community in Hebron was attacked by Hamas terrorists who shot a lot of the settlers. A mother was swinging her two year old on a swing in the playground and both of them were killed. Her husband, a doctor, came running from the clinic and he was shot in the arm and chest. He had been a surgeon and now could no longer operate. At Ilse's hospital in Jerusalem, they asked for nursing volunteers to go to Hebron to treat the many wounded. Ilse went. She was a nurse in critical care for this doctor, Uri, who had lost a great deal of blood. She also took care of his four year old boy who'd been shot in the leg and his three month old baby who had slept through the attack. After more than a year of care, Uri and Ilse realized that they had feelings for one another and Ilse loved the children. So they married and have raised the children together.'"

"The children who just ran through here?"

"'Yes, the two younger boys are Willemina's who married a printer. And the tall teenage boy and girl belong to Uri and Ilse. Life is a strange adventure, is it not?'"

"I hugged Barta and Margolit and thanked them for sharing their remarkable story with me. It would be published in a follow up book about survivors, I assured them. Stories about survival during the Holocaust were stories of courage and resilience and often amazing cleverness. I would always remember Barta and her family."

THE EIGHTH MONTH OF PREGNANCY

"In November, my eighth month of pregnancy, I visited my obstetrician and shock! 'I don't really think that natural childbirth would be your best option,' he said.

"But it would give my baby the best chances. No drugs. And you promised me."

'I'm sorry, Valerie. I've given it a lot of thought and it would be best if you're not aware during childbirth. Just trust me. I've delivered hundreds of babies.'

"Well, you're not delivering mine. My one question to you when I became your patient was your promise that I could deliver naturally. And now you want me all drugged up and the baby would be drugged, too? And you tell me this so close to the due date? I've taken a ten week natural childbirth course to prepare for a natural birth. Would you tell your nurse to prepare a final bill?"

"'You should discuss this with your husband and not act so impulsively, young lady.'"

"I gave them a check and left."

"At home Alex said, 'All right, darling. What's your plan now?'"

"I'll find another doctor tomorrow. I"ll go to the UCLA Medical Center. I was right, wasn't I, Alex?"

"'Yes. I think you did the right thing. I was very impressed by that lecture on natural childbirth at the Paul Popenoe Clinic. Natural childbirth gives Jonny the best chance.'"

"I met with a very nice obstetrician at UCLA and together we filled out my Birth Plan. I would have natural childbirth unless some unexpected problem occurred. Then Alex, the doctor and

I would confer and decide. As a student at UCLA, I had a special financial discount. I signed papers and went home happy and relieved."

"A week later, the UCLA doctor called me. My former doctor, well known in Beverly Hills, had refused to release me or send my medical records." "But he's all paid up."

"'However, due to medical ethics, we can't accept you. UCLA is a public institution and there are laws.'"

"I called the previous doctor and yelled and screamed and threatened a lawsuit. He refused to talk to me so I spoke to his nurse. 'He will not release you and he doesn't have to,' she said."

"I went in search of another obstetrician. I spoke to eleven doctors and none of them could or would accept me due to "medical ethics." Alex called Mr. Kugler, the attorney, who explained that we could file to subpoena the medical records from Dr. Zeiss but it would take six to eight weeks. By that time I was beginning my 9th month."

"Jeanette was beside herself. 'She's going to have the baby right in the street,' she wailed. 'Who but you would start your 9th month with no obstetrician? Just go back to Dr. Zeiss and let him put you under. That's what I did and all my friends, too. You wake up and there's the baby.'"

"After my class, I left UCLA and walked down Westwood Blvd., stopping in every medical office. If they didn't do obstetrics, I asked for a referral. Finally, after going to seven offices, a receptionist said to me, 'Why don't you try Dr. Behne? I bet she would do it. Her office is three blocks over.'"

"I reached Dr. Behne's office at 6 pm and she was just leaving. Still, she agreed to talk to me and I explained my situation. Dr. Behne was a tall, very plump lady in her sixties at least. She was a refugee from Germany and had come to the United States, via Cuba, in 1940. She had four daughters, she said. 'Ach, I take you,' said Dr. Behne. 'So, no medical records. My life in Munich showed me that records are not always important. You'll take some more tests and I'll examine you now..'"

"Three or four weeks was her diagnosis after the exam. 'You'll come in every week. And the hospital where my babies are delivered is only maternity. Small and nice. Natural childbirth? Of course. Rooming in? Yes. Your husband with you? No problem.'"

"I can't deliver a baby unless Alex is there," I said."

"'Don't be silly. Throughout the ages, many women have delivered babies without their husbands. But if he's here, he can be with you. You're right about natural childbirth. Your baby will do better with the least amount of drugs.'"

"And um, marital relations. How long can we still do it?"

"'Another two weeks, I'm sure it helps childbirth. In two weeks I can tell better how close you are to delivery.'"

"Now I had the right doctor——totally by chance."

"Your true stories are scary and amazing," said Sister Mary Louise.

I HAVE TO PREPARE FOR EVERY EVENTUALITY

"This is a story about Alex," I told the nuns, "and what I overheard him telling his Mother on the phone. I was taking a nap in the bedroom. Alex was speaking in hushed tones on the kitchen phone."

"If the baby dies, I want to take Valerie to the Balboa house for a week."

"So I'll talk to my professors. They'll understand."

"Mother, I have to prepare for every eventuality."

"I certainly realize that my education is important. But I have to think of Valerie. This would be such a blow to her. She'll need comfort and distraction."

"It's a one in four chance that the baby will be impaired or not survive."

"God damn it, Mother, why can't you just give me the goddamn keys without all these accusations? Oh, shit. I'll just find a way to go to a hotel. I've spent all my money on a neonatal specialist."

"I know. I know. And what about my feelings? It's my baby, too. I'll also be heartbroken. Do you think I would be able to sit at Caltech and concentrate on lectures?"

"Okay. Thank you, Mother. I'll come for the keys tonight. Don't mention this to Valerie because I want her to be positive and think the baby will be alright. But I have to prepare for every eventuality."

"Sisters, that conversation tells you all about Alex."

"Yes, Valerie, it does," said Sister Cordelia.

WHEN?

"Our careful planning and timing had placed our baby's birth right in the middle of Alex's Winter Break. Alex planned small daily excursions for us as we waited—-walking on the beach, gentle hikes in Griffith Park, Descanso Gardens, the Zoo.

"The due date came and went. Chanukiah came and went. Friends invited us to a Christmas dinner and that came and went. New Year's came and went. Alex had only one more vacation week. Every day we practiced all the childbirth exercises we had learned together. I had promised him that this baby would not interfere with his school work—-the very essential Senior year."

"This baby was to be my project—-he would be able to participate only occasionally. And he couldn't miss even one day because everything was so fast paced. I have to deliver while he's still on Winter Break, I told myself every day."

"We went to the hospital twice with false labor. The nurse said that walking would help so the next day we walked for hours, ending up miles away in Santa Monica. No way could I walk back to Los Feliz so Alex called Geoffrey to come and get us. 'My Mom and I are praying for you and the baby,' said Geoffrey.'"

"On Monday of the last week, I could see that Alex was very anxious and so was I. Was something wrong that the baby wasn't coming? But I did feel the baby kick."

"'Valerie, would you mind if I went on a short hike with Sebastian? Just an hour and a half.'"

"Poor Alex had been my shadow. This was not an exciting vacation for him. "I don't mind. Go."

"Alex dropped me off at my mother's house and she and I had tea in her cozy living room. Watching TV was such a treat since we didn't have one. An hour and a half passed with no Alex. Then it was two hours. I was so on the edge of panic these days that I paced back and forth in the living room. Lucky was concerned for me, a worried look on his freckled spaniel's face. How could Alex have left me for so long? I was ten days overdue. I could go into labor at any minute. My mother couldn't drive and didn't have a car. How would we get to the hospital?"

"'We'll call a cab,' said my Mom. I paced more."

"Finally, after another half hour, Alex and Sebastian came up the stairs."

"How could you be late when I could go into labor?" Even I was shocked at my shrill voice. "How could you do that to me?" I shrieked."

"Alex looked at me, surprised. 'It was just two hours and fifteen minutes, darling.'"

"Sebastian stared at me in disbelief. 'Where is my unflappable friend? So sweet, so calm?'"

"Alex quickly stepped over to me and took me into his arms. 'I'm here, honey. It's okay.' Turning to Sebastian, he said, 'There's no calm when a woman is ten days past her due date, Sebastian. Uncle Ted told me that.'"

"'I'm sorry, Valerie,' Sebastian mumbled."

"Alex kissed away my tears. 'The baby will be here soon, I'm sure. And I won't go back to school until you've given birth and are all settled.'"

"If you're nearby I feel safe," I whispered."

"'I know, I know,' said Alex, smoothing back my hair."

"'Kinderlach, come to the table for lunch." I sat down."

"'So what do you do for her?' Sebastian asked in a low tone."

"'Whatever she wants. Anything.'"

"'Anything?'"

"'Anything. I'm on her like glue.'"

"The food looked and smelled delicious. We sat at the table, everyone smiling now. Alex was my everything and he knew it and he loved it.

MARISA

"Alex was by my side for most of the arduous twenty four hour childbirth. When he wasn't there, I lost it completely, screaming out for him. He had gone to his car for a brief nap when I was sleeping and my heavy contractions had woken me. For eight hours, I had been in intense pain but refused all the medication the nurses offered me."

"Suppose this is all for nothing, Alex? Suppose the baby dies?"

"'I just felt your contraction, darling. This baby is vigorous. He's not going to die.'"

"As soon as Alex would come into the room, he'd take over. He directed my breathing, encouraged me and rubbed my lower back. He had me try to sit up in a straight chair which helped. The nurses were impressed with him. 'You'd better not leave any more,' one nurse told him. 'She falls apart when you're gone and does everything right when you're here.'"

"'She's my brave and beautiful girl,' said Alex. He wiped my forehead with a towel and kissed me. 'I'll just be gone for two minutes,' Weeks later, Uncle Ted told me that Alex had phoned him around 4 pm. 'She's suffering so much. I can't stand to see it. What can I do for her, Ted?'"

"Uncle Ted told him to just keep praising and encouraging me. Uncle Ted told him that he'd done the right thing to hire a neonatal specialist for the birth in case the baby was in distress."

"Why is it taking so long, Alex? Is it that there's something wrong, the baby is dead already?"

"'Darling, I told you, I've hired a neonatal specialist. He'll give the baby every chance. He's an expert in problem births. He'll be here soon. Dr. Behne said it was time to call him. I think you're in transition now.'"

"Soon the neonatal specialist arrived and he checked the baby's heartbeat. 'Very strong, Valerie. This will be a live birth. Natural childbirth was a very good decision for you kids to have made in this case. You're giving your baby all the best chances. And your obstetrician, Dr. Behne, is one of the best.'"

"And can Alex stay with me during the delivery?"

"'Of course, of course,' soothed Dr. Behne. 'I promised you this. We all need Alex, don't we?' The two nurses laughed and then it was time to take me to the delivery room. Alex was holding my shoulders, echoing the doctor's instructions. 'Push, darling, push. Great, great job, Valerie. You are amazing.' He was all gowned in green but when I looked up at his face, tears were streaming from his eyes.'"

"Don't cry, honey," I whispered."

"'I can't stand to see you in this much pain,' he said. 'Isn't there something we can give her?'"

"'Look!' said Dr. Behne. 'The head is coming. Come here, Alex, and see.'"

"'Amazing!' said Alex. The baby was crying, a faint, mewling sound."

"'This is a good sign,' said the neonatal specialist."

"'And now the shoulders! Such a little peanut! You have a beautiful little girl. Alex, would you like to cut the cord?'"

"They cleaned up the baby and the neonatal specialist did some tests. 'Her eyes seem to be tracking well. I can't tell about her hearing yet. But all in all, a healthy child, good lungs, strong heart. Congratulations, Mr. and Mrs. Berk. I'm so happy it turned out this way.'"

"'Darling,' Alex said to me. 'I'm very proud of you. What a brave girl you were. This was worse than getting you across the chasm.' He left to pay the specialist. They placed the baby in my arms and I nursed her. She nursed happily and vigorously. "

"Dr. Behne patted my hand. 'Your first milk, colostrum, makes the baby very strong. She is tiny but seems healthy. Five pounds, two ounces.'"

"Then we took the baby into my room. "Welcome to the world, Baby," I told her, kissing her small head with strands of blond hair. We undressed her and examined her. Alex clapped his hands loudly and the baby startled. 'Her hearing seems okay.'"

"Alex, look at her. She is identical to your newborn baby picture. Could you stop at your Mom's house and borrow it? The one on the mantel."

"The next day Alex brought the picture. "It's amazing," I said. "She's totally you. Her hair is blonde and her eyes are blue. And she has exactly your face."

"'I see that,' said Alex."

"A nurse came in and looked at the baby and the picture. 'Well, you can't deny that baby! That's your clone,' she remarked."

""I would never deny her,' said Alex."

"Remember you told me the baby would be 50% you and 50% me? Instead she's 100% you."

"Alex laughed, pleased. He'd brought me a dozen pink roses. 'And look, darling.' He handed me a pink cylinder. 'Unwrap it.'"

"What is it?"

"'It's a chocolate cigar. I bought two dozen. Real cigars are noxious. I'm going to pass them out at school.'"

RUSHING TO GET READY

"The morning after the baby was born, a nurse came to check on us. I'd refused to put the baby in the nursery and she was in a little crib right by my side. She woke up to nurse and then went right back to sleep. 'I'll bet you have lots of darling clothes for her,' commented the nurse."

"Actually, I have nothing, just two little baby shirts," I realized. After I'd had the diagnosis of German measles, I'd stopped buying anything. If the horrible happened and I came home with no baby, I couldn't stand the thought of seeing baby things. I'd said no to any baby showers. The baby was sleeping peacefully so I sprang into action. I called Suzanne, an officer of the Caltech Wives Club. The Club had an entire basement filled with baby furniture. Members could borrow items for as long as needed and then, when you returned them, you were expected to add at least one thing. What a gracious system."

"I told Suzanne that the baby was okay and asked if I could borrow a crib, a chest and a changing table, all in white. 'It will all come this afternoon,' said this lovely lady."

"Then I called my excited mother and asked her if she would go shopping with Alex to buy baby clothes. From my baby care book I read her a very long list of things the book said were necessary, such as five receiving blankets, four onesies, little hats, warm outfits. "Please get everything in pink," I asked her. Now my mother told me that she'd saved the pink fleecy outfit that she'd taken me home in. Alex would bring it."

"The maternity hospital had a rule that only the husbands could visit and this cut down on any infections from the outside world. The husbands had to scrub their hands to their elbows in a special room. So there were no other visitors."

"My mother called me three times from Sears. She took my list so seriously. She said a very nice sales lady named Judy had been assigned to help them and she was enchanted with the story of a baby who might have been born dead but who was alive and fine. Alex took a picture of my mother and this saleslady, beaming over the huge stack of pink cotton things. 'They only have one pink long gown,' said my mother anxiously. 'The others have to be yellow.'"

"That's fine, Mom. Whatever you can get. And you'll meet Marisa tomorrow."

"Alex took my mother to lunch and when they got home, Jeanette was outside waiting for them. She had brought her cleaning lady, Ida Mae. My mother described the scene. 'Poor .Alex. As I was putting away all the baby things, his mother sat in the living room and directed Ida Mae and Alex. Alex was so tired from not sleeping Thursday night and then our shopping trip. Jeanette said, 'We have to get this place cleaned up.'"

"'It's clean,' said Alex. 'It's not sanitary enough for a newborn baby,' said Jeanette. 'You're lucky the baby was born alive. You don't want to kill her now with germs.' She insisted that Alex wash all the walls with a special brush while Ida Mae sanitized the blinds and double mopped the floors. You know I'm very clean and my house is clean but this was excessive. Finally it was all done and Alex drove me home. He's on his way to see you now but don't expect him to be too chipper.'"

"My mother was right. After a brief kiss and a look at the baby, Alex lay down on my bed and fell asleep. 'He's not allowed to sleep on your bed,' said a nurse.

"Please let him sleep," I said. "He's just exhausted."

"'He was attentive during the childbirth. Unusual for such a young man. So concerned about you.' She let him sleep. I looked from him to the sleeping baby, so similar. I kissed his darling face softly. I knew that he was disappointed that we hadn't had a boy but he'd said nothing about that. Instead we had said a Shehechianu Prayer of gratitude for new life and that we had arrived at this wonderful day.'"

"Now the hospital doctor came in to tell me that my five pound baby had lost two ounces and should stay in the hospital nursery for another four or five days. I could come and visit her."

"I am NOT going home without my baby."

"'If she's here she'll be getting professional care around the clock.'"

"I'm going home and I'm taking my baby."

"'Sir, let me appeal to you as a reasonable father,'"

"'You heard my wife. We're signing her out 'Against Medical Advice.'"

"The next morning I showered before going home. I hurried out of the bathroom when I heard my baby crying. 'Let her cry,' said the nurse. 'She's only been crying for five minutes. Babies should cry for one hour every day. It's good for their lungs.'"

"That's just bizarre," I said, beginning to nurse the baby. "I'm never going to do that. If she cries, I'm going to meet her needs."

"'You're a foolish young mother. You're going to spoil her. She should be on a strict schedule, not this 'on demand' theory. Otherwise you're going to go crazy.'"

"No, I don't think so," I said. "And many experts agree with me."

HOME WITH THE BABY

"'One last time I'll advise you to leave the baby in the hospital.' the doctor said to Alex. 'Try to convince your wife.'"

"'My wife is the mother and I trust her instincts. Whatever she decides goes.'"

"We signed the baby out 'against medical advice.' It was not the first time we'd challenged an established expert, and wouldn't be the last time."

"Alex drove us home, the baby sleeping peacefully in the baby car seat. As soon as we were settled, Alex went to pick up my mother so she could see the baby and give her her first bath. My mother came with lots of food; matzo ball soup, roast chicken, rice pilaf, and vegetables. She showed me how to bathe the baby, reviewing what I'd learned at the Paul Popenoe Clinic with a plastic doll. She also brought adorable birth announcements made for me by my father's printer friend, George. They were exact copies of the birth announcements my father had printed for me, little cards with two doors which, opened, revealed the baby's name, her parents and the date. She brought fifty announcements and I was thrilled. After a lovely two hours, Alex brought my mom home and we got ready for Jeanette's visit."

"Jeanette bustled in and sent Alex down to her car to bring up heavy boxes. She had brought a baby scale and a bottle washing sterilizer and twelve bottles as well as a case of baby food in little jars. I thanked her but told her to take the sterilizer back. "I'm nursing," I said."

"'Well, that won't last long. It never does. I bottle fed and it's much more scientific. You know exactly what the baby is getting and how much. That's why you have to weigh the baby after every feeding, But breastfeeding is so old fashioned. Bottle feeding is scientific. Breastfeeding! It's a wonder that Alex, a scientist, allows it.'"

"She went on to tell me the latest news of the other newly born Berk cousin. I had been delighted that, if all went well, I would be giving birth to Grandmother Berkowitz's first great grandchild. Instead, in a complete surprise, Alex's cousin had become a father of a baby born three weeks before Marisa. He was a year younger than Alex and the families never socialized for some terrible reason that had happened in the past. He wasn't married and now his girlfriend (whom he MIGHT marry) had given birth to a little Berk. It was a BOY and he weighed EIGHT pounds. We'd been married almost three years but I'd only brought forth a GIRL and a puny five pound girl at that. Clearly, an out of wedlock eight pound boy trumped a tiny girl. The boy was named after Alex's grandfather."

"'And she's NOT nursing.'"

"Well, whoopee for her," I said."

"Jeanette held the baby. 'Last week I bought a chicken that weighed more than this. But she does look like Alex.' She turned off the stereo playing *An American In Paris*. 'Babies need it to be quiet.'"

"I don't think so."

"'Well, you don't think about a lot of things. You have a lot to learn'."

"You don't think I do anything right, do you?"

"'Precious little, the way things are supposed to be done.'"

"But that's just your opinion and...."

"'NAPTIME.' boomed Alex. 'Valerie has to nap and the baby has to nap and we're so glad you came, Mother.' With his arm around her shoulders, he guided her out of the apartment, gave her a kiss and closed the door."

"But she didn't take that big sterilizer," I said."

"'Enough!'" said Alex. "

"Would you lie down with me and hug me?"

"'Yes, I will.'"

"We were hugging and kissing in bed when we heard loud knocking on the front door. Alex put pants on and answered the door. 'I forgot to tell you something,' said Jeanette. I could hear her from our bedroom. 'Why aren't you dressed?. Oh, I get it. Don't you have to study? You've missed several days of school. Nothing is more important than your education, you know.'"

"'I know, Mother. I feel the same way. Except that my wife and child are more important. But since you're here, would you take back this sterilizer?'"

"'I'm leaving it here. And how do you, a scientist, allow your wife to breastfeed when you can't measure how much the child is getting?'"

"'Valerie is in charge of all the feeding in this home, for me and Marisa.'"

"'So what are you in charge of? Nothing?' She left, her high heels clomping down the stairs."

"'DO NOT let anything my mother says bother you. We know that breastfeeding is best for babies. Now, where were we?'"

THE NEXT MORNING

"I nursed several times during the night and got up to change the baby's diaper. Each time, I gagged and twice I threw up as I removed and rinsed the cloth diaper. The second time, Alex came into the bathroom."

"'Darling, I don't want you to gag and throw up. If it's a bowel movement, call me and I'll change her. If I'm not home, put the poopy diaper in this bucket and I'll take care of it when I get home.'"

"Oh, my,' said my Mother, when I told her. 'He is a hero.'"

"He's wonderful. And he made me a chart and put it over the diaper changing table."

MARISA CRIES———REASONS

Hungry

Needs changing

Pin sticking her

Too warm, too cold

Bored

"For the first few days, a little nervous, I consulted the chart when she cried. She was a very good baby and usually only cried when she was hungry. Before she started to cry, she would vocalize for a few minutes and I tried to pick her up then so Alex wouldn't be disturbed."

"I was telling this story to Sister Agnes. 'So he was considerate of you as a mother and you were considerate of him.'"

"That's true, Sister."

But I remembered that I was upset about no sex for six weeks.

"I'll kiss Little Alex every night,"

"'I know. You're my precious girl. Remember Conrad, that grad student? You met his wife at The Caltech Wives Club. His wife couldn't bear to have sex during her pregnancy. He told me she said, "Leave me alone." Now their baby is five months old and she's still saying, "Leave me alone." He loves her and he's trying to be patient. He told me last week, kind of warned me about how my wife would react. I didn't want to tell him that we had sex all through the pregnancy. Because you, my hot little Romanian wife, were insatiable.'"

"I think I had raging hormones."

"'Do you really feel okay about my going to school tomorrow?'"

"Definitely. You made me the chart over the changing table. And Mrs. Holzberg will come at noon. The baby and I will be fine. Mrs. Holzberg will cook so I won't have to."

"You promise you'll rest? Whenever the baby naps, you nap."

"I promise."

"With my day camp salary, I'd hired a lady to help for two hours a day. I would have her help for four weeks. She was a refugee from Germany. She would prepare a simple lunch for me, tidy the small apartment and make dinner for Alex and me. I would take care of the baby and study for my two finals."

"Right after Alex left for school and I was nursing the baby, there was a knock on the door. It was Jeanette and a woman dressed in white. 'This is Mrs. Gibbons. She's an R.N. She'll be your baby nurse. I'll be paying her.'"

"Listen, I've already hired someone to help me."

"'Where is she?'"

"She'll be here from 12 to 2."

"'Two hours? You need full time help. I had a full time nurse for three months. This isn't a cat. You have a little human being here. She needs care.'"

(Oh, really? I thought she was a cat.}

"'You're going to have to bathe this baby every day. What do you know about bathing a baby? You're not even twenty-one. She's not even twenty-one,' she informed Mrs. Gibbons."

"My mother came over and showed me how to do it. And I took a baby care course at the Paul Popenoe Clinic. And breastfeeding is going great. Thank you both for coming. But I don't need a nurse. I need to go to the bathroom now." "'I told you she was a know-it-all,' said Jeanette to Mrs. Gibbons as I gently closed the door on them and engaged the lock."

"I loved being a mommy and I was blessed with a very good baby. But because she was so small, she ate every two hours almost around the clock. It kept me busy. Mrs. Holzberg would make me a lunch omelet and then make us a hearty German dish for dinner, left to warm in the oven. Alex loved the meals. I was hurt because he loved them so much."

"'Maybe we should keep her to cook,' he said."

"Just until February," I said. "Then I'll cook."

"'Your meals are delicious, darling,' he said quickly, realizing that I was insulted."

"After a week, I took the baby around the block in her stroller, but otherwise was home. When she was three weeks old, I said to Alex, "Do you think we could go somewhere, just us? I really feel claustrophobic in the apartment."

"Alex called my mother and asked if she would babysit for two hours. "

"We dropped Marisa off and Alex took me for a long walk in Descanso Gardens. Azaleas and rhododendrons were in full bloom. We held hands, stopped to kiss, and as before, he bought us hot chocolate. Then we picked up the baby and I was completely refreshed again."

"After that, I hired a practical nurse every Saturday night for three hours so we could have date night. I didn't want Alex to feel that we weren't still a couple in love and still the best companions, having fun together. I pumped breastmilk and put it in a little bottle and that gave us a three hour window. "I'm sorry we can't be as spontaneous as before," I told him." "'Our love for our little baby makes that all right,' Alex said. 'We can have fun in three hours.'"

MY PROJECT

"In the first weeks of the baby's life, Alex would come home and kiss me. He'd look in on the baby as she slept and occasionally hold her. He changed her diapers and talked sweetly to her as he did. I did everything else."

"As we had agreed, the baby was my project with the exception of Alex's volunteered diaper duty. That he would change her dirty diapers had surprised me and made me very grateful. One night when she was four weeks old she wouldn't stop crying and no offered breast feeding would calm her. After two hours of pacing with her and trying to comfort her, I was crying also. I woke Alex, sleeping in the living room."

"'It's 3 am, Valerie, and I've got Demonstration Exams tomorrow. I'm sorry but I have to sleep'."

"He didn't say "your project" but I knew that was our deal. I got her to sleep by myself, eventually."

"Fortunately, she didn't have colic and didn't cry again for no discernable reason."

"When the baby was five weeks old, I looked at my hair with dismay. Way too long, split ends. I asked Alex if he could babysit on Saturday morning while I went to the hairdresser. I would feed her and put her down to nap and leave a bottle of breastmilk in case she woke up."

"'Sure, darling, go ahead. I'll sit and study.'"

"I should be back in two hours. I think she'll sleep the whole time." It had taken just a bit longer than I'd thought and I was nervous as I got off the bus and ran down the street to our apartment. I hope she's still asleep, I thought."

"When I got home, to my surprise, I heard Alex laughing and the baby gurgling. He was holding her and bouncing her up and down. 'She really is adorable, darling. See, I think she's smiling at me. She knows who I am.'"

"Of course. She's noted the resemblance. Has she been up long?"

"'Right after you left. I've been explaining my quantum physics chapter to her and she listened with rapt attention. She's much more fun than the cat.'"

"I read that babies love their daddy's deep voices."

"'Well, she is one cute kid. Your hair looks nice.'"

"Now they'd bonded. Alex came home from school, kissed me, and then took the time to play with the baby. He'd lie on the floor and exercise with her as his weight, up and down, side to side. The baby loved it. "

"'You knew all along when I said it was your project that I'd soon get involved.'"

"No, I couldn't guess that. But I'm glad it worked out that way. I did know that you'd be a strong loving father. I saw how you were with my cousins. I knew that you'd set boundaries and give love. I always knew that."

MY LITTLE COUSINS

Uncle Ted's little boys were five and six. They were born when he was forty two and forty three and Ted was thrilled with them. More than a year ago, after we'd moved to the Los Felix area, my uncle had asked me for a favor. Would I be willing to supervise my little cousins for five days so that he and Aunt Viv could have a vacation in Las Vegas? They had not left the boys to go away together before. A housekeeper lived in their house so Alex and I just had to move in and be present. Since my camp was now over and Uncle Ted had always been so good to us, Alex and I said yes.

"It will be fun," said Alex. "I like things that little boys do. "He was still working at JPL and the boys went to day camp in the mornings. The housekeeper did the cleaning and I cooked.

On Sunday, we took the boys to the Zoo. They glanced fleetingly at each animal but demanded all sorts of toys and gadgets at the gift stands. Alex told them that we would buy each of them one thing so they should see what they really liked. The boys whined and coaxed. I'd never seen Alex with children for more than a little while. He repeated one sentence over and over and it was "Mind your manners!" The boys zipped around with no regard for who was in front of them. They very nearly brought down an elderly woman with a cane but Alex ran to help her balance.

The next late afternoon, when Alex got home from work, we took the boys on a hike in Griffith Park. Kenny, overweight at six, could not be urged to walk for more than ten minutes.

Robby wanted to go home and watch cartoons. Energetic Alex couldn't understand these boys. He'd brought his small telescope to Ted's house to show the boys the night sky. He tried to interest the boys in the stars and the constellations.

"What do they do?" Robby asked. "They just are up there."

By Thursday night, Alex told me that we had to have a serious talk. He took me out into the backyard after I put the boys to bed. "Valerie, I think we have to rethink about having children. We're extremely happy just the two of us."

We were sitting on a glider. Oh my God, my future family was in jeopardy! After planning to have four children in a few years, Alex was very seriously telling me that we should not have children!

"They are completely self centered and greedy and lazy. They're a lot of work with very little return."

I thought fast and, taking Alex's hand, I told him what countless women have told their husbands for many years. "But honey, our children will be different. You're going to be a great father, patient but with rules. You'll train our children to be active and interested in the world around them and to be thoughtful. Uncle Ted had his children later in life and doesn't really discipline them too much. And Aunt Viv is in graduate school and doesn't have time to give them loads of attention.

Believe me, Alex, we'll do things differently. Our children will behave. You'll be crazy about OUR children."

"Do you promise, Valerie? We won't have a bunch of brats?"

"I promise. Our children will give us no grief at all."

"All right, Valerie. Don't ever forget what you promised."

OKAY

"I went to the doctor when the baby was six weeks old. Geoffrey drove me and Jeanette waited in the car, holding the baby."

"'Is everything okay?' she asked when I came out."

"Everything is okay."

"We came home and I finished the very special dinner I'd planned. Alex ran up the stairs, home from Caltech. 'What did the doctor say?'"

"The doctor said "YES!."

"'We can make love?'"

"It's fine and I made a romantic dinner with wine and candles."

"'Candles, shmandles. I want you. Could the dinner wait? Will the baby stay asleep for a while? '"

"Yes to everything. " I reached up to kiss him and he put his arms around me. We smiled at each other."

"'Hungry and not for food,' he said, picking me up and carrying me to the bedroom."

FAREWELL TO ARMS

"Alex's English class had to read Hemingway's *Farewell To Arms*."

"'I've got so many midterms. Couldn't you read it and give me a synopsis?'"

"You know that I promised Dr. Crawford that you would do your own English assignments."

"'But I'm so busy.'"

"Just read it, honey. I read it in Freshman Lit. It's a good story. Men like it."

"'Why can't I read Ray Bradbury or Isaac Asimov?'" he grumbled.

"Alex read it during lunchtime at Caltech. A few days later I'd finished my Social Psychology homework and, since the baby was still sleeping, I picked up my copy of *Farewell To Arms*. I skipped over the early war chapters. Frederic Henry was an American volunteer ambulance driver in Italy during World War I. Hemingway was one of my favorite authors and the scenes were written skillfully. Maybe I could help Alex write his report by discussing it with him.

"I skipped to the part in the book where Frederic meets Catherine, the beautiful English nurse. They fall in love. He has a leg wound and she is a nurse in his hospital. She sneaks into his bed every night. Then she tells him that she is pregnant with his baby. They escape the war and go to Switzerland.

"Marisa woke and I diapered and nursed her and then, while she looked at her hanging toys, I read on. Frederic and Catherine await the birth of their baby in Switzerland and are absorbed with one another. I paused the story to hold Marisa and sing songs to her. She loved the "Itsy Bitsy Spider" and watched fascinated as my hands made the motions. Then she was ready to sleep again. My dinner was almost ready so I read on. And then I arrived at the woeful end. And I couldn't help the tears from falling.

"'Nookums! Valerie!'" Alex was home and I hadn't run to the door to greet him. He loved that greeting kiss. My sweet guy drove two hours a day to support my education. The least I could do was greet him.

"He walked across the living room. 'You're crying. Why are you crying?'"

"She died."

"'Who died?'"

"Catherine, the English nurse."

"'She dies in the end?' I nodded. 'You're crying for a fictional person? And you knew she would die, you read it a few years ago.'"

"But now it really hit home. Three months ago we were in the same situation, in love and waiting for our baby to be born. And their baby dies first."

"'Oh, darling.'"

"Suppose our baby had died."

"'But she didn't.'"

"But suppose she had."

"Alex held my shoulders and propelled me into the bedroom. 'See, she's fine. Her little chest is going up and down. Her arms and legs are plump with your milk. She's a happy baby.'" "But why did Hemingway have Catherine die at the end? And the baby, too?"

"'Dr. Kopeck said that Hemingway's message is that one should recognize the brevity of life and take advantage of life's joy while it's still possible.'"

"I think the message is that everyone has the desire to fall in love."

"'That, too.'"

"But promise me that Marisa won't die and you won't die and I won't die. Until we're really old."

"'If only I could promise you that.'"

THE PROM DRESS

"I was nursing Marisa in the living room and heard noises coming from the bedroom. "Alex, what are you doing in my closet?"

"'Looking for something. Oh, here it is.' He came into the room carrying my plastic enclosed yellow prom dress. from our Senior High school prom. 'We just got this flier about the

Caltech Senior Class Ball in June. I would really love it if you wore this.'"

"Alex, that's a size seven. I don't think I could get into that."

"'Well, why have you saved it all these years? How much weight did you gain with the baby?'"

"Thirty one pounds. And when I came home from the hospital I was twenty three pounds over. And now I've lost another two pounds but I don't think I could lose twenty one pounds by June."

"'Of course you can. It's just February now. You can exercise every day with that Jack La Lanne record and do a few sit ups with me every morning. And on the weekends we'll all go for little hikes and walks. Just watch your carbs and sweets a little.'"

"But suppose I can't lose, Alex? Suppose I can't get into that dress?"

"'I am still going to love you like crazy.' He paused to give me a deep kiss. 'But if you get into the dress, I'll dance two dances with you at the Ball.'"

"Three dances."

"'A deal. But this isn't for me, it's for you. You'll feel so much better when you're your normal weight.'"

"Are you going to weigh me every week?"

"'Don't be ridiculous. This is your project. Do it or don't. It's up to you.'"

"So the next day I started the Prom Dress Campaign. One other thing Alex had done was to tape a picture of us at our High School Prom to the refrigerator. GORGEOUS he wrote under my picture. This was to remind me of my goal before I opened the refrigerator and gazed and grazed in it. I didn't say a word about it. The picture seemed annoying but I knew that Alex was right. The first month I lost six pounds and that was heartening. The first night of the "campaign", I dished up Alex's favorite ice cream, Jamoca Almond Fudge.

"Do you think I should give up ice cream?" I asked him."

"'Not at all. Did you know that regular sex uses up 320 calories. That's 2/3 of a cup of ice cream. Vigorous sex uses up 360 calories. Vos vilst du, Vibila?'"

"Vigorous sex."

"'Fine. Eat your ice cream.' His grin turned into his intense stare. I knew that in five minutes I would be canceling out 360 calories.

PANIC

"My spring semester as a new mother was well planned. I was only taking my last two classes and had to go to UCLA one morning a week. So mostly I was home with Marisa and did my school work while she napped. I hired a babysitter for Tuesday mornings. But for my midterm exams I had to go to UCLA on a Thursday morning. My babysitter was busy so

Jeanette and Aunt Henny had agreed to stay with Marisa for this one occasion.

"I had a ride to UCLA, took the exams, and got a ride back home. Marisa was three months old and I was nursing her. By the time my friend dropped me off at my home, my breasts were overflowing with milk. There were two round wet spots on my blue sweater. I needed to nurse her. I ran up the steps to our apartment, not having seen Jeanette's car. The apartment was empty! No baby in her crib! Panicked, I ran around the four rooms. On the second run through, I found a note on the refrigerator. WE'VE TAKEN THE BABY TO CEDARS.

SOMETHING IS WRONG WITH HER EYE. MOTHER

"I didn't know what to do. I didn't have a car and Alex was at school. There was no way I could contact him. I called a taxi and waited a half hour for him to come, expressing my milk into a bottle as I waited. Then the taxi rushed me to the hospital. The receptionist had never heard of Marisa Berk but she gave me directions to Pediatrics. No nurse knew anything. Frantically, I ran down endless halls which turned and led to other halls. Finally I came to a waiting room with dancing animals painted on the walls and saw Jeanette and Aunt Henny reading magazines.

"Where is Marisa?" I shouted."

"'Marisa had something oozing out of her eye so we came here at once. Fortunately, Henny is on the Auxiliary Board as a volunteer and so Dr. Garbel, the Head Pediatrician, agreed to see her since it was such an emergency.'"

"I sat down and waited fearfully for the Head Pediatrician to come out with my baby. At last, a tall and broad man in his fifties, wearing a white lab coat, strode into the room holding Marisa. I ran to them."

"'Are you the baby's mother?' he asked angrily. 'THERE IS ABSOLUTELY NOTHING WRONG WITH THIS BABY!'"

"I grabbed my baby away."

"'Well, doctor,' said Jeanette. 'What about that discharge coming from her eye?'"

"'It's normal. Now, young lady, your mother-in-law here tells me that you want me to be the child's pediatrician. The first thing we want to do is put her on cereal, twice a day. And then we'll add fruits, one at a time.'"

"I already have a pediatrician. And I'm nursing her. I have no intention of giving my baby cereal at three months old."

"'Why don't you listen to the doctor?' said Jeanette, red faced and embarrassed.' 'He's the Head Pediatrician at Cedars. And I'll pay his bill.'"

"I have a pediatrician. He believes in nursing."

"Now the doctor was angry. 'I interrupted my day as a special favor to your aunt here. She said it was a real emergency.'"

"I was really angry also but needed to be calm to nurse the baby. The baby was rooting around in my arms, showing me that she was hungry. I took her to the far side of the room and sat facing away from everyone. I started to nurse her. I hadn't brought a sweater or any little blankets. I glanced at Henny and Jeanette and saw that they were shocked. Jeanette took off the pink jacket of her suit and draped it around me so no one could glimpse this appalling display."

"'Well, let's go.'"

"Marisa's not done nursing yet."

"Finally we were all in the car, driving home in complete silence.

"As Jeanette pulled up to my apartment, she said, 'We were only trying to save the baby. She might have had a dreadful infection, like pink eye.'"

"I am certain that both of you meant well. Thank you." I took my baby and went upstairs. Alex had just gotten home. 'Where were you?' I fell into his arms, crying with the relief of his strong arms around me. I told him what had happened.

"Is she going to interfere all our lives?"

"'I'm afraid so, Nookums. At least she'll try. Darling, don't ever use either of them as babysitters again.'"

"But what should I do when I have to take the final exams?"

"'You've got more than two months to find someone, If you absolutely can't, I'll stay home with her. It will only be one day.'"

"I don't want you to miss school. But I should never ask them to babysit again?"

"'Well, I wouldn't, And I'm glad that nothing is wrong with Little Pooh. Do you want me to hold her while you make dinner?'"

"Is that a hint that you're starving?"

"'It is.'"

"Would you hold her in the kitchen and talk to me? I need a little sanity right now."

"'Sanity coming right up, Mrs. Berk. Imagine, Marisa, that big, mean doctor wanted to give you CEREAL at your tender age. When you're doing so well on Mommy's milk. Look at these chubby arms and legs. Look, she's smiling at me again. She definitely knows who I am.'"

"Of course. You're the man we wait all day for, to come home and bring sanity."

"He smiled at me, holding the baby high in the air while she giggled and gurgled."

AN ORDINARY LUNCH

"Anneliese called. They had finished filming in Canada and were shooting scenes at her studio. Today she'd be through at noon and wanted to come over to see the baby."

"'I can't believe that she's four months already and I missed the early months. She's really cute.'"

"I served Anneliese lunch and she told me about the movie. It was a western and she played one of the five bar girls. And she had lines to say. She was really making progress. And she had insider gossip about Blakely Finn (a heart throb but sadly for the women on the set, he enjoyed men) and Angela Montgomery (her trailer was rocking back and forth every day and she might have slept with every actor and stagehand and production manager in Alberta.)"

"At 5:15, Alex came home with two pizzas. 'I knew when you told me Anneliese was over that you'd want to talk to her.' We all ate and had the best time. 'I'll take the baby for a walk in the stroller,' said Alex. 'You ladies relax.'"

"A half hour later, he and the baby were back. I fed her and he took her into the bedroom to diaper her. Soon after, Anneliese and I hugged and said goodbye. I went into the bedroom to tell Alex the interesting movie star news I'd been hearing. He was fast asleep in the middle of the bed with Marisa sleeping right on his chest. He had placed pillows on either side so she wouldn't fall off the bed. I stared at them. My family. My thoughtful husband. My trusting baby. I was so lucky. Quickly, I got my camera and took four pictures of them. I would keep these pictures forever, I vowed, to remember a moment of love and innocence and the beauty that chokes you in the throat.

PERMISSION FOR SEX

"Jam?" asked Alex. "Because you're making jam?"

"Well, what did you think I was going to do when we bought all those strawberries at that stand yesterday?"

"Please, Valerie. Come on. The baby just went down for her nap."

"But I'm right in the middle. Can't you wait a half hour?"

"I don't want to wait. Little Alex doesn't want to wait. Say yes, darling. I'm done putting the oil in the car. And I've showered."

"So you're done with your project. But you don't want me to finish my project."

"Oh, forget it."

I looked at the six mason jars, all set up. The smell of the bubbling, sugary strawberries was all through the kitchen. I never said No. And I wasn't saying No, I was asking Alex to wait.

But he wanted A.W. Available Woman. NOW.

"Your face is all flushed and you look so rosy." He was giving it one more chance.

"Remember that guy at Caltech? A.W. Available Woman has to be available."

"I don't think of you like that. To me A.W. means Appealing Woman or Adorable Woman. Like you."

"I think I can turn off the strawberries and get back to this later," I said, doing that and following him to the bedroom.

"You can buy strawberry jam in any market. But you, you can't buy anywhere," Alex said, grinning. "Although I know that your jam will be excellent."

I had finally realized that Alex felt that our bedtime love making was in his total control. We went to bed usually between 10 and 11 and he orchestrated the scene, sometimes asking "rough or gentle?" or "Are you very tired?" (brief sex) and occasionally saying, "You choose. Whatever you want to do." I often chose the Ben-Wa balls.

However, morning sex or afternoon sex was unscheduled and then he felt he had to ask, abiding by my decision.

But he didn't just ask. He coaxed, he charmed. He sang me romantic songs.

I smiled at him. To be so wanted, to be needed—-wasn't that one of the best things about marriage? And he was so cute. His look was intense as he undressed me. And I did what I always did. I responded Completely

WEEKEND IN PALM SPRINGS

"Jeanette called. 'I have an idea for Mother's Day, yours and mine. Why don't we all go to that resort in Palm Springs? We had so much fun there two years ago. I'll take care of the baby so you and Alex can go to that jazz club or whatever.'"

"What a nice thought. I'll ask Alex."

"'Don't you ever make any decisions on your own, Valerie?' delivered sarcastically."

"He wants me to consult with him."

"'Okay.'"

"We all drove to Palm Springs on Friday evening and I remembered two years ago when Alex had scolded me and made me cry as a young bride and Jeanette had comforted me and advised me. One of the few times she had treated me as a person and not the one who'd stolen her son."

"I fed the baby, we had a lovely dinner in the café, and then Alex and I went to hear jazz in the jazz club. When we went to get the baby from Jeanette's room, she said, 'Why don't you leave the baby with me overnight? So she won't see something she shouldn't.'"

"Alex laughed. 'Mother, we live in a one bedroom apartment. She's already seen everything.'"

"Alex! She has not! We have a portable crib in the living room. We put her there. But I do nurse her around 3 am so we'll keep her. Thanks, though."

"The next morning Alex ate lightly and went for a long hike in the surrounding hills, saying he'd be back by 2. Jeanette, the baby and I headed for the swimming pool."

"'Where did you get that white bathing suit?' asked my mother in law."

"Jacques, the designer at The House of Nine, sent it to me as a baby present. Also one in red. They're made by De Weese, samples."

"'You've lost a lot of weight.'"

"Nineteen pounds."

"'Did Alex make you do it?'"

"No, he sort of suggested that I might want to. If I can fit into my high school prom dress, he'll dance three dances with me at the Caltech Ball. And you know how he doesn't like to dance at these things."

"'Hmmm,' said Jeanette. 'The Berk men like their ladies thin. How did you lose the weight?'"

"I was happy to tell her. "You know that book you let me borrow that had belonged to Alex's dad? The Ice Cream Diet. I followed that."

"'Really?'"

"And it was so cute. Some of your husband's notes were on the recipes, like 'Don't eat this one—-terrible.' Basically it's protein and vegetables, one fruit per day and one cup of ice cream. I eat cottage cheese too since I'm nursing. And I exercise a half hour every day."

"'Maybe I should borrow the book back,' mused Jeanette. 'I'm sure that Saul would be happy that you're using it. It worked for him, too. He ate a lot of cooked spinach and spinach salad.'"

"She held the baby and I swam laps and then had a wonderful hour reading a magazine. Waiters and bartenders came to ask me for orders but I was fine with water. A middle aged couple came over to Jeanette to admire the baby."

"'Yes,' said Jeanette. 'She looks just like my son did as a baby except that she's thin. My son was very plump.' Then in a confidential whisper, 'All she gives this poor child is banana and avocado and breast milk. No cereal at all and she's five months old. And my son seems to feel that she knows what she's doing.'"

"'Children!' commanded the woman, with a shake of her head. I did what Alex told me to do, ignored her and didn't get upset."

"Jeanette then signaled a waiter to come over with lunch menus and told me to order anything I wanted. She told me to order a cream puff dessert because it was special and I'd already lost nineteen pounds."

"I still have four or five pounds to go if I want to get into that prom dress. And I want Alex to say,' Wow, you did it.'"

"I ate a half cup of ice cream and then we went to our rooms. I nursed the baby and she fell asleep in my arms. I heard Alex's jeep pull in and then overheard the most amazing conversation, right outside my open window."

"'Have you seen your wife in that white bathing suit?' asked Jeanette angrily.

"'No, why?'"

"Now she was going to say mean things about me."

"'Well, everyone at the pool saw her. All the men from twelve to sixty were looking at her in that white bathing suit.'"

"'Really? Well, she's a beautiful girl and her figure is back. Was she looking at them?'"

"'No. She swam. She read. I will admit, she's not a flirt. But whenever she walked she had that swishy walk and all eyes were on her. Listen, Alex, you do not leave your wife alone at the pool while you go to hike! You're asking for trouble.'"

"'What kind of trouble?'"

"'Don't make me say it. You're being very foolish when your wife's body is so—-so....'"

"'Attractive?' Alex filled in. 'Don't you have faith in my husbandly skills?'"

"'Whatever, Alex. Don't be foolish. That's all I'm saying.'"

"Wow! I hadn't noticed anyone looking at me. What would Alex do now? It would involve our bed, I was sure."

"'Okay, Mother. I'm rarely foolish. Thanks for the warning.' He kissed her and came into the room and kissed me."

('Can you put her in her crib? I'm sweaty and need to shower and your presence is urgently required in the shower,' he said in his Commando Sex voice.

Oh, the shower. This was the part of the story I didn't share with the nuns.

He washed me, I washed him. His hands caressed me and then he said, "I can't wait any longer. Hold on to this shampoo shelf. Don't let go." and he was behind me and very insistent.

"You have one hell of a body, Mrs. Berk." "You like it?" I said, shyly but smiling.

"I like it very much."

I came, shuddering and all wet hair flying around and Alex held me so I wouldn't slip and he came too.)

"'We can rest and then go for a swim before dinner,' he said. When he saw me in my bathing suit, he whistled. 'Very nice. Do you love me, Valerie?'"

"I am madly, madly in love with you."

"At dinner, with Jeanette, I said innocently, "Are you going hiking tomorrow, Alex?"

"'No, let's go horseback riding together. You brought your boots, right?' Alex and his mother exchanged glances. So at times he listened to her suggestions."

"'Do you want to go to a movie or the jazz club?' he asked me."

"Let's hear some more jazz for a while." After an hour of jazz, we collected Marisa and said good night to Jeanette. I nursed her and put her to sleep."

"'Let's play Silent Strip Poker,' said Alex. 'Since my Mother's next door.' We played and he kept winning. He pointed to what I should take off. If I hesitated, he smiled and said, 'Do it!'"

"When I was in a bra and blouse only, I was nervous. 'Your mother will remember to tell us something and come in.'"

"'Shut up and deal,' said Alex with his wicked grin. He loved living on the edge. Then I was only in my bra. Sure enough, Jeanette knocked."

"'I forgot to give you the baby's pacifier.'"

"Alex now smiled the I so own you smile but then took pity on me and stepped outside. Only his shirt was off. He came back with the pacifier and we went to bed, giggling and hugging and making love."

"In the morning , after breakfast, we went horseback riding. Alex asked for a docile horse for me. We climbed up a mountain trail, Alex leading."

"As we rode, Alex explained to me the various terms for the layers of rock we passed: sedimentary, "The further down, the older it is.", quartzite, fault lines, structured geography and so on. Alex loved to teach me things and it was usually interesting. We rode up the narrow mountain trail, my horse following his. The sun beat down on me and all sorts of bugs buzzed around the horse and me. Birds called harshly in the distance. I wiped the sweat from my face. In a flash, a large gray snake crawled before me across the road."

"The horse bolted and threw me off, then he turned and trotted off back to the stable. I was thrown into a deep ravine and, panicking, grabbed onto a short tree, three feet below the road. I was clinging frantically, afraid to call or speak. Above me, I could see Alex riding up the trail talking and gesturing at the mountain. "

"When will you notice that the horse and I are not following you? I asked in my mind. I was shaking and my hands were sweating so much that I feared I would lose my grip on the branch. A black bird swooped down near my head. I clung to the tree. Is this it? I thought. Does your life really flash before your eyes? I thought of my baby. Now Jeanette would raise her. She would switch to that pompous pediatrician and feed her formula. My mother would be devastated. After a few years of mourning, Alex would marry again. Maybe he would marry Jocelyn Lerner. This superficial girl would influence my child. Marisa would never remember me. I would be dead at 21, from crashing down the mountain."

"Finally, Alex looked back and quickly turned his horse around and galloped toward me. He must have seen me because he shouted, 'Hold on!' He threw his reins around a post and climbed down the ravine and grabbed my arm. 'I've got you. I've got you.' Now his arm was around my waist and he carried me up to the road and still held me closely."

"I couldn't stop shaking. "

"'Okay, darling, get on the horse and we'll go back to the resort.'"

"No."

"'Valerie, I'll hold you on the horse or I'll lead the horse.'"

"No."

"'Valerie, get on the goddamn horse.'"

"I can't."

"'When you fall off a horse, you get back on.'"

"No."

"A deep sigh from Alex. Together, we led the horse down the mountain path. Soon two horses met us. The manager of the stable looked concerned.

"Timbo came back alone. Are you guys all right?'"

"'The horse got freaked by a snake,' said Alex. ' He threw my wife down a ravine and she's quite shaken.'"

"'Do you want to ride this horse, Ma'am?'"

"No, I want to walk."

"'You remember you signed a paper that you can't sue the resort?'"

"'I'm not going to sue you. I'll sue the snake if I can find him,' said Alex."

"The manager's face showed relief. 'The resort owner wants to treat the three of you to a fine dinner, anything you like. Would you like to get checked out by a doctor, Ma'am?'"

"No, I'm okay. But it was scary."

"'I'm sure it was, Ma'am. How about a few drinks at the bar?'"

"'Would you like a drink, darling? You can have your favorite Grasshopper. Or a Brandy Alexander or MudSlide.'" "I want to go to my baby. I thought I'd never see her again." "Jeanette was back to nasty. 'She got thrown off a horse? Where were your reins?' She went on to remind us that she had grown up in Connecticut and had her own horse, Big Bob. Every day she rode around with her friends who also had their own horses. She'd taken lessons since she was four.

She and no one she knew was ever thrown off a horse."

"I lay down with my baby and Alex and Jeanette went off to drink for free. I slept. After some time, I felt Alex next to me. 'Will making love comfort you or annoy you?' he whispered, his hands stroking my hair."

"Comfort me."

"'Let me bring the baby to my mother and I'll bring this banana also.' Soon Alex was back. 'No more shaking from fear. Shaking from ecstasy now.' he told me."

(He took off my clothes and kissed my forehead, my eyelids, my nose, and my mouth. He went on to kiss my neck and spent a good deal of time licking and kissing my breasts. He held himself over me, supporting himself on his strong arms and I could see the muscles in his arms and chest.

"Please, Alex. Now."

"No, darling. We're taking this slow. I was so excited when I saw you in your white bathing suit and when I saw you clinging to that little tree, I died a thousand deaths. I could never bear to lose you. I'm going to kiss every inch of you." He kissed my mouth again and I could taste the beer he'd just had.

"How many free beers did you have?"

"Just two, so I still have my control and my focus. Now I'm going to taste you down there." He went on for a long time, it seemed, until I squirmed beneath him.

"Please, Alex."

"You want me inside you? Are you totally convinced that I adore you?" And now he made the ecstasy he'd promised come true. Then he held me for a long time.) 'Darling, I have another job interview next week. In a few weeks will be graduation and then I'll pick the best job. Once I have a job I'm going to buy us a house. One with a swimming pool. You'd like that, wouldn't you?'"

THE CALTECH WIVES CLUB DINNER

"Every June the Caltech Wives Club had a dinner, especially honoring the graduating seniors and their wives. It was held the week before the Caltech Ball. I wore a new black dress and Alex looked at me with pursed lips. 'My, you look good. Very sexy, baby.'"

"After dinner, each of the twenty three married seniors got up on the stage with a speech of appreciation and thanks for their wives. They then awarded their wives a PHT diploma.

This meant Putting Hubby Through." "Do you want to hear Alex's speech?" The three nuns and Mrs. O'Dell nodded.

"I decided to keep Alex's hand written paper. I will keep it forever."

"'My wife is the speech maker in our marriage. She was a California Debate Champion. So I am going to read some notes. I wouldn't be up here, happily about to graduate in two weeks, if it was not for Valerie. Valerie was my rock. She encouraged me, listened to my complaints, spurred me on, and was always there for me. She had such faith in me that she sometimes made me believe that I'd make it. She endured three years of no TV for me, three years of quiet from 6 pm to 10 pm. I've had four and a half years of her giving me joy as a wife and best friend. She typed all my papers and sometimes even a little more than that. Some others of you may have experienced a little help in that way. (applause from the audience.) She was an adorable ghost writer!

"While Valerie was doing all this, she maintained a 4.0 average in college, taught 5th grade one morning a week, directed two summer day camps, endured a very high risk pregnancy and, thank God, is now a great mother. Throughout everything, she was her usual positive, smiling self.

"Valerie, please come up here. Valerie, when we were married we promised each other that we would support the other's dreams. Thank you with all my heart for supporting my dream of a diploma from Caltech. I now award you your PHT, Putting Hubby Through, diploma. The words thank you seem inadequate for what you've done for me but thank you."

"We hugged briefly. "Oh, Alex," I whispered in his ear."

"'Wow, Berk,' said Jason, sitting at our table. 'Look at my wife's face. She's mad because my speech for her wasn't that flowery.'"

"'Well, you could have said more than two sentences. Here's a man who notices what his wife does and appreciates her.' said his wife.'"

"'Are you really such a paragon of virtue?' Jason asked me."

"No. My closets are a mess. My desk is a mess."

"'That's Number twenty two on the Twenty five Wifely Traits I require,' said Alex, grinning."

"'What's Number One, ha ha?' asked Jason."

"'You know what Number One is,' said Alex."

"'And? You didn't mention that in your speech.' said Don."

"'I have no complaints in that regard,' said Alex, giving me his I so own you smile."

"'You really could have put some effort into your speech about me. You said only two nice things about me,' said Pat, Don's wife."

"Barbara faced her husband. 'Two nice things! And you managed two words! 'Thanks, honey!' Four years of putting up with you as a student and 'Thanks, honey.' And this guy wrote a whole page!'"

"Embarrassed, we used the baby as an excuse to leave. The four of them were still arguing as we left the room.

THE CALTECH BALL

"Alex was shaving in the bathroom. "

"Don't come into the bedroom for ten minutes," I called. "I want to surprise you." I had not gotten down to my weight of 120 but had reached 122. The zipper of the strapless yellow chiffon prom dress went up without effort. That Saturday morning I'd gone to the hairdresser and my hair looked pretty good, I thought. I came out of the bedroom and Alex's eyes widened"

"'Darling, you look spectacular. And you did it!' He walked to me and hugged me. 'Like the Prom but four years later. I think you're prettier now. And we're graduating from college and have a baby. I would say that we've done well.'"

"Alex looked broad shouldered and handsome in the white dinner jacket he'd worn at our wedding. "You look handsome, too," I told him."

"He went to the refrigerator and took out a wrist corsage of tiny yellow roses. 'Let's dress up like this for our 25th anniversary,'" he said.

"Thank you for the corsage. And don't forget, you promised me three dances."

"'Three dances? I never said that,' he joked. 'How about compromising at one dance?'"

"Three."

"'Okay, three. And you get more than that, Mrs. Berk. I have a little surprise for you.' He reached into his pocket and took out a small, black velvet box. I gasped. He's gotten me a ring with a larger diamond, I thought. I opened the box to find two diamond earrings shaped like leaves. I would never show Alex that I was disappointed with his gift."

"Honey, they're so lovely."

"He smiled and took one out of the box. 'This is your reward for getting into the prom dress. And this earring is a thank you for giving me a lovely child and never ever saying No to me.'"

"I took off my small gold earrings and put on the diamond leaves."

"'Don't lose them. They're the real thing. I've insured them.'"

"Now Alex had told me that the diamonds were real and expensive. Why hadn't he gotten me a larger diamond engagement ring when he'd told me that he would in the future?" I was telling this story to Sisters Agnes, Cordelia and Mary Louise.

"Did you ever tell Alex that you wished for a larger diamond ring?" asked Sister Cordelia.

"No, I guess I never did."

"Why not?"

"I thought it would seem like I was sort of a gold digger. I didn't want to disparage his ring that he'd earned with his own money."

"But if you never told him. You can't expect the other person in a relationship to be a mind reader, you know."

"I know, Sister. You're right."

"So how was the dance?"

"The babysitter arrived and we left. The dance was held in a room that was decorated to look like an under the sea fantasy. We sat at a table with our friends Nathan and Bobby and their dates."

"'You look gorgeous, Valerie,' said Bobby."

"'And she's in her prom dress from Marshall, four years ago,' said Alex."

"'Berk, you're so cheap you didn't buy your wife a new dress,' said Nathan."

"'This is better than new," said Alex.

"I resented that Nathan, always sarcastic, had called Alex cheap."

"Look, he bought me these beautiful earrings."

"'So how does a humble, unemployed student afford such sparklers?' Nathan was always nosy."

"'I cashed in a Bar Mitzvah bond. She's worth it. I think it was the one from you and your family.'"

"'You didn't use all your summer earnings from JPL? That's how I financed this suit.'"

"'I used all the summer earnings to pay for a neonatal specialist. So Valerie hopefully would come home with a baby.'"

"'And is the baby okay?' asked Bobby."

"'Seems to be. Maybe a small hearing problem. She's really cute. And happy all the time. That's because Valerie meets all her needs. Some people call it spoiling but we don't. And now, Mrs. Berk, it's time for your first dance. It's Elvis, 'I want you,
I need you, I love you.'" *Hold me close, hold me tight.*
Let me thrill you with delight.
Let me know where I stand from the start.
I want you, I need you, I love you.
With all my heart

"We danced, had refreshments of all appetizers, and danced again. "Two more?" I said after the third dance."

"'One more,' he said. 'Then we'll celebrate more at home.'"

"At home, the babysitter left and Alex put records in the record player and we danced some more. He held me close and kissed me several times. Then the baby began to make noises from her crib. Alex went to diaper her and the three of us danced together. Marisa laughed and I viewed the reflection of us in the curtainless windows, dancing, man, woman, child, a moment in time, joy in the air."

GRADUATION LUNCHEON

"Everyone came to Alex's Caltech graduation. It was so joyous and such a deep relief to Alex and me. His mother treated everyone to lunch at Musso and Franks. There was wine and Sebastian stood up to offer the first toast."

"'To Alex, the greatest friend a man could have, for this wonderful achievement. And it wasn't easy. So what did Alex do? Had two majors, in physics and electronic engineering to add more challenge to the mix. You did it, Buddy. Raise your glasses for Alex.'"

"Around the table were Alex's mother, my mother, Grandmother Berkowitz, Aunt Henny and Uncle Leon, Aunt Viv and Uncle Ted, Claudia Clemons and our friends, Sebastian and Sebastian's debate partner, Teddy. Other friends were having their own graduation celebrations. Our five month old baby, Marisa, dressed in pink, was being passed from lap to lap."

"Alex stood up. 'First of all let's raise a glass to Sebastian, our friend of many years, and to Teddy, our new friend, who both graduated from USC yesterday. To Sebastian and Teddy! Thank you all for coming. It is a very meaningful and happy day for me! Now, you all see my diploma. I would not have THIS if it were not for HER (putting his hand on my head.)

"Valerie has been my rock. She encouraged me, had faith in me, was never sulky or moody, even through a difficult pregnancy. She typed all my papers, she did without TV so the house would be quiet and she was sunny and cheerful, the person you want to come home to. So please raise your glass to my beautiful wife, Valerie.'"

"I almost cried. In the space of one week my husband Alex, never a public speaker, had delivered two rather involved speeches, both praising me. I was wearing a new lavender linen dress and before we had left for the graduation, Alex had told me I looked sensational."

"After his toast, I whispered "Thank you," very touched. Then I looked across the table at Jeanette. She also was ready to cry but I quickly realized why. He hadn't thanked her. I stood up."

"I know I speak for Alex also as I say thank you to everyone here for your help during the past four years. I especially want to thank Alex's mother and my mother who did so much to help us, cooked so many meals and were so generous and wonderful. All of you fed us, encouraged us and made it possible to arrive at this happy day. To family and friends!"

"Now the plates were being served and due to the clatter, Alex whispered in my ear, 'Had to upstage me, Miss Debater!' I blinked at him, alarmed, but then saw that he was smiling, not upset."

"You forgot to thank your mother."

"'Thank you for all the nagging, all the interference, all the...'

"Alex, stop it! It's your mother."

"'And the major excuse for all she does, SHE MEANS WELL!'"

"'What are you two whispering about?' asked Aunt Henny."

"We're going to share our lunches half and half," I told her. "Now you have to give me half of your New York steak," I said with mischief. He shook his head, laughing, and handed it over.

BRUNCH AT CANTOR'S

"After the graduation ceremony, Alex came running across the grassy field holding his diploma. He kissed Marisa, then took her from my arms, handed her to my mother and grabbed me and twirled me around. 'We did it, darling. We did it!' The joy on his face was precious to see."

"Then Professor Ron Nelson came running up to us, his gown fluttering.

"'Valerie, Alex, congratulations. I am so happy for both of you. And this is your cute little baby. Listen, now that you've graduated, Brenda and I want to take you all out. We want to thank you for your splendid matchmaking. We want to thank you for everything. Would you like to go for dinner? Or a brunch with our two babies along? Chad is fifteen months now.'"

"'That's not necessary, Professor,' said Alex."

"'I insist, Berk. You two took two lonely people and caused us to become a family. And Brenda is expecting again. We felt we couldn't reciprocate while you were a student. Come on, make a choice.'"

"I was so happy that Jeanette was listening intently since she had told me not to interfere with our two teachers, that no good would come of it. It felt great to prove her wrong."

"'Decide,' said Professor Nelson."

"Alex looked at me. 'Brunch would be fun.' I smiled in agreement."

"'How about that famous Jewish deli, Cantor's? I ate there once. This Sunday at 11? We'll get our two babies together,'"

"We'd thanked him and now the four of us and our two babies were sitting around the table looking at the extensive menus. Brenda looked great, her blond hair in a ponytail, smiling and very obviously proud of her handsome little boy. As she fed him, she took out a notebook and wrote down what he'd eaten. 'Would you say that the scrambled eggs were one or two tablespoons?' she asked her husband."

"'Berk, let's take the babies into the restroom and diaper them. We'll let the ladies talk. After all, Brenda told me that your friendship began over breakfast in a diner.' Professor Nelson and Alex left the table, holding their little ones."

"'Ron is right, here we are again, at a restaurant eating brunch, just like two and a half years ago,' said Brenda. 'Except then I was a bitter and frustrated divorcee and now I'm a fulfilled wife and mother. Due to you.'"

"I'm so happy you're fulfilled. Are you still writing screen plays?"

"'Oh, no. The baby takes up so much of my time. And I love it. And Ron is such a sweetie, as happy with our son as I am. When I saw him with his collie, I knew he'd make a great father.'"

"Do you still have Oscar?" I blushed as I recalled Sebastian's steamy jokes about a threesome with that dog.

"'You remembered his name. Yes, Oscar is fine. One thing I want to apologize to you about is when I gave you my opinion that Alex was a rich boy who didn't want to go to college alone so he took you. And you told me off and said that you two were in love and had a happy marriage. I didn't know what 'being in love' was then. And now I do.'"

"I'm glad, Brenda."

"'And just think, you were only eighteen then. And you invited both of us for dinner and made all that Greek food.'"

"It was our pleasure."

"'And remember you told me that you two made love every night? You're not still doing that, are you?' So the newly fulfilled Brenda was just as nosy about sex as she'd been then. But then Alex had been angry with me because I'd confided in my creative writing teacher and he told me to say, 'I have no complaints in that regard.' I was about to say that when the men returned."

"'Did he have a BM?' asked Brenda. 'I'll write it in the book. 12:15,'"

"'Do you write everything in that book?' Alex asked her."

"'Yes, he's on a strict schedule and that way I have a record. And we'd better go so he'll be home for his 1 pm nap.' she told Ron. We all hugged and we thanked them and they left. The waiter came over."

"'How about some slices of Cantor's remarkable cheesecake?' he asked."

"'Yes, two slices. We're celebrating,' said Alex."

"Graduation?" I asked."

"'No, the fact that my wife doesn't write everything down and just flows.'"

"I laughed. Our coffee cups were refilled. 'Do you have two pens in your purse?' Alex asked me. I took them out and also a string of colorful plastic keys which I handed to Marisa. She shook them and threw them on the floor. Alex picked them up. "'Write down that she threw her keys down at 12:30.'"

"Why do you want a pen?"

"Alex handed me a napkin and took one for himself. "'I'm going to write the 5 best things about you and you write about me. ' He picked up Marisa's keys again."

"I wrote, "I love our romantic evenings. I think you're very sexy. I think that you're brilliant. I love your sense of humor. You make me feel secure and confident. You make me so happy that I dance around the house." I handed the napkin to Alex who read it with a smile."

"Then he handed me his napkin."

1. Sex

2. Sweet

3. Great mother

4. Great cook

5. Patient and unflappable

"We both put sex first. So is it true what you say, Alex, that it always boils down to sex?"

"'In a good marriage it does.' He picked up Marisa's keys but put them in his pocket. "'See, Marisa. We're still in love. Write this down. When we get home, she'll nap. And we'll be in each other's arms.'"

JEANETTE'S BIRTHDAY

"That's so charming," said Sister Mary Louise, listening to my story about brunch. "What happened next?"

"The morning after our brunch at Cantor's, I reflected as I tidied up the house. My Alex had so validated me. I was pretty much what he wanted. And he was certainly what I wanted. Why had fortune smiled upon me so graciously? I smiled at the baby, miniature Alex, and she smiled back at me. Enough cleaning! I swept up my Marisa, put on a merry record and danced her all around the apartment. She now knew enough to put her arm up in the dance position, the little darling. She gurgled and smiled and said "Dah!". She understood that this was fun and love. After a lot of whirling, I sat down in the rocker and nursed her.

"And I thought back to Friday afternoon at Alex's graduation lunch. In my mind, I could see the stricken face of Jeanette when Alex thanked me and gave me credit and not her. I was a mother now. A mother's child meant everything to her. Had she rocked Alex and sang to him? She must have. She really was thrilled with him in most things. The only grief she'd had from him was when he brought home a girl 'not of their station'. And then he married this girl who almost never took her seasoned advice. And her really brilliant son was bewitched by this girl and told everyone about her.

"It was the sex. She bewitched him with sex. Jeanette had told me exactly that. But what about her sex with her wonderful Saul? Had she had rapturous nights with Saul, the way I had most nights with Alex? At least in the beginning of their marriage? Poor lonely woman, in that grand bedroom all alone at night. Yes, she was meddlesome and jealous but it probably stemmed from her grief about her widowhood.

"Jeanette had told me that Saul was twenty seven when they married. She had been twenty five. And she told me that she had expected that Alex would be about that same age, not get married so precipitously at age nineteen. She felt cheated. She'd told me that she thought that during his college summer breaks they might have traveled to Europe or Alaska.

"As I nursed my happy little baby, I began to feel sorrow for this miserable woman, sorrow with a tinge of guilt. Had I really tried, really tried hard to win her over? I was polite but never companionable. A few times she'd asked me if I wanted to go shopping with her. I'd gone once, she shopped as a recreational activity. Actually, I hated to shop. I took my checkbook into a store, found what I wanted as quickly as I could and got out of there. So the next few times she'd asked me, I'd said I was too busy. (Of course, Jocelyn Lerner would have shopped all day with her, stopping off at a marvelous café for lunch.) I just wasn't Jeanette's type.

"And then it came to me. I would do something nice for Jeanette. Her birthday was in two weeks. I would make her a surprise birthday lunch, like Sebastian had done for Alex two years ago. I was excited, planning it. One of Jeanette's four close friends was my classmate Alan Berg's mother and I had her phone number. I called her and invited her for a surprise lunch for Jeanette, at my apartment. It would be on a Friday, the day before her actual birthday."

"'Well, aren't you sweet,' said Mrs. Berg. 'You can call me Pearl, dear. And I do have Sylvia and Birdie and Betty's phone numbers.'"

"I called the three ladies and they all said yes. Now I took out cookbooks and planned my special ladies luncheon. Chicken parmigiana? One of the women might be kosher. Rock Cornish game hen? Hard to cut. Little filets? Let's face it, I wanted to wow these women. I took out a butter press that I'd gotten for our wedding but never used and made little butter flowers with half the butter in the refrigerator. These went into the freezer. I would make a fabulous salad, with candied pecans and strawberries and blue cheese. I would cut the cucumbers the fancy way my friend Kay did. I'd prepare an interesting jello mold. In my cookbook I found the perfect dessert, Baked

Alaska. It could be made ahead and stored in the freezer. Then four minutes under the broiler, it could be brought to the table with the merengue brown and the ice cream still solid. That would be impressive. I was still planning when Alex got home."

"'I don't know, darling.'"

"Why not? It will be a token of my esteem in front of her four friends."

"'Well, it's nice of you. I guess my mother would like it.'"

"Alex and I discussed it and decided on poached salmon and asparagus with hollandaise sauce which I made really well. I would make an assortment of little rolls to go with the butter. And I would make large chocolate truffles with brandy and stick candles in them, instead of a birthday cake."

"Does that sound all right to you?" I asked Alex as he drove me to the market."

"'It sounds wonderful. A lot of trouble, though.'"

"I think she'll be thrilled," I said."

"For the next two weeks, I did whatever I could do ahead. I ironed a beautiful yellow tablecloth with matching napkins. A day before the luncheon, I asked Alex to carry our table from the kitchen to the large living room so there'd be lots of room. I'd cleaned and cleaned and bought little soaps and hand towels for the bathroom. I bought little real flowerpots of miniature roses as place holders and they were in my color scheme of pink, yellow and white. Still the day before the luncheon, I set everything up and stood admiring how nice it all looked. A pleasant luncheon in June."

"I sat in my chair nursing and told the baby, 'It looks like a French bistro, very summery.' Marisa agreed. Then I heard the familiar clattering of Jeanette's high heels, coming up the stairs. Oh, no, this would ruin the surprise. But I could tell her that this was a luncheon for my friend Arlene, just back from a semester in London."

"'JUSTWHATDOYOUTHINKYOU'REDOING?'

Jeanette shouted. 'Birdie called me and said you were having a surprise lunch for me. What do you know about doing a luncheon? My friends have certain standards. The last thing I want is all of them up here eating God knows what. If things go wrong I'll never live it down.'"

"I think it will be nice," I said evenly. "Do you want me to tell you the menu?"

"'There's not going to be a luncheon. I've called all four of them and canceled it. No way am I going through any embarrassment. And if you were planning a lunch for me, you know my favorite color is blue, not pink and yellow.' The last said dismissively."

"My perceptive baby looked at my stricken face and started to howl."

"'You should be devoting your attention to this baby, anyway.'"

"I picked up the baby and took her into the bedroom. "Just go," I said to Jeanette. She clattered down the stairs. I cried into my child's golden curls. Then I put her in her stroller and took her for a long walk."

"When Alex came home, I started to tell him. 'I heard,' he said. 'She called me at work. How DARE you do something nice for my mother!' he said, trying to get me to smile. He hugged me and kissed me. 'This looks like a charming little French bistro. I saw them when I was in France. Someday, I want to take you to Paris and the French countryside. Listen to me, darling. She's fucked up. I can't control her. Ninety nine out of a hundred women would be thrilled that a daughter in law would do this for them.'"

"Maybe it wouldn't have turned out well," I said mournfully."

"'No, Nookums, it would have been spectacular. And you've made most of that Baked Alaska which I really want to try. It will be, what did your designer Jacques always say, 'to die for'?

This is not all going to waste after you bought all that food and I carried that heavy table in here.' Alex picked up the phone."

"What are you doing?" I asked him."

"'Hello, Arlene,' he said. 'Valerie's planned a little dinner to welcome you home from London. Tomorrow night? Good. She doesn't need any food. You could bring wine if you want.' He then called Sebastian who said he would bring Kay. 'Bring wine also,' said Alex. Then Bobby called."

"'Can I come? I'm at Sebastian's house.'"

"'Absolutely. I was just going to call you,' said Alex. 'Bring some brandy.' He hugged me and grinned. 'See, your hubby can fix anything. This meal is going to be amazing. Your delicious food, two bottles of wine plus brandy. We'll get a little smashed. Who's a good husband?'" "Alex is a good husband."

ON THE TRAIN TO PHOENIX

"The next week, Alex interviewed with four companies and also had an offer from JPL. Three companies in Arizona wanted to talk to him. 'It isn't the money, Nookums,' he explained to me. 'It's the chance to be creative and have autonomy in my work, possibly invent things. Let's just take a trip to Phoenix and Tucson, scope things out.'"

"So now, at 6 pm, we were on the train in a green plush roomette. Alex wanted to sleep on the train because he'd never done that. 'Whenever I have a new experience, I like to have you with me,' he'd said, enchanting me with that thought. 'Do you think the grandmothers could take care of Marisa for two days?' he'd asked."

"So I tried to make that happen and five women, in shifts, would care for our baby. My Aunt Anna was visiting my mother for a few months so she and my mother would stay overnight and then Jeanette and Aunt Henny and Ida Mae, the cleaning lady, would do a shift. I had stored many bottles of breastmilk in the freezer and the baby was eating other foods also. So we would have a brief but purposeful honeymoon."

"We ate dinner in the formal dining room. 'We'll get into Phoenix around 6 am and check into a motel. Then I'll leave for the first interview at 8 and at 9 I've arranged for a real estate lady to pick you up and show you three or four homes. We can afford a much larger home in Phoenix than in L.A. So if we decide to move to Arizona, we'll have a house. The second day we'll drive down to Tucson, interview with a firm there.'"

"I think that's great, Alex, but I don't understand how we can afford a house at all. Don't we have to have a down payment?"

"'We have a down payment.'"

"But how? We haven't saved."

"'Well, Nookums, this is all my Bar Mitzvah money. When I had my Bar Mitzvah my father was building the Brentwood houses and the little shopping center. So a lot of contractors and builders came to my Bar Mitzvah and people from Temple Israel, some of them producers and directors and some other affluent people. And many of them gave me checks. I had to write a lot of thank you notes. So I bought my small telescope and my parents bought the large one for me. Then I put some money aside in a bank account so I could buy a car when I turned sixteen. Of course, I didn't know that my father would die when I was fifteen and I would get his car.'"

"'So Claudia Clemons told me that she would be happy to invest the rest of the money for me, in safe stocks. So that was eight years ago and the money doubled. We have $9000 for a down payment and I told the real estate lady not to go over a certain amount in the houses she'll show you. But all the houses will have pools, just as I promised you.'"

"I know how amazing you are, Alex, because Mike Stein once told me that his Bar Mitzvah was two months before yours and by the time he was seventeen, he'd spent all the money."

"'On this and that?'"

"I guess. But MY husband saved his money. MY husband is careful with money." Alex laughed, pleased."

(Making love in the little roomette with the train clicking and swerving was exciting. 'An Arizona fuck,' said Alex. 'Part Phoenix sophistication, part Navajo artistry and part prickly cactus.')

"He interviewed while I looked at houses. The real estate lady, Kelli, drove me to the first house which was modern and beautiful. I loved it and at the end of our walk through, I checked on the price. It was $10,000 more than what Alex had stipulated."

"That's not the price my husband set."

"'Usually what a husband says is more of a suggestion,' said Kelli. 'Your husband wants you to be happy, doesn't he? If you're all excited about it, most husbands will stretch their stated limits.'"

"Not my husband. He told me what to spend and he told you what we can spend. I don't manipulate him. What about the three other houses? If they're over the limit, then the tour is over."

"'They're in the price set that your husband told me. I felt it was important for you to see what only $10,000 more could get for you. I'm sure you and your baby would be a lot happier in this more modern house.'"

"Let's see what else you can show me." Kelli showed me a three bedroom house and two four bedroom houses. All, like the first, had swimming pools and all three were the correct price. I eliminated the three bedroom and focused on the other two. One was about five years old and was in a modern subdivision. Vegetation seemed scanty but there were many children around, riding bikes and trikes down the sidewalk. Young women held strollers as they chatted with one another. It was located on the outskirts of the city. The other house was thirty years old, located in a grapefruit grove in the center of the city. There were two large eucalyptus trees, in the front and back of the house. The owners had added a large family room onto the back of the house, with a brick fireplace. I could make it charming, I thought."

"This will be it if my husband decides to move here," I told Kelli."

"The second day we drove to Tucson. He explained to me the pros and cons of each engineering company and I told him that I would be happy whichever one he chose. "

THE REAL WORLD

"For four years we'd been preparing for this, when all our hard work and sacrifices would pay off and we'd be living in the wondrous Real World. We were flying home from Arizona and would be home and with our baby by 8 pm."

"'So we agree that we didn't like Tucson that much so that job is out,' said Alex."

"I agree so that leaves the three Phoenix offers. But what if we don't like Phoenix?"

"'All the contracts are for two years. If we don't like it, then we'll move back to L.A. Now Knight Engineering is too small, I think, even though the money is good. So the choice is between Motorola and Kavanaugh Engineering. Kavanaugh is offering $200 more each month. But Motorola has a large amount of government contracts so there's more opportunity for creativity. I could invent things. What do you think?'"

"Alex, I just want you to be happy and fulfilled. Accept the job where you'll be happiest all day."

"'Okay, it's Motorola then. And I'll have a staff of two junior engineers working for me and a secretary. Motorola will move all our furniture. They send movers to pack it all up. And out of the four houses the realtor showed you, you narrowed the choice to two?'"

"Yes, they both have four bedrooms and a swimming pool. One is in a neighborhood called Maryvale. It's a tract house, five years old and nice but the trees are kind of small and it's not very near shopping. The other house is a ranch house in a grapefruit grove so there are lots of trees. The house is about thirty years old. And a block away there's a small market and a drugstore and a hardware store. And the realtor said it's in central Phoenix."

"'So where would you be happiest?'"

"I think the house in the grapefruit grove, on Palos Verde Drive. But after two years, we'll discuss moving back to Los Angeles?"

"'Absolutely.'"

"Now came the bustle of moving, a goodbye party hosted by Sebastian, a family dinner at Grandmother Berkowitz's house, and dinner with my family at Hung Far Chin's."

"'I'll drive the car on Monday and on Wednesday you and the baby will fly in.'"

"No, we want to drive with you."

"'Nookums, it's July and it's an eight hour drive through the desert. If the car breaks down or something, it would be too hard for you and the baby. Or the air conditioning could break. I'll let the movers in and I'll buy us a washing machine and a stove. I just have to go to Motorola to sign a lot of papers.'"

"I want to drive with you."

"'No, Valerie. Just follow my plan.'"

"With a flurry of activity I packed for the baby and myself and then four movers came and packed everything in our apartment in blue paper. My Uncle Ted drove us to the airport for the one hour flight to Phoenix. My mother was sad but we agreed to visit one another often."

"I looked out the window as the plane descended into the green world that was to be my home for two years. The baby had been alert and happy on the flight. Soon I was walking down the steps of the plane, holding Marisa and gasping as the dry heat enveloped me. It was like walking into an oven, though it was only 10 am."

"And there, in a light blue polo shirt and shorts, was Alex, waiting for us behind a gate. He spread his arms out to welcome us and I ran into them. The comfort of each other's arms. Two whole days of separation and we kissed and kissed. Soon Alex whisked me to an air conditioned restaurant and we ate brunch and talked. Now we were going to begin life in the REAL WORLD, what we had often promised each other would be the reward for diligent studying. We walked in the air conditioned mall, actually skipping with our baby, so happy were we. "

"Next we went to our house. It had been empty when I'd seen it before. Now Alex had had the movers place all our living room furniture into the back family room and our bedroom furniture in our room. A small bedroom held both our desks and our stereo. Today we'd go out and buy new furniture for Marisa since I'd given back the Caltech baby things. Later I would rearrange our bedroom. I would decorate Marisa's room in a circus theme and paint a jolly clown on her wall. I wanted to swim in our pool but Alex said that the water was too hot in the summer days. It will cool down around 6 pm."

"'This is the very latest model of washing machine,' said Alex. "It has a dryer as part of it so you put in the dirty clothes and an hour and fifteen minutes later when you take them out, they're dry. I thought this would be much easier for you. And this is a convection oven which the salesman told me is the best.'"

"I walked around the large house, marveling that this belonged to us. I had never lived in a large home, besides my few weeks as a nanny in Beverly Hills. Our whole apartment as I'd grown up would have fit into this family room. And there were thirteen grapefruit trees, a lovely patio and backyard and a turquoise blue swimming pool. I am now living in a palace, I thought. "Where are the polo ponies?" I asked."

"Alex thought it was great also. 'Behind the stables and the tennis courts.' he joked."

"You know what we'll do," I said, looking at the completely empty living room. "We'll save some money every paycheck and gradually buy one piece of furniture at a time."

"'Here is my final surprise,' said Alex. 'This is for the living room, the last of the House Money.' And he handed me a check for $1000. 'I think you can buy some nice things with this.'"

"Oh, my gosh. Alex, this is wonderful. Let's go and look."

"'I'm thrilled to see you this happy,' he said. He drove me to a nice, large furniture store. He had no interest in picking out furniture, he said. He would take the baby home and let her nap, unpack some of his records and pick me up in two hours."

"I bought a nice sectional couch and end tables and lamps. I bought us a new bed and drapes for the living room. It would look lovely with our pictures by Van Gogh, Monet, Bruegel and Mary Cassatt. I bought teal blue and yellow throw pillows for the couch."

"Every evening, we had fun in our pool, with and without the baby. When the baby was sleeping in her crib, I got out of the pool every ten minutes to check on her. So Alex invented a device which amplified the noise in the baby's room and blasted it out to the pool. If we were swimming and she woke up, we could clearly hear her. We swam laps and splashed each other and made love in the pool. The REAL WORLD was as magnificent as we'd thought it would be."

THE REAL WORLD, REALLY

"Well, not quite so magnificent. For three days I unpacked, arranged furniture and knick knacks and then rearranged them. I took out the decorating notebook that I'd assembled over three years. It had charming ideal rooms and color schemes in it. I marveled that I was a homeowner at age twenty one."

"The washing machine which Alex had so proudly bought for us to make life easier for me was annoying. It washed and dried the clothes in one machine. What it did was make the laundry process much longer because I couldn't wash one load while drying another. But I didn't say anything because he'd wanted the best for me. Same with the convection oven. I burned several dinners because it was hard to figure out the new way to time the meals."

"Then I realized that after Alex ate breakfast and left for work in Scottsdale, I had only spoken to a cashier until Alex came home. Marisa was seven months old, cute but no conversationalist."

"I went next door to our elderly neighbor, Mrs. Swift, to thank her for the cookies she'd sent over to welcome us. She invited Marisa and me in for tea."

"'I noticed your husband nailing some little thing by your front door. And our neighbor Susie O'Neill says it's some kind of Jewish religious thing. Are you a Jew? Good,' she continued, 'because I've never met a Jew before. Is that thing to ward off evil? And however do you celebrate Christmas?'"

"The neighbors had been scoping us out already! But I was on a mission."

"Mrs. Swift, are there any young families with children around the neighborhood? I've been to the mini market and I haven't seen anyone as I walk there."

"'Well, we all were young when we moved here. The development was brand new thirty three years ago. All our kids are grown up and gone now. There is a family at the end of the block in the light blue house. She has two little kids but she works and the kids go to daycare.'" Daycare said with distaste."

"Early the next morning as soon as Alex left, I walked to the neighbor's blue house. And there the young mother was, putting her two children in her car. I introduced myself and said I was new to Phoenix and she put her coffee cup on the roof of her car to shake hands with me."

"I'd love to invite you over for coffee and to swim. We have a large shallow end," I said."

"'Honestly, Valerie, I'd love to but I'm very overwhelmed right now with my kids and my job and a sick father. And I just can't be late to work another time,' she said with panic in her voice. We said goodbye and she quickly drove off with her coffee cup still on the roof of her car, tottering and finally shattering, like my hopes. Marisa and I went to visit the goats at the neighboring goat farm and then to the drug store. I bought myself a magazine for solace."

"When the baby napped, I called the four synagogues that were listed in the Yellow Pages. I asked if any of them had an opening for a religious school teacher. The first three synagogues had no available jobs but invited me to come to services with my husband. The fourth synagogue said that they were small but they did have an opening for an 8th grade teacher who could teach Holocaust. I gave them my former director, Abe Raffner's number for a reference. Later that afternoon the Rabbi called me back and offered me the job. The Rabbi and his wife would drive me. School started in four weeks. I now had a part time job but would have to wait four weeks."

"I spoke to my mother every day and finally told her how lonely I felt."

"'Well, what were you thinking when you left your family and your childhood friends and moved to a city where you knew no one?' My mother was now voicing her disappointment. It was probably an awful thing that Alex and I had done. We were only children and we'd moved away from widowed mothers and taken their only grandchild, too. My mother had often said she'd like to live next door to me."

"'I'm sure you'll make some young friends soon,' said my mom."

"I hung up, realizing that I wasn't going to school, so stimulating, after being a student for sixteen of my twenty one years. And I wasn't going to work. Being alone in a house all day without homework or phone calls from friends was something I'd never experienced. And the other problem, I understood, was that I could not drive and had no car. I'd soon found out that the bus service in Phoenix was not like L.A. Buses ran only every hour and only north and south. If the destination was east or west, too bad."

"Do you think I could learn to drive?" I asked Alex. "And we could get another car?"

"'I'm not sure that you have the coordination to drive a car,' he said. 'Remember we tried with the jeep?'"

"But that was a stick shift. I think I could drive an automatic."

"'Well, we don't have the money for an automatic right now. I thought you wanted living room furniture so the last of the money went for that.'"

"When Jeanette called, I admitted my distress to her. She, of course, echoed my mother. 'What do you expect? You moved away from everyone you knew, excepting Alex. But I'll tell you what to do. You'll have to become a joiner. Join the Sisterhood of that small synagogue. Most of my friends I made at our Sisterhood. Join a fundraising committee, help them set out the Oneg Shabbat food. But don't go whining to Alex about all this. He needs to focus on his new job.'"

"The next morning.at the market, I spotted a young woman wheeling a baby stroller. She left while I was still in the checkout line. As soon as I paid for my food, I followed this woman, now a block ahead of me. She looked behind her and walked faster. Did she think I'd hurt her with my baby in the stroller?"

"I caught up with her and said, "I'm new in town and thought maybe we could get together and our little ones could play."

"'We don't play,' she said and quickly slipped into her house, locking her door with a loud click. I shook my head to clear my dismay. I'd actually been stalking someone. I turned and walked home."

"Later, when the baby was napping, I called Alex at work. I started to cry. "I'm so lonely," I told him. "No one here wants to be friends." Silence greeted me."

"Finally, 'Well, Valerie, a lot of people in Phoenix take vacations in August. Once your new job begins you'll make some new friends. I'm certain of it. Why don't I pick you up after work and we'll go to that pizza place that has a band.'" "What a twit I had been. I'd cried to my husband who was miles away, during his work day. I'd disregarded Jeanette's advice."

"That sounds great, Alex. We'll be ready."

"And things were less than magnificent for Alex at work also. He soon discovered that the Motorola plant had no windows, with the exception of the executive offices. He hated working under fluorescent lighting all day and shortened his lunch hour to a half hour so he could come home sooner. During the half hour lunch break he walked around the block, even in the broiling sun. And his two technicians had not been well trained and were holding up his project with their mistakes. "

(We put the baby to sleep and then consoled each other in the way we knew best, a long session of making love.)

"Alex had his own grief and I would not complain to him again. Certainly I could solve this loneliness by myself. The next morning I decided to cross the major street and look for a young mother in that neighborhood. I realized that I'd made a big mistake. When I'd looked at the newer subdivision house there had been children riding tricycles on the sidewalk, a woman with two children in a double stroller and a woman holding a baby, chatting with a woman cutting her hedge. I'd assumed that all neighborhoods had young families. Unwittingly I'd chosen an older neighborhood."

"One block down, I saw what I'd been searching for. Two preschool children were splashing in a little wading pool under the watchful eye of a young woman holding a baby younger than mine. I introduced myself and she smiled at me very hesitantly."

"'I'm Abigail,' she said. Even though it was already quite warm at 10 am, she was wearing a long skirt and a long sleeved blouse. She was a redhead with pale freckled skin. Maybe she had to be careful about sunburn. I extended my invitation. Coffee? Swim in my pool?"

"'I don't know,' she answered me. 'I have an awful lot of housework to do. This baby wants to nurse all the time and I'm getting so far behind with the house. And my husband wants the house just so. He just wants me to be friends with women from our church.' Abigail had a sweet shy smile. She asked me how old I was and said that she also was twenty one. Her children were two and four so she'd had her first child at seventeen. 'My husband might not approve of our being friends.'"

"Seeing my disappointment, she said, 'I'll tell you what. Tomorrow is Saturday and my husband is home. And you look nice and live on the next block and all. Why don't you come by in the morning and meet him? I think he'll like you.'"

"WEIRD! But I agreed to walk over and meet him the next morning."

Part Three

CHRISTIAN DOMESTIC DISCIPLINE

ABIGAIL AND OTIS

"On Saturday morning when the baby went down for her nap, and Alex was installing a garbage disposal, I went to visit Abigail and her husband."

"'Hi, I'm Otis,' said this tall, and somewhat good looking guy. He looked very Scandinavian or Germanic with straight sandy hair and a small pinched mouth. He immediately handed me a coke and took a beer from his refrigerator for himself. 'Have a seat, Valerie.' He pointed to a kitchen chair. Oh, I was to be interviewed. 'Abigail is vacuuming,' he said and I could hear the whine of the vacuum cleaner in another room. 'Abigail said she asked you and you said you're Jewish.'"

"Yes."

"'And do you believe that every word in the Old Testament is true and to be truly observed?'"

"Well, I teach the Bible. I'm a religious school teacher."

"Now I received a stiff smile from him. 'That's good,' he said. 'We're Christian but I don't mind if you're Jewish. I just want Abigail to associate with God fearing women, women who follow the ways of the Lord. I don't want her spending time with any of these modern women who think they're in charge of everything.'"

"Wow! "Well, I always consult my husband," I said."

"'Is your husband religious? Does he know the Bible?'"

"My husband studied the Bible for years and he reads Hebrew also. He can read all the prayers."

"Now Otis was visibly impressed. 'Does he believe in the ways of the Patriarchs? I'll bet he knows a lot about the Old Testament and I'm very interested in that.'"

"I believe he does."

"'Our church has great respect for the Old Testament. We believe in Christian Domestic Discipline. Have you heard of that?'"

"No, I haven't." (Weird and getting weirder.)

'"Like in the days of the Patriarchs, we believe in the natural order of the family. The husband is the head of the household and he is to be respected and obeyed. Our wives feel protected and safe performing their womanly roles.' He looked at me with piercing eyes. 'Does your husband ever spank you?'"

"I blushed deeply. "My husband and I talk and work things out. We're very much in love." Could I derail him with that?"

"'See, Valerie, we believe that in a marriage, there can only be one leader. That way, the marriage isn't going in all different directions. And the leader, the husband, has to be loving and compassionate. We believe in love, too. But the woman has to know her place and if she transgresses, she requires discipline.'"

"I stared at him, fascinated."

"'Now this is from Ephesians, 5th Chapter, Verse 22. 'Wives, submit yourselves unto your own husbands, as unto the Lord. For the husband is the head of the wife even as Christ is the head of the Church.' That's our firm belief in our church. But I'd love to talk to your husband, show him some of our writings. How about this? Tomorrow we go to church in the morning. How about you both come over for Sunday dinner, at 4 o'clock? We can get to know one another. Really, I'd love to hear the Jewish viewpoint. Someone told me that some Jewish wives take charge of the whole marriage, instead of their husbands taking charge.'"

"I'm sure we'd both like to hear more about Christian Domestic Discipline. Thank you for the invitation. I'll bring dessert."

"Abigail came into the room with her crying baby. 'She needs to nurse. Do you think Valerie could come into the bedroom and talk to me while the baby nurses?'"

"'All right. Only nurse her for a half hour though, she's got to learn, she can't nurse all day.'"

"We settled into their bedroom. a rather austere room done in brown and tan with some touches of yellow. Abigail leaned against pillows on the bed and I sat on a chair. I tried for a safe subject. "So how did you and Otis meet?"

"'Well, I'm the oldest of six children. And I had to do a lot of the childcare in my family. If my mother wasn't feeling well, which was often, I had to stay home from school and watch the little ones. So sometimes I'd be out of school for three days or a week so my grades weren't that good. And my mom would say, 'Stop that studying and come here and do the dishes.' (My Mom would say, "Valerie, I'll do the dishes so you can study.")

"'And my Dad told my younger sister and brother to watch me at school and make sure I wasn't talking to a boy. Sometimes

I was just saying like how was your weekend? And my crummy sister would tell my Dad. And sometimes she just made it up and there was no boy. Becky was always out to get me in trouble. So one morning she ran into my parents' bedroom, she and I shared a double bed in our room, and she said, 'Abigail's rocking the bed again and doing it.' And my mom came roaring in and caught me—-you know. I knew I shouldn't but——So this was the second time they'd caught me doing it. The first time my father had hit me with his belt and said it was against God's wishes and dirty."'

"'This time my father took his cigarette lighter from his pocket and held my arm and burned the tips of my fingers on my right hand. I was screaming and all the younger children ran in and my Dad told them, 'Don't ever defile yourself with your hands like she did. This is the consequence.'"

"'Even my Mom got a little shocked and said, 'Ed, stop it. Stop it.' and she put my hand in a bucket of ice water. She wrapped my hand in a large white bandage and my Dad got close to my face and said, 'Now try to stick your hand in there, wicked girl.' In the morning my Mom said, 'If they ask you at school, say you touched a hot pan by accident.'"

"'My typing teacher, she was a nice lady, asked me what happened to my hand because for sure I couldn't type so I told her about the hot pan. But right away she sent me to the nurse. And the nurse, she started asking me all these questions and I stuck to the pan story. Then when I got home, I found out the nurse had called.

'That's it,' said my father. 'Nosy bitch. Abigail is sixteen, get her a work permit.'"

"'So they made me quit school and my father got me a job with his friend in his 99 cents store. The man said he couldn't pay me until the bandages came off because I couldn't fully help. After my hand healed, my Dad collected my wages every two weeks, for room and board, and gave me $7 for me"'

"'And then Otis came into the store and I helped him find things. And I was pretty then, not like now.'"

"You're kidding. You're very pretty now."

"'No, back then I was really thin and I had time to fuss with my hair, not stick it in a ponytail. Anyway, Otis kept coming in and he was tall and had a really good job. He was twenty four. He's twenty nine now. He's the Finance Manager for his car company,' she said very proudly. 'All day long he does all that math and deals with difficult people. That's why he has to have peace when he comes home and a clean house.'"

"So you and Otis dated?"

"'Well, he took me to a social at his church. He asked my Dad first and my Dad said yes. And the church ladies were so nice to me. It's the same church we go to now. They told me that Otis was a really fine person, very responsible. And they explained about Christian Domestic Discipline which is just a traditional marriage with the man doing what he's supposed to and the woman doing what she's supposed to. And then, since the ladies had explained it to me, Otis asked me if I thought I could live that life, which also meant never working outside the home. And I didn't have to think long before I said Yes. So he talked to my father who said we'd have to wait five weeks until I was seventeen. And my father said that the other problem was that the family would lose my wages which helped them make ends meet.'"

"'So Otis said, 'I'll come up with something.' And he gave my family a second hand station wagon, just two years old, from the lot where he works. And then my father said okay.'"

"Otis bought her with a used station wagon, I thought."

"'Then we had a real nice wedding at our church. The pastor's wife had a closet full of wedding dresses that other girls had donated and we picked one and fixed it up for me and all the ladies and my mom made food. And how did you and your husband meet, Valerie?'"

"We were high school sweethearts." My heart sang as I remembered our romantic courtship and our magical Prom and two exceptional weddings. And my loving, encouraging husband. This poor girl."

"'A half hour is up, Abigail,' yelled Otis."

"Abigail disengaged from the baby who started to protest. We went back to the living room."

"'It was awfully nice talking to you,' whispered Abigail."

"Thanks for inviting us for tomorrow. See you then."

THE DISCIPLINE PART

"'No way am I going over there,' said Alex. 'They sound like sickos.'"

"Please, Alex. I've never heard about stuff like this. It's like extra research from my Marriage and the Family class. It's like fieldwork in anthropology."

"'Sociological studies, huh?'"

"Please, Alex. We'll only stay an hour and a half, And she seems so nice. And she lives only one block away."

"'All right. I'm doing it for you since you're lonely.'"

"The reluctant Alex and I walked over with the baby in her stroller. I wore a floaty skirt instead of shorts. 'In honor of CDD?' asked Alex. We brought chocolate chip cookies that I'd made and a bag of grapefruit from our trees. Otis and Abigail welcomed us and seated us at their family room table. Otis asked if we would all hold hands, including their two small children, and he gave a short thanks for the food and a welcome 'to our new neighbors.'"

"'Abigail!' he said sharply.' Where's the salt and pepper?'"

"She sprang up and brought them from the kitchen. Throughout the meal, which was good, he gave Abigail orders. 'Can't you see we need more mashed potatoes?' and to the silent children, 'Use your fork!' 'Don't spill that milk!'

'No talking during dinner!'

There was an awkward silence and Alex decided to break it. 'Abigail, this is the best chicken fried steak I've ever eaten. They serve it for lunch at Motorola but not with this light and tasty gravy.'"

"She flushed and smiled with the compliment. Otis said nothing so Alex went on. 'Darling, you have to get this recipe.'

Next he praised her blueberry pie which really was good."

"'She uses suet in her crust,' said Otis. 'So you've just eaten some pig fat. As a Jew, does that bother you?'"

"'Doesn't bother me,' said Alex."

"Then Otis said, 'Well, Alex, why don't you and me grab some beer and go into my den? We can talk while the ladies clean up.'"

"'Yes, I'd love to hear about your church,' said Alex, giving me his wickedest grin with raised eyebrows which meant, 'Go do your women's work. I get to hear about CDD and you don't.'"

"We cleaned up. I nursed Marisa and put her down for a nap in her stroller. Abigail busily wrote out the recipe I would never make. But I wanted to know."

"Does Otis actually spank you like he said?"

"'Well, he has to. It's his responsibility. When I don't do what I'm supposed to.'"

"Does he give you a smack?"

"'Always over his knees. And much more than a smack. Sometimes it lasts a long time. He doesn't want me to cry but sometimes I can't help it. And he says, 'If you wake up the children, I'm going to explain to them what a bad girl you are.' So I put my hand over my mouth and pray that it will be over soon.'"

"What do you do that makes him so mad?"

"'Usually it's what I don't do……the house, the laundry. I can never seem to catch up. And Otis works so hard and buys all the food and pays the house payment and all. The least I can do is take care of my home.'"

"But you have three very young children. And you're nursing a new baby."

"She gave me a panicked look. I was offering a different side of things. Then her eyes and mouth became resolute. This new woman was not going to crumble her carefully built façade. There was too much comfort in believing that she was wrong and Otis was right, that she was weak and he was strong.

"'God demands this of women, that she cares for her house hold.'"

"But he's hitting you maybe once a week....."

"Her eyes flew open in surprise. 'Once a week? It's every night.'"

"Every night?"

"'It's a program that they have at the church. Not every family follows it but a lot of families do. It's called Maintenance Spanking. It's not only to punish you for what you did or didn't do but to remind you to be good the next day. Sometimes he's so tired he doesn't want to do it. But he has to because he's the head of the household. It's his job to train me.'"

"Does he just use his hand?"

"'Sometimes the hairbrush or a paddle. Once he was really mad and he used his belt.'"

"Oh my God, I thought."

"'You know what hurts the most?'"

"No,"

"'The hairbrush.'"

"I should change the subject. "Abigail, would you like to bring the kids to swim tomorrow?"

"'No thanks. Otis was very clear on this. No going nowhere until I get control of the house. Only with him to the market on Saturday and to church on Wednesday and Sunday. And he's put a lock on the TV so I don't watch it during the day and waste all my time.'"

"We don't have a TV. Alex says there's too much silliness on it. We want Marisa to love books, not cartoons."

"'Does he make all the rules, too?'"

"Alex? His rules? Hug him hello. Go to bed together. No name calling. I heard his voice in my mind. 'Vos vilst du, Vibila?' He really meant,' What can I do to make you happy?'(I had a mental picture of him hovering over me in bed, his mouth open a little, his eyes boring into me, wanting me and ready to bring joy to my body as I brought joy to his.)

"He does make rules," I said and she gave me a satisfied nod. All husbands made rules."

"'Does he spank you?'"

"No." I thought of when we had rough sex.

"'Never?"

"Never."

"'How does he discipline you then?'"

"We talk. He suggests things." I blushed, thinking of the night before, a rather wild night in the pool."

"And now Alex appeared. 'Valerie,' he said firmly. I knew that tone meant he'd had enough and so I gathered up the baby and her things."

"We gave profuse goodbyes and the two men shook hands. We walked down the street holding hands and pushing the stroller."

"What did you do in the den?"

"'Oh my gosh. He showed me all this scripture that said God demanded this crap. And he had other books, too like The Man Must Rule, The Submissive Wife, and Punishments That Are Effective In A Family. He treats her like she's a child.'"

"But why?"

"'He probably has low self esteem and he gets off by bossing her around. And he's probably also sadistic. He enjoys inflicting pain. Maybe that's the reason he joined that church.'"

"Ours, what we do, is very different, right, Alex?"

"'What we do sometimes is sexual spanking. It's very different. You have to be in the mood for it and say yes. So it's consensual, exciting to both of us, doesn't hurt you and you can always say Stop. Can she say Stop?'"

"No, I'm sure she can't. He doesn't let her cry out, she said."

"'What we do is kiss, hug, spank. I ask you if you feel like rough or gentle and it's always up to you. I'm not out to dominate you and the Bible never told me to. I'm trying to make you happy and to excite you.'"

"You do excite me. But a lot of times when I pass by, you smack my tush."

"'Well, it's a very appealing tush. Do you like it?'"

"You know I like it." We were home and put the baby in her crib. "So how would you classify what they do?"

"'I'd classify it as abuse. He's trying to dress it up by making it Holy Abuse.'"

"I feel like taking a shower to wash away the CDD."

"'Let's go swimming, Nookums. The water will be cool now. And you're the one that made me spend Sunday afternoon with those meshugganah.'"

"We swam and I checked the baby. "Still sound asleep.""

"'We could also take a nap,' Alex suggested."

"Good idea."

"He removed my bathing suit and held my shoulders. 'Gentle or rough?'"

"You're the head of the house. You decide."

"He smiled. 'I decide gentle. I'm sorry it didn't work out for you to have a neighborhood friend.'"

"Well, she may still be."

"'No. That would disturb his balance of power.'"

"You know, she said he doesn't just use his hand to hit her. He uses a hairbrush."

"'My Lord.'"

"And she can't leave the house. Just to go to church twice a week or buy food with him. He keeps the checkbook."

"'Well, he's not letting her near you. You're too emancipated. The hairbrush ,hmmmm?' looking at mine."

"Don't even joke about that."

"'Will you be good?'"

"I'm always good."

"'You are, in lots of ways. And you know that I cherish you, don't you, Valerie? The cherishing is going to start RIGHT NOW.'"

"The next morning my mother called me.' Aunt Anna and I will be there tomorrow, sweetheart.'"

"What, Mom?"

"'Aunt Anna and I will arrive around dinner time. Didn't Alex tell you? Oh, I think he wanted it to be a surprise. He bought us tickets and they're at the Southwestern counter. See you soon.'"

"I called Alex."

"'They'll be here until Sunday afternoon, darling. You'll all have a nice time. And then it will be only one lonely week and your school will start. I think you'll meet some nice people then.'"

"I'm overwhelmed by you, Alex. You...you....."

"'I care about your feelings, darling. I don't like to see you miserable. Have to go to a meeting now. Love you.'"

"I was so glad that I had a day to make everything special for the company. I cooked some meals for the freezer and some baked goods also. But where had Alex gotten the money for their tickets? He said there was no money for a car. And he deposited his entire check in the bank every week. Oh well. I wouldn't worry about it. I sang as I prepared for my relatives and once again danced around the house with my baby. That evening Alex came home to Miss Cheerful."

"After dinner that Monday, I asked Alex if he would stay in the kitchen and talk to me while I baked goodies for my relatives."

"I can't stop thinking about Abigail. Did Otis tell you he makes her write out 'lines', like 'I will keep my house clean,' ten times? So she's pressed for time and she has to sit down and write these sentences like some child from the 18th century."

"'The whole thing is sick, darling.'"

"But Alex, do you think we should call someone, like a hotline, to report that Abigail is being abused? She's getting hit every night."

"'Darling, we can't do anything. There's nothing we can do. I didn't like it either. When he ordered her around, so crudely, I just cringed inside. But let me ask you, did she ever work before she got married?'"

"She worked in a 99 cent store."

"'And how about her family?'"

"They've moved to Texas and she hasn't seen them in years. They've never seen her children."

"'But did abuse go on when she was growing up?'"

"She intimated that it did. Certainly her father was abusive if he burned her fingers."

"'Because she masturbated?'"

"Yes, I told you."

"'Okay, here's how I see it. One, she has no reliable way to support herself, let alone three kids. Two, she witnessed and experienced abuse as a child and teen. Three, her only support group is this Christian Domestic Discipline church which gives her the message that punishing her is normal. So really, I think she's stuck. You can't help her.'"

"Alex sliced the freshly baked cranberry walnut bread, buttered his slice and ate it. 'Mmmm, I love this bread.'"

"I know. But I feel so sad for Abigail and worse because I know you're right. Do you think she'll wake up sometime in the future?"

"'I doubt it.'"

"You know, I definitely don't appreciate you enough. My childhood as a loved child and then with a great high school situation that made me feel competent, those things were just good fortune. And then the good fortune of you, wonderful, amazing you. I don't appreciate you enough."

"'No, you don't,' Alex said solemnly, his eyes twinkling. 'What can you do to appreciate me more?'"

"I'm going to take this honey cake out of the oven and then I'm sure I'll think of something. And," I said in the Commando Sex voice, "you will like it."

"I greeted my Mother and Aunt joyously. They loved playing with the baby. I decided to have a little luncheon and invited my neighbor, Mrs. Swift. I also called Abigail and invited her, fairly certain that she wouldn't be allowed to come."

"'Otis says I'm not going nowhere until I get this house in order. He's very rightfully provoked by it.'"

"Okay. Poor lady. I thought of him coming home, making his inspection and then using the hairbrush on her. But there was nothing I could do."

"Alex took us out to two restaurants and to a Navajo pow wow. On Saturday, he took us all to Nogales and the relatives were thrilled to be in Mexico. He bought all of us sombreros."

"'Alex, a wonderful week. Thank you for this marvelous gift,' said my Mother."

"Alex put his hand on my head. 'Thank you for this marvelous gift. The best wife.'"

"On Sunday morning we all put on our sombreros and Alex took us to the desert to shoot cans and targets. Neither my Mother nor my Aunt had ever held a pistol or a rifle. Alex took pictures of them which both later loved and showed to everyone. We drove them to the airport on Sunday night."

"'Will you be all right for one week, darling?' asked Alex."

"Oh yes. I bought five yards of that Egyptian cotton in Nogales and I'm going to sew two desert shirts for you." We could no longer find the shirts that Alex loved for hiking."

"'You'll make me cotton shirts? Fantastic."

Part Four

ACCLIMATING TO PHOENIX : LETTERS TO MOM

"Dear Mom,

Alex and you were right. I went to the Teacher's Orientation at the Temple and met a lovely girl. Her name is Erica and she is the First Grade teacher. She is married to a doctor at Good Samaritan Hospital and they just moved here from Boston. We already made plans to get together as couples next Saturday night.

Dear Mom,

These are pictures that I just developed. This is another new friend, Martha. Her son is in my 8th grade class at the Temple, She also has a baby girl just a little older than Marisa. The morning after we met she picked me up and took Marisa and me to the park to play. And the other picture is of a clown that I painted for one wall of Marisa's room.

Dear Mom,

Here is a picture of Alex in the Egyptian cotton shirt that I made for him.

Alex told me that we are starting VNO, his idea. What does that mean? Valerie's Night Out. One evening a week he said I should go out and he would babysit. So I went to a Sisterhood meeting (after being amused for years with Jeanette's obsession with her Sisterhood.) I enjoyed it a lot and Erica and Martha were there also. And I met another young mother, Ruth. Erica works during the week but Martha and Ruth call me with plans to go places with our little girls, to the mall, to a children's music class, to a little nearby Zoo. I have to tell you, I'm very happy.

Dear Mom,

Next week I am going to a lecture by Leon Uris about his book *Exodus* which I loved. This will be my Valerie's Night Out adventure. I am going to bring my copy of the book and ask him to autograph it. Love, Valerie"

ALEX'S NIGHT OUT

"Valerie, now we have Valerie's Night Out. So. I'd like one. too."

"A night out? What will you do?"

"When I gave that talk at the Community Center on the Night Sky, I saw a flier about guitar lessons."

"Really? You want to play the guitar?"

"I've always wanted to play an instrument. My parents offered me lessons but I didn't have that much time. You could take guitar lessons with me. We could get a babysitter. It's one hour on Tuesday nights."

"No, you go. I'll go with you to buy a guitar, though. Do you want to play jazz?"

"Maybe. Some jazz. Some regular songs. Some show tunes. The love songs of our marriage."

The night of the first lesson, Alex came home and played 'The old gray goose. She's not what she used to be.' "Easy chords," he said.

Two weeks later, he came home. "Sit down, darling. Listen." He sang:

Put your head on my shoulder Whisper in my ear, baby Words I want to hear, baby. Put your head on my shoulder.

"I love it. Who sings it?"

"Paul Anka. He's only eighteen. It just came out."

"It's wonderful, honey. I'll whisper the words you want to hear. I am amazed at how much talent you have in so many ways."

"Let me demonstrate some other talents."

Part Five

RUBY AND ISAIAH WINTERHILL

"So life was again enjoyable. I had fun with girlfriends who mostly had babies about the same age of mine. I was very engaged teaching about the Holocaust to 8th graders. And my evenings and weekends with Alex were sparked with love and the magnetic force that drew us together always."

"So how did you get started working on civil liberties and editing that book?" Sister Agnes wanted to know.

"About a month after my mother and Aunt Anna visited, I got a phone call from my cousin in Los Angeles."

"'Did you know that your mother has no social life at all? All she does is walk the dog, go to work, then rush home to walk the dog again. If she didn't have the dog, she could go to meetings at the Community Center, meet some people her own age. She's still a very pretty woman.'"

"But she loves the dog."

"'Maybe, but she needs more. Why don't you take the dog now that you have a backyard?'"

"Of course I'll take Lucky. But how can we get him to Phoenix?"

"'Maybe we could send him by Greyhound. Do you think they do that?'"

"A week later, my mother called. 'The problem has been solved. Ruby and Isaiah have been wanting to take a road trip now that they got their new Buick. Ruby offered to take Lucky and me to Phoenix and then they'll go on to the Grand Canyon.'"

"Ruby had been a playmate of my mother's since their childhood on the Lower East Side of New York. Ruby's mother had been the janitor of the six story tenement apartment building. My grandmother, Brucha, who ran a daycare in her apartment on the 5th floor, had taken care of Diamond's three daughters and gotten in trouble because of it. The entire thing was a fascinating story which I'll tell you sometime. So Diamond named her three daughters after gemstones; Sapphire, Pearl and Ruby. Ruby moved to Los Angeles as a young girl and worked as a cleaning lady for several movie stars. After we moved to L.A. my mom and Ruby reconnected."

"So I worked very hard on the dinner which would greet them all (including a beef bone for Lucky) because Ruby was a fabulous cook and catered parties and weddings. After she and Isaiah became wealthy, they moved into a huge house in Inglewood next door to the man who played Jack Benny's butler on the radio. Every New Year's Day, Ruby would give an open house party in her home attended by about a hundred friends and members of their church. She served platters of roasts and casseroles and desserts on gold plates. Every year, my mom and uncle and I would go and it was interesting and wonderful. Famous people like Nat King Cole and Lena Horn would drop by."

"I described to Alex the tables of roast beef, turkey and ham and fried chicken and the tables of vegetables and side dishes, the perfect biscuits with butter and the tables of pies and layer cakes and puddings. Because Ruby had been the cook for a Jewish producer, she had also learned to make noodle kugel and apple strudel."

"I made my mother's recipe for brisket with potato latkes and salad and chocolate chip cookies. "

"'Sweetie, this is all just excellent and tasty. Alex, you got you a fine cook,' said Ruby."

"'I know it and I appreciate it,' said Alex. 'Isaiah, your achievements just fascinate me. Would you mind telling us how you did it?'"

ISAIAH

"Isaiah's white teeth sparkled in a wide smile. 'For sure I'd love to tell you my tale. I was brought up in Harlem and graduated high school and got me a job as a conductor on the railroad. A cousin got me the job. So we started out in New York City, had a short layover in Chicago and then went all the way to L.A. At first I was more a porter and helped people with luggage and such but after a few years I got to be a waiter in the dining room. That was me ringing that dinner bell. Well, I loved working in the dining room with those crisp white tablecloths and fine silver and nice dinner ware. And most of the people eating were pleasant to deal with. But even if they weren't, I didn't care. See, these were the "roaring twenties" and if I had a table of gentlemen, soon enough they would be talking about their investments and stocks. I listened intently and since I was a smiling colored waiter, they paid me no mind."

"'So one man would say, 'I just bought 100 shares of A.T.and T or Kodak or Westinghouse and it is doing really well.' So I would hustle into the pantry and write this all down on my pad. Then I would buy maybe five or ten shares. Before the stock market crash in 1929, several tables of gentlemen were sounding the alarm so I sold out what the gentlemen called 'my portfolio'. I came away with a nice chunk of cash. Ruby and me had just gotten married then. And Ruby has always been a real hard worker, haven't you, darlin? So she came from New York like me with nothing and she got jobs in Hollywood cleaning houses. And she was reliable and honest and after a while she got that job as a cook to that producer. Ruby and me, we met at church and we got us a little apartment. But you want to know the secret to our success?'"

"'Here it is, kids. We never threw money around. We didn't drink much, we didn't gamble and we went dancing in neighborhood places. We didn't go eating fancy food because both of us had access to fancy food that they were going to throw away anyway so we took it home. In other words, we lived modest. We lived on my salary and saved hers. And not in banks neither because I didn't trust no banks.'"

"'So then came the stock market crash and Ruby and me had enough money to buy a two bedroom house down near the airport. Houses were selling cheap then because a lot of people lost their jobs. And that's where Jerome was born. And Ruby and me, we had a talk and decided to have one child and really do right by him, give him all the advantages. So it was the Depression and we're both working and saving, but still giving 10% to the Lord and active in our church. I was a deacon by then and Ruby headed up this committee or that. Times were hard for some people and we were able to buy two more houses and rent them out.'"

"'We were able to put Jerome in private school and then he went to Columbia and then on to medical school to become a radiologist. And Shaina here knows, he did us proud. So I'm still on the train and listening to the conversations of these well dressed men and they said, you never go wrong with real estate and then some said, the new big thing is going to be television. So I invested in RCA and bought some more houses. In 1949 we were able to buy our present house, bigger than we needed really but very fine with the kitchen and dining room that Ruby always wanted. And it has lovely trees and a gazebo and a pool. And we're retired now, able to travel around and do things we like. Yes, the Lord has been good to us.'"

"'So you might say you made your fortune by eavesdropping.' said Alex. 'This is a really impressive story.' Both Isaiah and Alex were laughing and Isaiah offered Alex a cigar."

"Ruby, an ample woman, always dressed in long colorful dresses. Today she wore a print in autumn colors, brown and orange and green. Isaiah was well dressed as well in casual clothes which featured a soft tan sweater."

"Did you stop for lunch in a nice restaurant off the highway?" I asked."

"'Oh no, sweetie. We can't go to no restaurants that we don't know. And we never know what reception we're gonna get. So I fried up some chicken and sandwiches and jugs of iced tea and we had us a nice picnic at the rest stop near Yuma.'"

"Alex and I looked at each other, thinking, we knew, the same thing. Here, in America in 1959, was a prosperous couple, hardworking and worthy in every respect, driving a large 1959 black Buick and fearing that they would be denied entrance to some restaurant."

"This just isn't right. We've got to make it better somehow," I said. I had known Ruby since I was a little girl and I hugged her now."

"'All in good time, darlin. Things will get better and you and Alex and our Jerome and Audrey, you're all well educated and yours is the generation that will improve things.'"

"Ruby and Isaiah left for the Grand Canyon and my mom stayed on for the weekend and then flew back to Los Angeles. Lucky was very eager to watch baby Marisa and he loved the backyard which, as an apartment dog, he'd never had. Alex installed a doggy door for him which he loved. Peaches, the cat, totally ignored him."

PACE

"Several days later, I went to Temple Beth Israel to hear Leon Uris talk about his beautiful novel, *Exodus*. It was exciting to hear him tell us about his research for the novel and to answer questions about Israel and about the writing process. Leon Uris signed my copy of his book."

"Then two gentlemen stood up. They introduced themselves, two law partners, Eugene Silver and Brad Goldberg. They were disturbed, they said, by the lack of uniform public accommodations in Phoenix. Some people of color were denied access to some restaurants and hotels. So they were forming an organization to be called PACE, Public Accommodations for Everyone. As Jews, we knew what discrimination was like and it was important for us to fight prejudice wherever it dwelled. "

"They passed around a sign up sheet to become a member of PACE and help in the struggle for civil liberties. Remembering Ruby and Isaiah, I signed up and gave my telephone number."

FIGHTING FOR CIVIL LIBERTIES

"A few days later, Eugene Silver called me and invited me to the first meeting, in his office in midtown Phoenix. Eleven other people were there including another Jewish lawyer, a black lawyer, a black minister, a black undertaker, two Hispanic secretaries, a female lawyer, a native American teacher and me. I, really a housewife, was impressed to be in the company of such a varied and accomplished group. Elections were held and Eugene Silver, a tall, very handsome man, was elected President. An hour later, when I left to relieve my babysitter, I had been elected Recording Secretary. This was because no one else would take the job. 'It will only take about an hour a week,' Eugene told me."

"You know," said Sister Cordelia, "I joined PACE a few months later than you. But I couldn't get to the meetings at noon, I had to work at that time. But I sent in my dues and a few times on Saturdays I'd do voter registration."

"All very important," I said. "So I did voter registration also and helped write the newsletter that went out to all the members. We began meeting twice a month at my house on Palos Verde Drive because it was more convenient for most of the members and Eugene and Brad's office was too small when more and more members joined. And I always served cookies and coffee."

"When someone would inform us of a restaurant or hotel or motel refusing to serve black or brown persons, Eugene or Brad, Herb, Larry or Donna, the attorneys, would go and visit the restaurant or hotel. Although there was no public accommodations law at that time, the lawyers would use persuasion techniques which sometimes worked. But some restaurants or hotels were stubborn and refused. We had about 50% success. The whole prejudice thing was so surprising to me."

"Didn't you experience prejudice growing up in Los Angeles?" Sister Agnes asked.

"No, not at all. Growing up, Ruby and my mom were close friends, confiding in one another and my Uncle Ted hired African American workers in his art gallery. John became a personal friend and often joined us for dinner at Hung Far Chin. And then I became a camp counselor at Camp Universe, run by the Hollywood-Los Feliz Jewish Community Center. Their mission was a 'universe' free of discrimination and there were many campers who were black or brown. I told you that in my own 1st grade group I had the daughters of Nat King Cole and Harry Belafonte and also a janitor's son." "I remember that you told us that," said Mrs. O'Dell.

"Then something interesting happened. Alex had a friend Eric. Their family was friends of the Berks and went to Temple Israel of Hollywood."

"They were lovely people and owned a series of bookstores around Los Angeles. They'd given us certificates for many books as a wedding present. So Mrs. Sternberg called me and said they'd never visited Arizona and would like to take a four day vacation for her and her husband and their two boys. She asked me if I would make reservations for the family at the famous Camelback Inn. She was having difficulty getting through on the phone. She didn't want to stay in the hotel but in one of the private casitas."

"I called the Camelback Inn and began making the reservations. They asked me to spell out the last name, Sternberg. Then they told me that the Inn was filled for that weekend. I called Mrs. Sternberg and she said to make reservations for the next weekend. I called the Inn and they were filled for that weekend also. And the weekend after that? Filled."

"And then I got it. The Inn was discriminating against Jews. I brought the matter up at the next PACE meeting and Eugene immediately arranged for me to go with him and visit the Camelback Inn. While still in my living room, he called the Camelback Inn and made arrangements for the Duffy family for the weekends in question. The Camelback Inn had casitas available for the Duffy family. So there was no doubt."

"The next week we visited the Camelback Inn. They told us that they were privately owned and were following the procedures set by the owner. 'There are many other resorts where your friends can stay,' they told us. Eugene told the Manager that this was a poor business decision. Many Jews in Phoenix and around the country would love to be their guests. They were closing their doors to weddings and Bar Mitzvah celebrations. 'Nevertheless,' said the Manager, 'we have to follow the policies set down by our corporate office.'"

"Eugene had one last thing to say. 'There is a member of our organization, PACE, who is a writer for the Arizona Republic. She will be writing an article tomorrow, an expose on the corporate policies of the Camelback Inn. I guarantee that you will be losing a lot of business because many people in Phoenix are fair. Why don't you take a few days to review your policies and I'll call you back one week from today.'"

"You were impressive," I told him as we got into his car."

"I played hardball but didn't raise my voice," he said with a smile."

"The following week, Eugene and I went back to the Camelback Inn. "Couldn't we just phone them?" I asked him."

"'No, this kind of sensitive thing has to be in person,' he said."

"The Manager got right to the point. 'Our owner does not want adverse publicity or a war with any minority group. So, last week he sold the Camelback Inn to a well known hotel chain. They have told us that they will welcome all guests who can afford to stay here.'"

"We shook hands and left. 'We've won,' said Eugene. He wanted to take me out for a drink to celebrate but I had to get home to cook dinner."

"Eugene was full of plans for projects. At our next meeting, he told us that he wanted us to write a book which PACE would publish. Various experts would write a chapter telling us the true picture in Phoenix of civil liberties in their fields: medical, mental health, education, voting, hospitality and so on. Eugene asked me to be the editor of the book and I agreed, He also asked me to interview Judge Hazell Daniels on the history of how the 'separate but equal' elementary and high schools in Phoenix had become desegregated only five years before in 1954. Judge Daniels, one of the first black attorneys in Arizona, had had much to do with creating the legislation as had Judge Bernstein. I was delighted to meet and interview Judge Daniels for our book. I was excited by these new challenges and Alex was proud of me. The book would be called "*TO SECURE THESE RIGHTS.*"

"Then at another meeting, Eugene announced that PACE should do a sit in at a place that refused to serve minorities. Some members said that a sit in would be too dangerous. But the members voted that we do it and the next meetings were given over to planning it. Where would we go, who would participate, when should we do it?"

"The Sternberg family came to spend a long weekend at The Camelback Inn. They invited Alex and me to dinner in their casita. The next night, Friday, I invited the four of them to Shabbat dinner. After dinner, as they were leaving, Mrs. Sternberg said, graciously, 'Well, I'll certainly tell Jeanette that you DO know how to entertain.' She seemed to think that she was paying me a compliment but I was offended. So Jeanette was still disparaging me."

"Alex was angry. 'Tell my mother that she knows how to entertain and that night after night she makes wonderful meals.'"

"'I'm sure she does,' said Mrs. Sternberg in a small voice."

SO SICK

"The next day, Saturday, Alex said he didn't feel well. I put my hand on his forehead. "Alex, you're burning up. Let me take your temperature. It's 103. You have to get into bed."

"It had been four years since our mountain wedding and Alex had not been ill ever. I had only had a cold once and then my bout with German measles. I took deep breaths to control my panic. He said he felt too weak to drive to the doctor's office. Suppose it was something serious? If only I could drive. I can't neglect this, I thought. I looked at my strong Alex, shivering under quilts on our bed. Think, Valerie."

"We had plans to go to dinner with our friends, the Singers, that night I called Erica to tell her we couldn't make it."

"Erica, I don't know what to do. He's never sick. Yes, he has thrown up and he feels so weak."

"'Valerie, they said on the radio that this is one of the coldest Novembers on record. Winters are much colder here than in L.A. Steve will be leaving the hospital soon and I'm going to ask him to swing by your house. Don't worry. He should be there in an hour.'"

"'It's definitely a bad flu,' said Steve. 'You'd better call his work and tell them he won't be in for three or four days. It just has to run its course. Extra strength aspirin will help make him more comfortable. And you should be careful because this flu is very contagious. Our hospital is filled.'"

"But Steve, he's so weak. I've never seen him like this. He could barely walk."

"'These are the symptoms. I'll come by early in the morning but if he's really worse, call me and I'll bring him to Good Sam's Urgent Care.'"

"Steve, I can't thank you enough."

"Alex was sleeping. The only thing I could think of to do was to make him chicken soup. When he woke up he had three mouthfuls and threw them up into a glass. 'Thank you but no food, darling. No food.' he said."

"A little after six the next morning, Steve was back. 'Valerie, you look awful. No offense. Let me take your temperature. All right. 102. Listen, I can call a nursing service to come in and take care of both of you. Don't shake your head. Okay. At least you should both move into your guest room with the baby. It's next to the kitchen and the other bathroom. You're going to need the kitchen. I'll push the crib in there.'"

"Steve pushed Marisa's crib into the guest room since Alex clearly was too weak to do it. He helped Alex lie down in the guest room bed and set extra quilts down on the floor. He checked the baby who had no symptoms. 'She's fine now. If she gets a fever, call me. Both of you, try to get as much rest as you can. That's all you can do now.' And with a wave he was out the door, running to be on time for his 7 am shift."

"For about an hour Marisa slept and so did Alex. Then she was up. At ten months old she was tapering off from nursing, interested in many other foods. Taking care of her was problematic. I felt too weak to hold her unless I was sitting in a chair."

"'She needs a bottle of milk,' said Alex. 'And some food. I'll go.' I watched Alex get up shakily and then he couldn't walk. He got down on his hands and knees and crawled into the kitchen. Somehow he warmed some milk and came back with a bottle and a small jar of peas. We took turns feeding the baby."

"Please hang in there, Marisa," I told the baby. "It will only be for a day or two. "She looked at me, smiling. Thoughtful Steve had thrown a bunch of toys and little books into her crib. She played with them. The next time she needed food, I insisted that Alex rest and I crawled into the kitchen. I could not stand up. I brought back water for Alex but neither of us wanted to eat."

"This terrible regimen went on for three days. I crawled to the nearby washing machine to wash Marisa's diapers. Alex and I alternated sleeping and bringing food to the baby. She crawled around the guest room and played with her toys and her forehead remained cool. On the third day, Alex was feeling a little stronger. When there was a knock on the door, he got up to answer it."

"'Where do you want it?' said a voice."

"'In here,' said Alex. A burly man wheeled in a TV on a stand. 'I rented it for a week since we're in bed.'" "I love it," I said."

"Slowly, we both got better and the baby never got sick. When she was up, we all watched The Howdy Doody Show and Captain Kangaroo. When she napped, we lay on the bed and watched Masterpiece Theater, I Love Lucy and the Late Night Show with Jack Paar, among other things."

"'Do you want to keep it?' Alex asked."

"Oh, yes."

"Two days later we were both alright and we went out and bought a new TV. The three and a half years of no TV so Alex could study were over."

THE SIT IN

"Tell us about the sit-in," said Sister Agnes.

"At 8 am, I walked into the downtown Woolworth's with the other members of our volunteer group, PACE. Larry and Preston were tall good looking black men around thirty. Eugene, Brad and I were white. Lincoln Ragsdale, a black war hero and the owner of a large mortuary, would join us soon."

"My stomach was churning with fear and my mouth felt dry. The smells of bacon and coffee hung in the air. At intervals on the green formica counter there were round plastic containers filled with slices of pies and cakes. I counted eighteen stools, all filled with customers, many of whom turned when we entered. Did they know what we were planning? Maybe a sit-in in downtown Phoenix was not a good idea."

"Eugene put a reassuring hand on my shoulder. 'Just remember everything we practiced yesterday.'"

"The problem is that we might not have thought of everything that could happen,' said Preston, a youth minister at a large Baptist church. 'And I certainly don't relish the idea of going to jail like those college kids last month in Baltimore. Although I do believe that God will protect us.'"

"'At least Larry and Brad and I are lawyers,' said Eugene."

"A seat opened up. 'Valerie, you sit down,' said Eugene. A pleasant young woman, her hair all covered by a net, took my order. I ordered one scrambled egg with toast and coffee. But the plan was not to eat it so I'd eaten it at home. My stomach was fluttering so badly that I probably couldn't have eaten anyway."

"A seat became available and Brad sat down and ordered. Eugene, Larry and Preston stood behind me with about six other people waiting for seats. A motherly black woman with curly gray hair came up to the counter and patted Larry's arm. 'You and your friend get served in the COLORED TO GO line,' she said to him. 'You can get coffee and some baked goods. They don't make you any hot foods but you can get you a hard boiled egg if you want. And then you gots to take your food out the door. You can eat at the bus bench. That's how it's run.'"

"'I know how it's run,' said Larry in his New York accent. 'But I went to law school so I could run it differently.'" "Eugene had told us all to dress professionally. The four men, three lawyers and one minister, were all in fine suits with white shirts and subdued ties. I was wearing a conservative plum colored dress with low black heels. I had pearls around my neck and pearl earrings."

"An older man in the COLORED TO GO line spoke to Larry. 'Listen boy, don't make any trouble for us now.' He was scared, his forehead wrinkled."

"The lady sitting next to me now got up with her little boy. Preston and Larry sat down in the two empty seats. All the people sitting at the counter and standing in line stared at them. A man eating a bagel shouted out, 'Hey, you guys can't sit there. Go to the COLORED TO GO line.'"

"My waitress, in her yellow uniform with her name tag, ELLEN, slid my plate of an egg and toast down and stared at the two black men next to me."

"'I'll just have oatmeal and whole wheat toast and coffee,' said Preston, casually."

"'You know you're not allowed at the counter. You get your food over there and go. I can't serve you nothing.'"

"'I'll have the $5.99 special, with ham, not sausage,' said Larry in his precise and cultured accent."

"Ellen's eyes darted around. Without another word, she walked to the kitchen and an older woman, her gray hair also in a net. came out wiping her hands. Her name tag said RONNIE."

"'We're not allowed to serve you men here. It's against the rules of Woolworth's and we have to follow their rules.' She turned to me. 'Ma'am, you haven't touched your food. If you don't want it, could you please give up your seat to them that's waiting?' Ten people were waiting."

"I'm going to just sit here until you serve my friends," I said."

"'You can't take up the seat, lady. We're not serving them and you'd be here all day.'"

"A pleasant looking grandmotherly woman behind me said, 'Yes, young lady, you're being very rude. I need to sit down. My legs are killing me.'"

"Another woman in a lovely brown suit walked up behind me. ' I have to get to my office. Get up!'"

"When I said nothing, she leaned over and hissed, 'Nigger lover!' And there it was. And it was not even 9 am yet. I kept my eyes in front of me. Eugene, behind me, stepped closer. Ellen and Ronnie went back into the kitchen and came out with an older man, his hair also in a net."

"'Look, I'm the cook here. We don't want no trouble. But we're not serving you and you're taking up three seats during our morning rush.'"

"'Why can't you serve us?' asked Preston."

"'Because you're black.'"

"Larry took out his wallet and waved several $20 bills. 'Our money is green. We're sitting here courteously, not bothering anybody. I'm a lawyer and he's a minister. And we want to eat breakfast.'"

"'We're not going to serve you. Our store manager comes in at ten and he'll take some action. Probably call the cops on you.'"

"There was muttering behind us. Two white men in telephone company uniforms said, 'Do you want us to drag them out? We could take them on.'"

"'These men are our colleagues,' said the six foot four, solidly built Eugene. The telephone company men looked Eugene up and down and sat way at the end of the counter as a couple got up."

"The middle aged woman sitting next to me said, 'Don't you have something better to do than causing a fuss? I see you have a wedding ring. Are you married to one of those Negroes?'"

"I thought, No, I'm married to Alex, a man I love desperately who has argued with me all week about participating in this sit-in. 'I don't want you to get hurt. Anything could happen,' he'd said. 'You have a one year old child. I know you want to stop discrimination but this stunt is too dangerous.' Finally, exasperated, he'd said, 'I can't stop you, I suppose. I agree with your cause, you know I do, but I don't want my wife doing it.'"

"And it was worse with Jeanette, my scrutinizing mother in law, visiting us from Los Angeles. 'This is one of the stupidest things you've ever done, Valerie. You want to change the natural order of things. You know you're only going to make colored people more uppity. I told you when you were registering colored people to vote that no good would come of it. Those colored people will not be content with just voting. They're going to want to run things, they're going to want to be all over the place. You're a Jewish girl. This isn't even your fight.'"

"It's 1960," I'd said. "It's every American's fight."

"The two women standing behind me seemed to echo my mother-in-law's thoughts. 'Be reasonable, dear,' one of them said to me. 'You're not going to change anything.' The other woman hit me in the back with her heavy purse and it was not an accident."

"Behind us, in a low voice, Eugene said. 'Calm. Non violent. Mahatma Gandhi,' reminding us of the training we'd had. It was now nine thirty and Eugene and Brad found seats at the counter."

"'We'll order when you serve our friends,' said Brad."

"Now Lincoln Ragsdale arrived and slipped into an empty seat. 'Sorry, we had an early morning funeral,' he said to Eugene."

"'Another black man,' said a man seated at the counter. 'Another one who thinks because he's dressed up in a suit, he can eat with us.'"

"So we sat there. About an hour later, a man in a rumpled suit came up to us. 'I'm the store manager,' he said. His badge read MR. TURLEY."

"'You can't just sit here. See our sign? We reserve the right to refuse service to anyone. If you're not out of those chairs, all six of you, I'm calling the police. We get a good crowd here for lunch and you all are taking up a lot of space.'"

"'Bring all of us our orders and we'll eat and go,' said Eugene."

"The lunch crowd seemed even angrier than the breakfast people. 'This is outrageous!' said one woman. 'I only get forty minutes to eat,' said one man. All of a sudden I felt a little thud on my head. Someone behind me had spit into my hair. I wiped it away with a napkin, shuddering."

"Two uniformed policemen arrived and Mr. Turley pointed out who we were. 'Arrest all six of them,' said Mr. Turley."

"One of the policemen, the very heavy one, leaned in to talk to Preston and Larry. 'Look, you've made your point. I'm talking to you, too, boy.'"

"His head jerked to war hero, businessman Lincoln Ragsdale. 'All three of you, get up now and go about your business before there's any trouble.'"

"'We're not causing any trouble, Officer,' said Larry."

"'We're just waiting for our food,' said Lincoln Ragsdale in a mild tone."

"Eugene gave each of the officers a PACE card. 'It's a non profit organization to provide equality for all, in restaurants, lunch counters and hotels. We want to end discrimination in Phoenix.'"

"'Have they broken anything, taken anything?' a policeman asked Mr. Turley. 'We can't arrest them unless they've done something illegal.'"

"'They're taking up our seats,' said Mr. Turley. 'If that's not illegal, it should be.'"

"'We have another call so we have to leave,' said one policeman and they left the lunch counter."

"Now in came a man carrying a large camera and a sign that said NBC NEWS. A blond woman, heavily made up, interviewed us. 'We're on the board of PACE,' said Eugene. 'We feel that all people should be able to eat where they wish as long as they can afford it.'"

"'Could you tell our TV audience why you're doing this?' she asked me."

"The lights were hot on my face but I looked directly into the camera. 'I have a little daughter and I want my child to grow up in a city where people can be served regardless of their color.'"

"'They've been here for seven hours,' said Mr. Turley. He turned to us in rage. 'Now you've brought the TV in on us. I'm calling our corporate office in Chicago.'"

"At four o'clock, I was tired and had to go to the bathroom. The crowd waiting behind us was growing exasperated. At 5 pm, Mr. Turley was back. There were about eight people waiting for stools behind us."

"'Serve them coffee,' said Mr. Turley to Ellen. 'From that pot from this morning.'"

"Sullenly, lips pressed together, Ellen gave all six of us a lukewarm cup of coffee. Larry put down a $20 bill. We took a sip of the awful coffee and thanked them."

"'Will I be served at Woolworth's tomorrow?' asked Lincoln."

"Corporate says yes. They said to allow it. Not at all their lunch counters. Just in Arizona and Illinois.'"

"'What is this country coming to?' wailed an older lady. 'We have to eat with colored people now.' A mixed sensation of exhaustion and jubilation crept over us as we exchanged victorious glances."

"Before we walked out we all took another sip of the coffee. It was cold, thick, grainy and tasteless."

"When we reached the sidewalk, Brad said, 'Worst coffee ever.'"

"'Are you kidding?' said Larry. 'This was the best cup of coffee I ever had.'"

"When I walked into my house, Alex was holding Marisa on the couch."

"'There's your Mommy, the activist,' he said. 'We saw you on TV, darling. Sit down, they're repeating it for the 7 pm news.' He handed me a taco from Taco Bell and soon I watched myself, looking tired and a little scared but speaking in my firm debate voice. "I want my child to grow up in a city where people can be served regardless of their color."

NEW MEANINGFUL JOBS

"So how did ON TO COLLEGE come about?" asked Sister Agnes.

"After the sit-in, I was offered two part time jobs in the most curious way."

"Eugene Silver asked me to come to his office to meet someone "very interesting." He introduced me to Joseph Choate, a short and frail looking man who seemed to be in his late forties. He spoke in a very pronounced Boston accent. 'Besides running my family's business, I am looking for ways to effect change for young people. Disadvantaged young people. And I had an idea which I've named On To College. Eugene here, whom I met at Yale, has recommended you to direct it. Do you want to hear about it?'"

"Of course I nodded yes."

"'It's simple really. We select 100 high school juniors and seniors who have been chosen by their high school counselors for their good grades and good conduct. I want us to pick 25 black students, 25 Hispanic students, 25 white students and 25 native American students. We'll rent three school buses and hire college students as bus monitors. Then every Thursday afternoon after school, we'll take the group on a field trip. The main emphasis is to make the students comfortable with the idea of college so you'd take them on various university tours but also to museums and other cultural places to broaden their horizons. Are you with me so far?'"

"Yes, Mr. Choate."

"'Call me Joseph. They'll tour for about an hour and then comes the irresistible reward. We take them all out for dinner! They don't pay for anything. I've already run similar groups in Boston and Baltimore. And I developed another incentive. If the student gets into a college, my foundation will pay the first year's tuition with a stipend for living expenses. If they do well the first year, we consider the next year. A few of my Boston students have graduated from college so we've urged them to sponsor and mentor another high school student. And most of them have. What do you think?'"

"I think it's a beautiful, well thought out plan to change many lives."

"'Would you be interested in running it? We'd pay you for eight hours a week. About four hours on Thursday night and four hours at your home to make all the arrangements. What do you say?'"

"I didn't have to think about it. "I would love to do it."

"At home I told Alex about it. "It would only be one afternoon a week. I'd have to be at this community center in South Phoenix at 3 pm and we'd be on tour until about 4:30. Then dinner would be about an hour and I'd be home by 6. Would that be all right with you? I'd have a babysitter here until you got home."

"Alex enveloped me in a hug. 'Such an enthusiastic Nookums! I'm proud of you. Of course it's all right.'"

"Two weeks later, we were all set up. High school counselors had recommended the students although only ten native American students were interested. We filled in with five students from each of the other three groups. It happened that Arizona State University was having a concert in their music building. We took them there and then out to a large Mexican restaurant, available because it was only 4:30." "When we arrived back at the community center, Mr. Choate wanted to talk to me privately. 'This was not at all what I wanted,' he said, frowning."

"What was wrong?"

"'Didn't you notice how the students got on the buses? You filled up one all white bus, one all black bus and one Hispanic bus. That's not the idea at all. We want the students to mingle, to make some new friends.'"

"Can we tell them where they have to sit?"

"'I'm buying them dinner. I'm paying for the school buses. If a student objects., he's out of ON TO COLLEGE. We have plenty of other students who'd like to join.'"

"I followed Mr.Choate's instructions and almost every Thursday afternoon went smoothly."

"I was offered another small part time job in an unusual way. A block away from the South Phoenix Community Center was a Safeway market and I stopped there to buy bananas for Marisa. At the produce department, a black woman and a white woman stood chatting. Both seemed to be about forty and both wore green uniforms of some sort,"

"So she declined to take the job?' said the black lady."

"'Yes, she said that three hours a week were not enough hours and the pay was not very good.' from the white lady."

"Shamelessly, I eavesdropped."

"'And now we're going to disappoint all those girls.'"

"'How many signed up?'"

"'About twenty five girls. And their mothers will be disappointed as well. They want their daughters to be Girl Scouts.'"

"Excuse me," I said. "I couldn't help but overhear you. Are you talking about a job working with Girl Scouts?"

"'Yes, were you a Girl Scout?'"

"I was a Brownie and I couldn't become a Girl Scout because my mother worked and couldn't help."

"'What a shame. They should have let you. Are you a college graduate?'"

"Yes."

"'What was your major?'"

"Social work." This entire interview was conducted in the produce department."

"'Sounds good. This job is as a Girl Scout professional developer. Right now, there are loads of troops in Phoenix but none in South Phoenix. You would work three hours a week. The idea is to start a. troop and for a half hour before the meetings, you would train the mothers. The hope is that in a year or so, three mothers will have been certified by you and us. Then they would take over the troop and you would move to another area and start a new troop. Would you be interested?'"

"Yes, I would. I have a little girl so three hours a week is fine for me."

"'I have to explain that the population is half Black girls and half Hispanic. Would that be all right?'"

"Of course. I'm the Director of ON TO COLLEGE which meets on Thursday afternoons and has pretty much the same population."

"'Great! Can you come to our office near Encanto Park and meet Miss Brunswick, our supervisor? If you have a resume and your college degree, please bring them. I think she's going to love you. Don't you agree, Rhoda?'"

"By the next afternoon, I had the job and would receive two weeks of training for three hours each week. They gave me seven books of ideas for art projects, music, camp cookery and developing fellowship. The girls would be from nine to thirteen years of age."

"Now I was working three part time jobs, including teaching 8th grade Holocaust class on Sunday mornings. I worked a total of fourteen hours a week and could do the organizing work at home while Marisa napped. I would be gone for eight hours a week. It was perfect, fulfilling and the majority of my week was spent with my baby and my new friends who also had young children. I also had time to work on PACE projects."

"'I'm thrilled with how happy you are, darling. I told you, it would just take time.'" said Alex."

A CALL FROM RUBY

"Do you want to hear how Audrey and Jerome came to town and what happened next?" The nuns and Mrs. O'Dell nodded yes. They all liked Audrey and Jerome.

"I was surprised when Ruby telephoned me and more surprised to hear in her voice that she was crying."

"'Hi. darlin'. How are you? How is Lucky doin' in your home? The reason I've called, darlin', is that we've had another disappointment in the family. My daughter in law, Audrey, a precious sweet girl, has just miscarried again. Her fourth miscarriage. And Isaiah and I were so hopeful that she'd carry to term this time. And she was nearly five months along.'"

"'So why I'm callin', darlin', is that she's so sad and discouraged that Jerome wants to give her a change of scenery from New York City. And he's been offered a position at Good Samaritan Hospital. You know that he's a radiologist. don't you? So I wondered if you could look around and see about houses for sale. Audrey can get a job in the District Attorney's Office, they have an opening for a lawyer. And with their two salaries, they can afford a nice house. But with all their salaries and all the money we've got, we still can't get us a child.' And Ruby cried some more."

"Ruby, somehow they will get a child. I just feel it. And meanwhile I'll go and see what nice houses are available."

"As luck would have it, a large red brick home was for sale a block away from me. The realtor showed it to me. It had four bedrooms and a glistening swimming pool like our house but other additions had been made. There was a cherry wood kitchen with the latest appliances and a large glassed-in sun porch with a built-in bar. The backyard had been beautifully landscaped. Jerome and Audrey decided to fly out the next weekend to see it. Alex and I picked them up at the airport."

"I remembered Jerome, who was ten years older than I, from Ruby's New Year's Day Open Houses. He was very tall, thin and pleasant looking. He wore a gray suit with a paisley tie. Audrey was striking, with a dark Egyptian looking face, huge brown eyes and numerous braids in a fancy design around her head. She had the type of beauty that looked gorgeous with her hair severely pulled back. She wore a fitted plum suit with matching shoes and a stylish black purse. Even her gold earrings were elegant. Her smile was wide and warm. "

"I had arranged to have the realtor show us the house. Both Jerome and Audrey loved it. They walked through the house twice and consulted quietly. Then Jerome gave the realtor a check for earnest money with his offer. He decided to pay full price."

"'In New York City this would go for five times as much,' he said. The realtor made a call to the owners and the house would be theirs. I was thrilled to have new friends moving in on the next block."

"'We have Happy Hour most nights around 6 so we want to see a lot of you both,' said Audrey."

"'I'm a fine bartender and Audrey makes the best fancy little snacks,' said Jerome."

"Alex and I took them out to dinner at a large popular Mexican restaurant in Scottsdale. It was crowded and we waited in their patio with drinks, sitting on the large stone fountain."

"An hour went by and I was hungry. Alex went to check on when we'd be seated. He came back with tight lips and said,

'They're too crowded. Let's go to another great place.' He drove us to the stockyards area where we all had delicious steaks, baked potato, Caesar salad and cheese cake. The four of us had so much to talk about and Jerome seemed to have a sense of humor like Alex. We laughed through dinner. Then we drove them back to their hotel."

"As we drove home, Alex said, 'At the Mexican restaurant I asked the Maitre D,' 'When will our table be ready?' 'Maybe never. Come back without your black friends.' I restrained myself from hitting him. Put them on your PACE list.'"

"A month later, Audrey and Jerome moved in and started hosting themed Happy Hours such as 'A Night In Austria' with wines and beers and snacks or 'Evening In Paris' with wines and cheeses and coq au vin in small bowls."

"A week later, a portly gentleman rang my doorbell. 'I'm your neighbor from down the block, Wayne. I'm circulating a petition about those niggers that just moved in. They're going to bring down the value of our entire neighborhood. And you know how they are. When one moves in, forty others soon follow. We're asking them to move. Sign here, Ma'am.' He showed me a petition with perhaps fifteen signatures."

"This is a lovely couple," I said. "He's a doctor and she's an attorney. They've already planted lovely rose bushes in their front yard and put in that fountain. They're enhancing the neighborhood."

"'You won't sign?'"

"No. You should be ashamed to spend your time this way. Has every neighbor signed?"

"'Not everyone. Some are nigger lovers, like you. I have nothing against them personally but they should be in South Phoenix, They have their own neighborhoods there.'"

"Alex and Marisa and I went to the Winterhill's Happy Hour and Alex asked Jerome if he had a gun and knew how to shoot. Jerome's answer to both questions was No."

"'I'd like to teach you,' said Alex. 'You're in the Wild West now.'"

"Now Jerome went to the desert with Alex most Saturday mornings. Sometimes Audrey and I went also. Alex reported that Jerome was getting good at it. Jerome bought a pistol and a rifle."

"About a week later on a Saturday, Alex parked in front of Audrey and Jerome's home and he saw Wayne, the portly petition passer who lived across the street. Alex took two rifles from his rack in the jeep and said 'Hi. Going shooting with the doctor here,' he said. 'Did you know that Doctor Winterhill is the finest sharp shooter I've ever met?' Alex told me that Wayne gulped and shook his head. No petitions for the Winterhills to move were ever circulated again."

RUBY AND CHLOE

"Several weeks later, Ruby called again. She thanked me for our friendship with Jerome and Audrey, which I answered was our pleasure."

"'I'm calling you because my ridiculous younger sister, Saphire, has called me for help once more. I don't know if your mother told you but Saphire has always had a drinking problem. So I've tried to help her with her two kids as much as I could. Her Chloe doesn't drink and doesn't do drugs but she is WILD. Dropped out of high school, running with all sorts of boys and men. Now Chloe is nineteen and, surprise, surprise, she's pregnant, living in Texas. So. five minutes after Saphire called, Chloe called and she wants me to send her $300 for an abortion.'"

"Oh, Ruby," I said, a light going on in my mind.

"'Sugar ,you're thinkin' the same thing I thought. Here she wants to kill a baby, a baby who has my blood, and my precious Audrey is yearning so desperately for a baby. But Chloe said firmly that she does not want to carry this baby to term. And I thought, remember when you were twelve or so and you used to write all those little stories and read 'em to me? I thought maybe you could think up somethin', like a story plot.'"

"What does Chloe like to do?"

"'She fancies herself an artist. Makes some nice jewelry with beads. I paid for two art classes she's taken.'"

"Well, could you have her come and stay at your place and offer her art lessons?"

"'She also asked me for a van that she could live in and go to art shows and sell her jewelry.'"

"You could give her a van, couldn't you?"

"'Yes, we could. But here's the problem. If she knows the baby has been adopted by Jerome, she'll be showing up at his house, maybe take back the baby. I know her. She's capable of causing all sorts of problems and breaking Audrey's heart again. Now, as a story writer, what scene could you dream up to solve this dilemma?'"

"I'll call you back tomorrow."

"On TV we watched the Ed Sullivan variety show and on it were three black British rock stars. I called Ruby. "I think you should tell her that you know of a really rich black rock star. He and his wife want to adopt and he, not you and Isaiah, will get her the art lessons and buy her a brand new van. Tell her the rock star lives in London and wants to remain anonymous. She never needs to know his name since he doesn't exist anyway."

"'That might work, darlin'. I'll talk to Isaiah and call Chloe.'"

"In days, Chloe was living with Ruby and Isaiah in their large home and taking private art lessons in the sun room that Ruby turned over to her as a studio. Ruby was making sure that she ate nutritious meals and had her own TV and record player. She said that Chloe slept a lot."

"How far along is she?"

"'She says four or five months, she's not sure. And she's also not sure who the father is. It could be any one of three men, all black, thank the Lord.'"

"Ruby warned me not to say a word to Jerome or Audrey. She had heard of girls who had decided that their babies should be adopted but then had changed their minds once the baby was born. 'Audrey and Jerome have been through enough and we don't want their hearts broken again,' she said."

My friends, the Romance Club, Sisters Agnes, Cordelia, Mary Louise and Betsy O'Dell, the convent cook ,were very familiar with adoptions since they all worked at the Good Shepherd Home for Girls. "Oh yes, so true," said Sister Cordelia who was the convent social worker. "About half of our girls who sign up to give their babies for adoption will change their minds. The disappointment for the adopting parents is harsh."

"So Ruby and Isaiah hired an obstetrician for Chloe who was a member of their church. She told them that Chloe and the baby were in good shape. But she also told them that Chloe was not four or five months pregnant but in her seventh month. The baby would come in about eight weeks."

"It was very difficult for me to keep receiving these updates from Ruby and not tell Audrey whom I saw every day.

Especially when twice Audrey cried in my arms because she'd gotten her period or her birthday had come. 'Now I'm thirty two and I'll never be a mother.'"

"Somehow I feel that you will and it will happen this year," I said. I was so tempted to tell her but I knew that Ruby was right. Losing this promised baby would fully depress Audrey."

"'Keep your mouth closed,' advised Alex, firmly. 'Until it's a done deal.'"

"'Sugar, I hope you don't mind that I'm calling you so often. There's no one I can talk to besides Isaiah and the doctor and the lawyer we hired. I oughtn't tell another living soul where this baby is going. We hope. Now Chloe told the doctor that she wants to be asleep for the birth because my dumb sister, Saphire, has told her about the terrible pains she had delivering her two kids.'"

"Maybe it's better if she doesn't see the baby or hold it," I said. "She can get on with her life."

"But Chloe seemed to be a slick manipulator. 'Does this British rock star and his wife really want this baby?' she asked Ruby."

"'Yes, they do.'"

"'Well, do they want this baby enough to support me for a year?'"

"'Chloe! The man is already buying you a brand new van. How can you ask for more?'"

"'Well, I have to live and my jewelry might not sell so well.'"

"'How much would you need per month?' I asked my niece."

"'$500 should do it.' she said. And you know, Valerie, not once has Chloe asked me about this rock star or his wife, how old they are, who will take care of the baby, how kind they are, nothing. Questions you'd think any girl in her position would ask. She did ask me, 'Are they really rich? Do they live in a big old house?' But the van! She peppers me with questions.' How big is it, what colors, how is it furnished?'"

"You know, Ruby, Chloe is still very young, only nineteen, and you've told me her childhood was rocky. So she wants an extra $6000. Do you think you could afford that, on top of the van and the doctor's bills?"

"Ruby thought for a moment. 'Oh, well. In for a dime, in for a dollar, my mama used to say. If this baby will make my Jerome a daddy, I guess we should do it. I could get a bank to set it up, some faraway bank, and she could get the money a month at a time.'"

WORKING THE THREE JOBS AND PACE

ON TO COLLEGE was going very well. As Joseph Choate had mandated, the ethnic groups were mixed up in the vans and the dinner tables and we could see that some friendships were forming. We went to Arizona State University often. On tours of various departments, I noticed that the high school students were attentive for up to an hour. After that, they started passing notes and whispering, so I kept tours to an hour. The exception to this was concerts and musical events, even classical music. One professor at Phoenix College told interesting stories about composers and showed them the many instruments. We also went to private Christian colleges and to museums.

I began to know many of the college administrators. One lovely lady at A.S.U. said that if we had students with good attendance, A.S.U. would honor them at a dinner on their campus. What a great incentive for the group.

"'Would you like to bring your high school students to Motorola?' Alex asked. I nodded eagerly.

"This is my husband, Alex Berk," I told the group as we entered Motorola."

"Janice, a Hispanic student, raised her eyebrows. 'Hey, you're in love with him.' she said. 'You look at him so nice.'"

"You're right, Janice. I hope that when you get married, you choose a nice young man."

"'How do you know if he's nice? Boys always promise you things to get into…you know.'"

"You take your time and get to know the boy. Alex and I were engaged for a year and a half before we got married." I didn't tell Janice that I'd been extremely lucky. 'Boys always promise you things.' And Alex had promised me quite a bit. Then he kept his promises. What if he'd listened to his mother who never lost an opportunity to bad mouth me? I knew that I wasn't that wonderful. But he was. How I loved that man!

"In PACE, all the Board members thought of local people who could write chapters for our book, *TO SECURE THESE RIGHTS*, to tell about discrimination and good progress in 1960s Phoenix. We had a psychiatrist and psychologist write chapters about mental health programs in Phoenix. And members from the hospitality sector wrote about hotels, motels and restaurants and the notable strides PACE had made in those places. "

"A realtor wrote about housing and a banker wrote about business and housing loans for minorities. A college professor wrote about hiring practices for college staff and an employment expert wrote about jobs. A public official did a chapter about the rise in voter registration since PACE volunteers had been actively promoting progress through voting."

"And I wrote about the history of the 'separate but equal' black elementary school. Judge Daniels had visited the school and told me about many torn or outdated textbooks he'd seen.

"As each expert wrote his or her five pages, they mailed them to me for editing, which I did carefully. Eugene, Brad and Larry wrote about the legal system and Audrey wrote about juvenile justice for minorities."

The Girl Scout troop was also going well. There were five mothers helping me and getting interested in leadership. They especially liked teaching the girls cooking skills and had wonderful and often unusual recipes. One woman knew dozens of songs and chants and clapping games to add to the standard Girl Scout songbook. Another woman was talented in crafts. I realized that the five women were my students too and it was my job to encourage their skills and interests. The girls were earning several badges which went on their sashes. They arrived at the Community Center laughing and eager for the meetings to start.

Chanukah

"We were excited because it would be January born Marisa's first Chanukah. Her blue eyes widened as we lit the Chanukah every night and sang songs. She soon got the routine of opening a present every night for eight nights. We followed the order we had established on our first Chanukah while we were engaged. 1st night, pajamas, 2nd night, books, 3rd night, records, 4th night, charity (which we couldn't explain to a one year old so we gave her a teddy bear.) On the 5th night we opened the box of presents that Jeanette had sent and on the 6th night, the presents sent by my mother. We designated the 7th night as "made by ourselves night". I made Alex a desert shirt and a 'feely box' for Marisa. Alex made Marisa a 5 room dollhouse. As the most sensitive and kind person towards me, he brought out his surprise for me. He'd made another 5 room dollhouse for me, remembering my story of the orange crate doll house that Uncle Ted had made me when I was five and how heartbroken I'd been that we couldn't take it to L.A."

"I kissed him again and again. "You listened to me! And I love miniatures."

"'I'm pleased that you like it.'"

"I love it."

"Marisa made both of us crayon drawings which were colorful abstracts that I'd framed. She seemed to get the idea that she'd given us something that she'd made."

"The 8th night was "The big present." I gave Alex the Remington rifle he'd been wanting and we gave Marisa a rocking horse. She got on it with no hesitation and much laughter. Then Alex said, 'Close your eyes, Nookums.' He went to his car and brought out a bicycle for me. I had always wanted a bicycle and my mother promised me a red Schwinn for my 12th birthday. Then she changed her mind because we lived on a very busy street and she was afraid I'd get hurt. So I 'd never learned to ride. Alex bought me a Peugeot Touring bike with extra sturdy tires."

"He immediately set out to teach me to ride it. Night after night we practiced with him holding onto the seat and running with me. I was scared."

"Don't let go of me until I'm ready," I told him."

"'I won't. I always know when you're ready, Valerie.'"

"Then, one day a week later, he'd let go and I was pedaling down the street. My elation was great."

THE WINTERHILLS

"A month passed and then I received a call from Ruby. 'The baby is here, darlin'. A boy, nearly eight pounds. And cute as a button. And you know Jerome's lips, kind of full on the bottom and thinner on top? Well, I tell you, that baby has the same lips! I'm callin' you from the hospital. We're waitin' for Chloe to wake up and then we'll see her reactions.'"

"Have you bought the van?"

"'Oh, no. If she doesn't give up that baby, the British rock star is not going to get her a van. No way.'"

"The next day Ruby called to say that all was good. Chloe had asked the doctor about the baby and the doctor, a member of Ruby and Isaiah's church, said 'A beautiful little girl.' So then Chloe said, 'She's going to live in a fine house in London. She'll have all the advantages I never had. And I absolutely don't want no baby cramping my style.'"

"'She did not ask to see the baby or hold her. 'Better if I don't.' But she had made the baby a lovely and intricate beaded necklace with a cross. 'Just tell her her birth mama made her this and I want her to have a happy life.'"

"Ruby cried as she told me this. 'See, Chloe has feelings but she knows the time ain't right for her to raise a child. Meanwhile, I called Jerome and Audrey an hour ago. 'Both of you, sit down 'cause I have something to tell you that will knock your socks off.' And both of them just couldn't believe it. A lawyer here, from my church, is making it nice and legal. But after all, Chloe is my niece and she could give me the baby to take care of, like they do in lots of families. But the rock star scene is better because then she won't come back in three years to claim her little girl.'"

"'Meanwhile, Valerie, Jerome and Audrey are flying in tomorrow to get their son. They're going to scramble all day today to get baby things.'"

"I can loan them our cradle. And I have a lot of little shirts and things stored in a box. Until they have a chance to buy things. And I have a birth to three month car seat that they should bring with them."

"'Well, thank you, darlin'. I'm going out to buy my grandson some outfits, too. Hoooeeee! This is all so wonderful!'"

"Alex and I brought the cradle and box of clothes and car seat over. Jerome and Audrey were floating in the air with excitement and happiness."

"'And Mama told us what a big part you had in this, Valerie, constructing a plausible story.'"

"Later that afternoon we walked back to their house because Jerome and Audrey were having a champagne Happy Hour to celebrate. Several of their friends dropped in and were sharing in the joy of the adoption."

"Alex and I walked home, pushing Marisa in her stroller. 'I'm so happy for them,' said Alex. 'But I'm still grateful that I could have my own child and that you got pregnant on our first try.' His pride was evident in his voice and his posture."

"Oh, so proud!(Because you have strong and cunning sperm)."

(Alex gave me a very severe look. 'Strong and cunning, huh? What? You're making fun of my sperm? Sarcastic, are we? Well, I know what to do with a sarcastic wife. This kid is going to sleep soon and then you'll be seeing my strong and cunning sperm.' I laughed. "I don't doubt that for a minute, honey.")

(He stared at me, his lips pressed together. Then his lips curled in a smile that I knew very well. I felt that same familiar thrill in my body. After four and a half years with Alex, he could still do that to me. Now we were home. Marisa immediately fell asleep in her crib. I quickly washed and put on his favorite nightgown, the lacy lavender one. I brushed my hair out the way he liked it. Then he led me to the bed.

"Strong and cunning sperm, hmmm?" he murmured.)

WELCOME HOME, BABY WINTERHILL

"Audrey had given me her house keys to let in the furniture men with the crib and dresser. So I arranged a short baby shower for them when they came home. Erica and Steve came and Martha and Sheldon and some lawyers from Audrey's office and two doctors from Jerome's hospital. Everyone brought food and a gift for the baby."

"'Did you know?' Audrey asked me. 'When you told me I'd be a mother?'"

"Nothing for sure. Ruby said not to say anything, in case... ..And here it's the best outcome."

"'And he's so precious,' said Audrey, rocking him in her arms."

"'What's his name?' asked Martha."

"'Isaiah James, for his two grandfathers. We're going to call him I.J.'"

"We all left so the new family could rest. 'Look up at the sky,' said Erica. as we walked to our cars. There was a beautiful and clear rainbow. 'God is welcoming the new baby, also,' she said. 'And I have happy news. I didn't want to step on Audrey's joy but we're expecting.'"

"'Tell them what we're expecting,' said Steve."

"'Twins,' said Erica."

EVALYNNE

"I still could not drive and had no car. "Since I have three little jobs now and I'm making some money, I could pay for car insurance and gas," I told Alex.

"'We'll figure out your transportation in the next few months,' he told me. For some reason, he seemed reluctant to have me driving. Meanwhile, I was lucky because one of Jerome's doctor friends had started a free afternoon clinic at the South Phoenix Community Center and she was happy to drive me there on Tuesdays and Thursdays at 2:30. Alex would pick me up at 6 pm."

"That Thursday, I entered the small office off the large meeting room where the ON TO COLLEGE students met. A small black woman with curly gray hair was asleep on the worn green couch. Since we were about to leave for our field trip, I decided not to disturb her. Two hours later we were back and she was still asleep."

"I had to wake her. "I'm sorry but I have to lock up the Center now.""

"She rubbed her eyes and then got up. 'Sorry. I'm Evalynne Stevenson. My grandson is in your going to college group. My husband died last year so I moved in with my son and his wife. His illness took up all our money. And the boys are in one bedroom and my son and his wife are in the other one. So I sleep on the couch. And when they want to watch the TV, well, I can't take up the whole couch and sleep. So it seems like I'm always tired.'"

"We walked out together. 'I'm a teacher's aide at my younger grandson's school. Mrs. Berk, is there anyone you know who needs some help with their housework? And I could have a room there? I'm sixty seven years old and I can't do a full eight hours like I used to. But I could do four or five hours. I'd sure like to get out of my selfish daughter in law's hair for most of the week.'"

"Then Alex drove up and I introduced him to Evalynne. He offered to drive her home but she said she lived nearby and she'd walk."

"Let me have your phone number, Evalynne, and I'll call you tomorrow. I might know of someone."

"The next morning, Marisa and I walked to Audrey's and I told her about Evalynne. Audrey had arranged to be working from home in the mornings for the next six months."

"'That might work out. But do we know her? Shouldn't we get some references?'"

"I'll call the school principal where she's been a teacher's aide."

"'Yes, I know Evalynne,' said the Principal. 'She's a fine woman, always on time, very responsible and kind to our students. You can also call our Pastor because we go to the same church.'"

"I called the Pastor. 'She's honest and has helped in keeping our Social Hall nice and clean. I surely recommend her.'"

"So Audrey and I formulated a plan. Jerome was using one bedroom as a music room, the baby had a room and they had a guest bedroom for Ruby and Isaiah who came to visit every other week. However, I had an unused guest room and Evalynne could sleep at our house. Evalynne would help Audrey with I.J. from 9 to 12 and then come to my house."

"All I needed was the laundry done and the floors. But if Evalynne was there to babysit in the afternoons, I could go on bike rides with Alex when he came home. This would make Alex very happy."

"I called Evalynne. "Work for you, the Sit-In Lady, AND an engineer AND a lawyer AND a doctor? I think I've died and gone to heaven.'"

"Are there any things that you need?"

"'Only one thing. A TV. I have one soap opera I've got to watch at 1:30 and another one at 2:30. Then at night I have to watch my wrestling. And for my peanut butter and jelly sandwiches, I don't care for grape jam at all.' The money for her salary was settled quickly."

"Alex had made his mother a Heathkit TV and he said that Evalynne could have it in her room. He'd make another one for his mother."

"I can't believe that you make TVs for fun," I told him, always in awe of his talents."

"You need a little help in the house since you have three jobs and cook and take care of Marisa and me."

"Did I ever tell you I was too tired?"

"No, you never did." (And then one of his skilled hands was on my breast and the other hand held my head firmly as he kissed me then swept me up and carried me to the bedroom. 'I love it that you giggle all the way to the bed,' he said.)

JEANETTE VISITS

"'I have to ask a favor of you,' said Alex. 'You know that my mother is coming for Marisa's birthday. And you know how she is. She'll be critical, she'll give you advice. I can't help it, that's my mother.'"

"I know."

"'So I want you to learn a mantra now and be ready for her. It's nine words. When she says something you don't like, and she will, you say, 'I appreciate your concern. I'll give it serious thought.' Nine words. Will you do that for me? Because you love me.'"

"I will."

"'Say it now.'"

"Maybe she won't say anything mean."

"'She will. I love her and she's been a damn fine mother to me. But she is who she is and I'm just being proactive.'"

"All right, Alex. I promise." He left to go hiking."

"Audrey, carrying I.J., and Evalynne walked in. 'Jeanette is visiting?' Audrey asked. 'I hate the way she talks to you. Such barely concealed scorn. My mother in law Ruby is a gem, like her name.'"

"Evalynne had only met Jeanette once on her recent visit from L.A. 'She was a tough one, for sure. She seemed to blow a little air of negativity into the house.'"

"'How could she have raised such a fine man as Alex and be so mean?' asked Audrey."

"She's only mean to me, or about me. I'm the lower class girl who stole her son and never does anything right."

"'Has she ever approved of anything?'"

"Only once. Even my baby was the wrong sex and the wrong weight. But once she came over to our apartment with a stack of six copies of the LA Times. Her friend Birdie had been reading the paper and there was an article listing all the students who'd earned all A's at UCLA. And my name was on the list."

"'You're bringing more pride to the Berk name,' she said. 'Saul would have liked that. You can keep these newspapers and give one to your mother and one to your uncle. I have some for myself to show at the Sisterhood meeting.' That was the only time. Other than that, it was all put downs."

"'What did Alex do about the put downs?'"

"He'd tell her to stop it. Once, before we got married, I heard him tell her, 'The more you put her down, the more I want her.' He always defends me. If we're at her house and she says something awful, he just says 'We're leaving,' and we do. If it happens at our house, he escorts her to her car. And he'll say 'Don't talk to my wife like that.'"

"'Sweet Jesus, why can't people get along?' said Evalynne."

"A Holocaust survivor just told my class that it's the classic battle between good and evil."

"Two mornings later, Alex left to pick up his mother at the airport. Before he left, he gave me either a tutorial or a test."

"'If she says, 'Put a sweater on that baby, it's so cold out,' what do you say?'"

"I appreciate your concern. I'll give it serious thought."

"'If she says, 'This food is so spicy. Alex wasn't brought up to eat such spicy food,' what do you say?'"

"I appreciate your concern. I'll give it serious thought."

"'If she says 'Why do you wear your hair so long? It's hard to keep it neat that way.' what do you say?'"

"I appreciate your concern. I'll give it serious thought."

"'Don't forget, darling. I don't want you upset and I don't want her upset.'"

"I know." Poor Alex. He was worried about keeping peace between the two women who adored him."

"As his car left, I continued the tutorial. 'If she says, 'You still haven't tidied up your desk' I will say, 'I appreciate your concern. Why don't you stow it where the sun don't shine!'

"But I knew, and Alex knew, that I'd behave because I loved him."

"We both knew that Marisa didn't realize that she was now one so we just invited Martha and Ruth over with their children for pizza and cupcakes and ice cream. Jeanette and I argued over the cupcakes. I had made healthy blueberry muffins and she felt that they should have icing for a birthday."

"'Lordy, Lordy,' said Evalynne. 'So put the icing on the cupcakes, Valerie. It's not worth the argument.'"

"It's not that I want to argue but I don't want Marisa to have so much sugar."

"'A little sugar once in a while won't hurt her. I'm sure she gave sugar to Alex and look how nice and fine his teeth are.'"

"Jeanette explained. 'What we want to do is give her the iced cupcake and let her eat it and smoosh it all around. And we take a picture of it. That's what we did when Alex was one. It was adorable.'"

"I don't want her to smash the cupcake all over her face!" I said."

"Alex had picked up Marisa from her nap, diapered her and was putting her into her high chair in the dining room. She was wearing her ruffled pink outfit."

"'Let her smash the cupcake, Valerie.' said Alex."

"No. She's wearing a pretty outfit and I want a nice picture."

"'It will be cute,' said Jeanette. 'I'll show it to all my friends.'"

"No. Turning one is an important milestone. I want to put a nice picture in her baby book."

"'Let her smash the cupcake, Valerie.' from Alex in firm tones."

"NO." Now it was a battle, with sides drawn."

"'LET HER SMASH THE GODDAM CUPCAKE, VALERIE!' said Alex. This was angry Alex, nearly snarling at me. And then he laughed. 'I can't believe I just said that sentence. Now there's a message I never thought would come from my mouth. Darling, just let her have fun with it.' He propelled me into the kitchen. 'Let's do this privately,' he whispered."

"You're siding with her."

"'No, Vibila. You know I never do. This is beyond silly. Let her have her moment, relive her past. Do it for me.'"

"Then how will you reciprocate?"

"'What do you want?'"

"Will you give me whatever I want?"

"'Not a car. But for most things, you know I can be very generous.' He said this softly, in my ear, and then kissed my ear, too. Like he usually did, he had charmed me into doing what he wanted. I put my arms around him. Let Jeanette think she'd won. But I had won because now Alex and I would have an exciting night. His being generous could mean 'items' but also often meant our intimacy. "

"Evalynne came into the kitchen to get the ice cream. 'Mommy and Daddy kissing is the best present for a one year old,' she said, smiling with her wide smile."

THE UNBELIEVABLY SCARY NIGHT

"A month later, I took Marisa to the doctor on the corner. "She's not energetic at all today and she has a fever. What should I do?"

"He took her temperature and said that it was a little high. He prescribed baby aspirin and told me to keep her hydrated. It was Wednesday and I didn't work that day. I gave her water and juice but she only accepted a small amount. She turned her head away from food, even her favorite grapes. Her nap seemed to be longer than usual."

"When Alex got home, he was concerned and we didn't go for our bike ride. He kept taking her temperature and it kept rising. We gave her a cool bath but a half hour later, the temperature had risen again. At 10 pm, he told me to call the doctor again. Maybe he should see her in his office."

"'Just continue to monitor her and give her the baby aspirin. If the temperature doesn't go down, bring her to see me at 9am.' Alex, listening in, took the phone."

"'Shouldn't we bring her in now, Doctor?'"

"'No. The morning will be fine.'"

"Alex took her into the shower with him for a cool shower. He kept reading his Merck Manual for information which wasn't there. By 1 am, her temperature was 104. Alex knocked on Evalynne's door."

"'Evalynne, I'm so sorry to wake you.'"

"'Not asleep, Alex. I'm praying for the baby.'"

"'You've raised three children, Evalynne. Would you look at her and give us your opinion?'"

"Evalynne peered at Marisa and shook her head. 'She don't look good, Alex.' Just then, Marisa began to shake. "

"Oh, Alex. Her fingers are blue!" We took off her onesie and her toes were blue also."

"'That's it! We're taking her to the Emergency Room. Get in the car, Valerie.'"

"'You're doing the right thing,' Evalynne called as we ran to the car."

"I don't know if she's breathing, Alex."

"'Breathe into her mouth, like we learned in that class. Remember? One, two, three, Puff. One. two, three, Puff.' Alex turned onto 16th Street and started to drive very fast. When he encountered traffic, he sounded the horn and went around the car. Beep, Beep, Beep. At the same time, he counted for me,

One, two, three, Puff, as I blew into my baby's mouth. Now her lips were blue."

"A siren sounded behind us and we saw the red flashing lights of a motorcycle. Alex pulled over and the policeman shouted at us. 'You're going 95 miles an hour!'"

"'My baby is dying and we're rushing her to Good Sam,' Alex said, frantically."

"The policeman peered into the car, nodded at me breathing into her mouth. 'Follow me!' he yelled. 'I'll call ahead and tell the hospital you're coming.'"

"The motorcycle rushed through the streets, siren on and colored lights flashing. Alex followed right behind. Cars pulled to the side to let us pass. He continued to count for me. When we pulled into the parking lot of the emergency room, a doctor and nurse with a rolling crib were waiting for us. The doctor looked at our baby and clamped an oxygen mask onto her tiny face. They ran inside with the crib. The nurse looked over her shoulder and said, 'Sign her in inside. We've got her,' and they disappeared inside the building. Alex put his arms around me as I sobbed into his face. "

"Will she die?" He shook his head. We signed Marisa in and gave them our insurance card and our permission for treatment."

"'Please wait in the waiting room, Mr. and Mrs. Berk. You can't see her right now and we have excellent pediatricians helping her.'"

"We sat on a small plastic couch, hugging tightly in each other's arms."

"But what's happening? Why can't we see her?" I cried as I spoke.

"'We have to have faith in medical science now. Do you want coffee?'"

"An entire hour went by. Then, Alex went up to the nurses desk. 'Any news about our baby?'"

"'They're treating her now. The doctor will come and talk to you when he's done.'"

"And another forty five minutes passed. The same doctor came up to us, rubbing his face tiredly. 'I'm Dr. Walavalcar,' he said in an Indian accent. 'She's going to be okay. But you came in not a moment too soon. Another hour with that fever and you would have lost her.'"

"I was now crying with relief. Alex grabbed the slight doctor's hand and shook it, 'You saved our baby's life. We can't thank you enough. But what was it?'"

"'A severe respiratory infection. It happens sometimes. We're observing her now. You can take her home in an hour. We'll bring her out. Watch her all day tomorrow.' He smiled. 'I hate it when I have to tell parents bad news. Good news I like.' He walked away."

"I hugged Alex again. "You also saved our baby's life. You make decisions so quickly."

"'We both did it, darling.'"

"Marisa was happy to come into my arms and her forehead was cool. We drove home, overwhelmed with how close we'd come to tragedy."

"It was 4 in the morning, still dark. When we got home, we went to Evalynne's room to tell her the baby would be okay. She was kneeling at the side of her bed. 'I've prayed to the Lord all night.'"

"Your prayers and your advice saved her, " I said. "We're not going to work today and I wish you would rest, too."

"'I will. I'll go over to Audrey's but she'll understand if I just take care of I.J.'"

"We put the baby between us in the bed and all three of us slept. After an hour, I woke and checked her breathing, nice and steady, and I slept again. I was awakened by the phone at 8 am."

"'What's the matter with the baby?' demanded my mother."

"Did Evalynne call you and tell you?"

"'Tell me what? No, no one called. At 1 am I woke up with a terrible feeling. like my throat was choking, and I thought, something is wrong with the baby!'"

"That's incredible, Mom. We had to take her to the hospital. Her temperature kept rising and then it was 104 and Alex said, we're taking her to the Emergency Room. And the doctor said that we got there just in time. But you're in LA. How could you have known?"

"'I don't know,' said my Mom. 'I'm just telling you what happened.'"

"Well, she's all right now. She's right here, breathing nicely and her body is cool."

"'Thank God!' said my Mom."

"Alex was exhausted and I let him sleep. About 11 am, he woke up and I told him about my mother. "How could that be, Alex?"

"'There are unexplained things that sometimes come about. The only thing I can think of is that you and your mom have. such a connection between you that she sensed your extreme distress, even in Los Angeles. Or maybe your Guardian Angel alerted her.'"

"Who could that be? My father, do you think?"

"Now awake, Alex did three things. First, he told me to find a new pediatrician. 'If we'd listened to him, we might not have Little Pooh here.' Then he went to the Central Police Department to find out the name of the motorcycle cop who had escorted us to the hospital. He left four six packs of beer for the police in this man's honor, with thanks. Next he went to the hospital. Dr. Walavalcar was off for the day but Alex left a large box of Miracle Mile pastries for the staff and wrote a note of commendation for the doctor. He came home with two large pizzas, one of them my favorite anchovy."

"'One last thing to do. Let's say the Hebrew prayer of thanks for deliverance from illness.'"

"Evalynne watched us say the prayer. 'A man who acts fast and then prays his gratitude is a very special man,' she said. I agreed."

MARTIN LUTHER KING, JUNIOR

"Eugene Silver was very excited as he opened the PACE meeting. "Guess what, everyone. Martin Luther King, Junior is coming to Phoenix in three weeks. There's going to be a big parade which he'll lead, from the downtown courthouse to the New Hope Baptist Church. And when we get to the church, Martin Luther King is going to give out twenty awards to the people who have been so effective for the cause. And all six of us who were in the Sit In at Woolworth's will be getting an award and shaking his hand. What an honor"

"Alex and I and Marisa in her stroller walked with hundreds of others, mainly black people but other races also. Audrey and Jerome, with I.J., and Evalynne and her son and grandsons walked with us. We walked from the courthouse to the church, singing the inspirational songs of our quest for civil liberties."

We shall overcome. We shall overcome.

We shall overcome someday. Oh, deep in my heart, I do believe That we shall overcome someday.

"When we all arrived at the church, the twenty people who were to receive an award were directed to sit in the first two rows. Alex and Marisa and our friends sat behind me. Then we lined up on the stage."

"Sister Berk," boomed Martin Luther King in a deep, sonorous voice. He shook my hand and handed me an award. FOR PARTICIPATING IN AN IMPORTANT AND SUCCESSFUL SIT IN."

"Newspaper cameras flashed, recording this moment and I sat down to applause."

"We were there also," said Sister Cordelia. "Sister Agnes and I marched. We didn't know you then but we were there."

MAKING TALIA

Another story I would not tell the nuns.

We were sailing in a large sailboat on a beautiful clear Saturday in March. Alex sailed expertly as always and Marisa was laughing at the soaring birds, strapped into a seat and wearing a baby lifesaver vest.

"Alex, do you think we should try for another baby?"

"Would it be too soon? The babies would be two years apart."

"Well, we're both only children and we want four or five children. If they're two years apart, they'll be friends. Which we didn't have growing up."

"Could you handle two babies?"

"Oh, yes." I was so confident and so oblivious about the hard task of a baby and a toddler.

"Okay." said Alex. "Do you want to make the new baby now? There's a little inlet up ahead and we can dock and set up the tent and bring out the ice chest." Early in the morning, we'd gone to the Miracle Mile delicatessen and bought all sorts of yummy foods packed in little white containers. We had rye bread and pickled herring and whitefish and stuffed peppers, and Romanian olives and roast chicken and grapes for Marisa. We'd also bought containers of custard and rice pudding and many bottles of juice. We enjoyed our feast and then Marisa fell asleep on a pile of quilts.

Sometimes Alex made love to me in two ways. Before he entered my body, he worked on my mind. He said lovely things and suggestive things and even as I knew what he was doing, it always worked.

"Today we could make a baby because your period was two weeks ago. You're ovulating now."

"It amazes me that you keep track of my periods. Do you

still have your little calendar?"

"Someone has to keep track. You don't. Your period is always such a surprise to you."

"It's good that you still like me with all my faults."

"You have very few faults, darling. Sometimes at work I think, this crappy day will be over in two hours and I can go home to my Nookums."

"You think that? But really, you're thinking about your dinner."

"That, too. Mostly I'm thinking of my girl, who has the face of an angel and the body of a devil. And such sweetness and appreciation."

Just this speech had warmed me a lot but he went on.

"Remember our gardener, Ito? His daughter, Serena, remember her? She's written an article on the attributes of Greek goddesses. Ito brought me a copy of it, so proud of her."

"Did you like Serena?"

"Well, she's older than me. The gardener's daughter."

"So I would be the printer's daughter."

"Would your father have liked me?"

"Of course he would."

"What was he like?"

"European, a bit formal, spoke seven languages."

"A bright man."

"Yes, and he would have loved that you're so bright and graduated from Caltech. So you learned about the Greek goddesses from Serena's article? Which goddess would I be like?"

"A few of them. First of all, Aphrodite, the goddess of love."

He paused to kiss me, long and hard. "And then you are like Demeter, who rescued her daughter Persephone from Hades for eight months every year. You are that sort of mother. You'll always rescue your children from various types of Hades."

"Really? Tell me more about Demeter."

"Demeter was the goddess of agriculture. After Hades, the god of the underworld, kidnapped her daughter, Persephone,

Demeter became unconcerned with the harvest and so widespread famine came about. Persephone had to stay in the underworld because she ate one pomegranate seed there. Finally, with no plants growing, Zeus, the King of the gods, intervened. Persephone had to stay in the underworld for four months a year and that would explain winter, when no plants would grow. Then for eight months, she could come home to her mother and food and flowers and trees would grow."

"So interesting, Alex."

"But you probably are more like Aphrodite, who was also the goddess of beauty and fertility. So we called her today. And how does a mortal man make love to Aphrodite? One hundred kisses all over her to start, I think. And a little touch here and a little touch over there."

The tent seemed warm and we could hear Marisa's soft breathing in her sleep. The lake lapped against the shore of our inlet and seagulls called in the distance.

"You're lovely," said Alex. "And you're mine. And we're going to make a very sweet, pleasant baby now." He partially undressed me and partially undressed himself. Then he said what he almost always said, in that tone of awe and satisfaction, "You are so goddamn beautiful."

Afterwards, I smiled up at him. "I feel like screaming I AM SO HAPPY! across the lake but I'd wake up Marisa.

"It's my job to make sure that you're happy," said Alex, smiling his beautiful smile.

Two weeks later, the doctor on the corner confirmed that I was pregnant.

"And once again, on the first try! Assisted by my strong and cunning sperm," said Alex, swaggering a little with pride. "We'll call this new baby Jonny and when he's born we'll name him Saul."

JEANETTE AND THE CIVIL RIGHTS MOVEMENT

The nuns and I were meeting at Irina's Café.

"Then it was April and Jeanette was visiting for her monthly three day inspection."

"'I certainly hope the new baby is a boy,' she stated. 'And that you don't come down with anything like you did the last time.'"

"I was about to say, "I got sick on purpose!" when Alex made a sharp gesture with both hands. 'Ignore her!!!' So I did.

"Jeanette paused in front of the three newly framed pictures in the family room. I had just put them up. One was of me, taken by Alex, shaking the hand of Martin Luther King, Jr. After many of us had marched from the downtown City Hall to a Baptist church, Martin Luther King, Jr. gave awards to twenty people who had been "active in the struggle" as he put it. The second picture was the award, for voter registration, participating in a sit in and as an officer in PACE. And the third picture was a newspaper photo of four of us sitting at the Woolworth's lunch counter. Visible in the picture were Eugene. Preston. Larry and I."

"Jeanette looked at the pictures and sniffed. 'You and all these do gooders are causing drastic changes. You couldn't leave well enough alone. I might not be here for these terrible changes, maybe in twenty years from now, but you both will be. There will be changes and more competition for this little girl here. I will look down from heaven and laugh at you, Valerie. You'll be so sorry.'"

"I was forming my reply. 'I CAN'T FIND THE LEMONADE', Alex called from the kitchen. I translated it as 'Get in here now!'"

"'When she goes on like this, don't waste your breath,' said Alex. 'You're never going to convince her. She's stuck in her provincial ways. Change the subject and don't let one word upset you. I've already told you this.'"

"It's fine for you to make suggestions, Alex."

"'This is not a suggestion. It's an order, Valerie. Change the subject.'"

"Oh, yeah?"

"'Don't start, Valerie.' He stared at me with glinty eyes and not a hint of a smile."

"I walked back to the family room. "Would you like to come with me to Marisa's music class? It's for toddlers ages one to two. She claps her hands and plays with some instruments." I still did not address Jeanette as anything. The word 'Mother' would not fall trippingly from my tongue. So I stood in front of her."

"'That sounds like fun and then we can go to that darling café after, my treat.' Jeanette smiled at me."

"Who's a good wife?" I whispered to Alex.

"'Valerie is a good wife.' he whispered back."

"At the music class, as Marisa shook little shakers in both her hands, I mused. Where had Alex come from? He had not one prejudiced bone in his body. He always made friends with people of all colors, all religions, as I did. Both of us invited them to our home. He had expressed great pride in what Jeanette called 'my do gooder work.' He had said, 'You're following your grandmother's example. She'd say, 'Let me have the courage to make my life a blessing.' And you're a blessing to me and others.' And then he would hug me."

"That evening, I asked Alex, "Regarding minorities, what was your father like?"

"'My father was color blind. He hired a black foreman, Justin, and gave him a lot of responsibility and they were great friends. When I worked with my dad in the summers, we'd go to a bar after work with Justin and with Hector, the contractor who was Hispanic. Everyone treated everyone with respect. Except treating me with respect because they wouldn't let me have a beer.'"

"'They'd all be joking and laughing. And they had this running joke. 'A black, a Jew and a Mexican walked into a bar...... .and they'd have different funny endings. One joke I remember. When the Jew was ninety, his two friends paid for a call girl to visit him on his ninetieth birthday. 'I've come to give you super sex,' the call girl told him. 'At my age, I'll take the soup,' said the old Jew.'"

"'And the summer I turned fifteen, Hector told my dad to get me a beer. My first beer. And I still drink Coors.'"

"So your mother is prejudiced and your father isn't."

"'My father was like your uncle. Help people whenever you can. Just disregard what my mother says about race.'"

"I thought men married women like their mothers."

"'I was looking for a girl who could be like my mother, loving and attentive to me. 'Did you get enough to eat, dear?' But then, for the rest of my perfect girl, she had to be the OPPOSITE of my mother. Interested in the issues of the day, feisty but sweet, talented in her own way. AND Jewish. AND beautiful. AND with a body you couldn't keep your hands off! And there you were, the total package, my Vibila.'"

"I was sitting on the edge of our bed. "Did you get enough to eat, dear?"

(Alex grinned and tipped me onto the bed and rolled down my shorts.)

"After three days, Jeanette was preparing to fly home. Alex thought he might impress her by showing her the magazine article of the ON TO COLLEGE Art Show, held at the Phoenix Museum."

"'A lot of the high school students are exhibiting their paintings and ceramics and other art works. It was all Valerie's idea.', he said, tousling my hair."

"'She's raising the expectations of these minority children and most of them are bound to be disappointed Making them think they should go to college. She should be steering the girls into typing and the boys into plumbing.'"

"'Plumbing is too good for them,' said Alex. 'They should be steered into construction labor and the girls should be taught to be maids.'"

"'Make fun of me, Alex. In twenty years you're going to see that I was right. People have to learn to accept their station in life.'"

"'Their station?' I said, remembering that term used against me."

"Alex rushed in to avoid an argument. 'Look, Valerie is doing all kinds of good for people. She's..........'"

"'Then she should spend her time organizing her closets,' said my mother in law."

COMMANDO SEX

Another story NOT for the Nuns.

Now it was May and Sebastian had flown from St. Louis to L.A. to spend time with his mom for her birthday. Alex had suggested a weekend camping trip in Flagstaff and Sebastian decided to bring Kay. After we arrived at the rustic campsite, we all went on an 'easy' one hour hike, Alex carrying Marisa on a seat on his back. Then Alex and Sebastian walked us back to our campsite and then they left for an arduous three hour hike. The easy hike had exhausted Kay and me. We relaxed on nice camp chairs while Marisa napped.

"Are things going well, Kay?" She knew what I meant.

"Wonderful." A pause. "Valerie, do you and Alex ever do Commando Sex?"

"Yes."

"Probably one of them taught it to the other."

"Probably."

"Do you do it this way? He tells you what you're going to do, then he gives you several directions. Then after a while he says, 'All right, Kathryn, come now.' He only calls me Kathryn in bed. Is that how you do it?"

I laughed. "Alex never calls me Kathryn. He says, 'Come, darling.'"

"I can only come with Sebastian," she said. "Is it that we're so used to following what they say for twenty minutes that our bodies just automatically listen to 'Come'?"

"I think so. Does Sebastian use a sexy voice?"

"Yes, very sexy, very deep and serious."

"Alex, too."

We smiled at each other and read our magazines.

That night in our tent, I asked, "Did Sebastian teach you Commando Sex?"

"No, I taught him."

"Where did you learn it?"

"From a book I bought while we still lived in L.A. Is that what you want to do tonight? Don't worry about being noisy. That's why I put their tent on the other side of the tables."

"Aren't you tired from your long hike?"

"Too tired to make love to my wife? Are you kidding? And the baby is fast asleep. Okay, darling. I'm going to make several suggestions now. Or do you want to direct things tonight?"

"No, I want you to direct things. I'd rather be the follower. It's much easier for me. I'm directing two programs for work. I don't want to direct you or us."

"You just want to lie here and be thrilled?"

"You've got it."

"Okay, my love. Lift up your leg, let me get your shoe. Now your other shoe. Down come the jeans and panties. Let's unbutton your blouse. Let me get the bra. Look at you. Seven weeks pregnant and so goddamn beautiful. You Are Lovely!"

Now he gave me little feathery kisses from my neck down to my stomach. He sucked my breasts. Then his fingers went to my clitoris and I was floating above the tent.

"Don't stop doing that," I murmured. After a while I said, "I'm ready."

"You're ready when I say you're ready," he said sternly. "This is Commando Sex. Do what I tell you when I say it." Then came the commands.

"Put your legs around me."

"Higher."

"Roll over onto your stomach."

"Sit in my lap now."

"You be on top now."

"Move, darling."

"Okay, darling. Come now."

My legs became stiff and then my body was shaking. I came and rolled over onto the sleeping bag.

"That was exceptionally good," said Alex, taking a thermos of water from the food chest. He gave me water and then drank some. He stretched out his arms. "We didn't even bother the baby. How do you see me when we do Commando Sex? What are you thinking about?"

"I think of you as the General and me as the soldier. I try to follow the orders quickly and efficiently."

"How does it make you feel? Emotionally?"

"Aroused. Excited. Peaceful, somehow."

Alex smiled. "Well, I think of myself as The Conductor. You are my musician and I urge you higher or lower. Or maybe you're my violin."

"You're creating a lovely tune?"

"A lovely symphony. Good night, Vibila. I love you." Then I felt his rhythmic breathing against my ear. He exercised hard, made love hard and now he looked totally relaxed. From forty feet away I heard a squeal. Kay and the Commando Sex. Then I heard a low chuckle. Sebastian. Proud of himself. He'd completed his symphony. Both guys had to have control. But oh, how charming they both could be.

Something hard was hurting my arm. I turned around and felt the bear that Sebastian and Kay had brought for Marisa.

It was not a sweet little teddy bear but a small realistic looking black bear.

And I remembered. In our first year of marriage we'd gone camping in Big Bear. We'd been sleeping in our tent when we heard a huge crash. Alex grabbed his flashlight and looked out the tent flap.

"It's a bear. He knocked the food chest off the table. He's grabbed the package of bacon." He looked at his watch. "2 am. God, he's huge. His eyes look so crazy. He must be really hungry to come so close to us. He's over by the latrines eating the bacon but I think he'll come back for more food."

Alex reached for his rifle and checked to make sure it was loaded. "Yes, he's back. Now he's taken the loaf of bread." Alex shot a blast up in the air. "He's only six feet away. I just want to scare him. If I wound him he might charge the tent."

"Don't kill him, Alex."

"No, darling. I'd only kill him if he tried to hurt you. You go back to sleep. I'll just sit here."

"Is he gone?"

"I'm not sure. It's hard to see, it's so dark out."

"So lie down and sleep, Alex."

"Shhh. It's fine. Sleep, darling."

I'd been exhausted from our long hike and our lovemaking. I closed my eyes and when I opened them, streams of light could be seen from our little plastic window. My watch said 6 am. Alex was sitting in the doorway of our tent, his rifle in his lap, his eyes open.

"You've been up for four hours?"

"I have to protect you. Who knows what a bear will think of doing? Keeping you safe is my highest priority."

"I thought giving me an orgasm was your highest priority."

"That, too. "

"I'll always remember that you sat with your rifle for almost all night to protect me from a bear. I'll tell it to our children when we have them."

"That I protect my family? All men do that. Real men."

Now it was three and a half years later, I looked at Alex sleeping but he would waken in a moment if I told him we were in danger of any kind. Determined, protective, loving and in his own words, a real man. Now Marisa was standing in her travel crib. We smiled at one another. "Good morning, honey. When you're older I'll tell you about how your daddy stayed up all night to protect me from a bear."

KAY GIVES UP

Sunday night we returned to Phoenix and Kay drove Sebastian to the airport to catch his plane back to St. Louis. It was raining heavily and the radio had announced that most flights would be postponed for one to two hours. "Just drop me off at the door," Sebastian told Kay. "I have to write a speech for the mayor and it's silly for you to wait around the cold airport." They kissed and agreed that it had been a wonderful camping trip. Sebastian said to think of a plan for them to get together again for July 4th.

Kay was back to my house by 9:30, her eyes swollen from crying, her face miserable.

"What happened, Kay? Why are you crying?"

"Sebastian. Why else do I cry? After our great weekend, after our Commando Sex, he shows me how he really feels. He said not to come into the airport, that he had work to do, so we kissed and then I drove away. But after one block, I reconsidered. If he had to be in the airport for maybe two hours, I could cheer him up. We could have a drink together. Maybe he'd read his speech to me, ask me for my opinion. So I turned around, parked and went to the bar. He wasn't there so I went to the coffee shop. And there he was at a table with some girl."

"What girl?"

"I don't know. Some girl. Some red haired girl. And they were laughing and she had her hand on the table and Sebastian put his hand over it. Typical Sebastian early flirtation move. He smiled at her in great delight."

"Did you confront them?"

"No. What would I say? That's the same smile he gave me after an hour of Commando Sex? No. Now I know who I am. I'm the west coast squeeze for when he comes to L.A. But only if Annaliese is on location. "

"Oh Kay. I'm so sorry."

"Don't be sorry. I'm giving up Sebastian forever. He'll never change. I'm going to take the correspondent job they offered me and go to London. I'll protect my sanity and my self respect. Maybe then I can fall in love with some other guy and obliterate Sebastian from my mind."

"I think you're right. Tell me about London."

"It's much more money, for one thing , and I can sublet the flat that Susan Minors is leaving. And there are several friends from college already living in London and writing to me about good times and interesting people to interview." "It sounds like just the right adventure, Kay."

OH, BEING A WIFE ISN'T GOOD ENOUGH FOR YOU?

A story NOT for the nuns.

Kay and I had a cup of coffee together and we talked. My life, her new life in London, her new life without Sebastian. No more Sebastian, ever again.

Then she got into her car to drive back to L.A. and I waved to her from the front door.

When Alex came home I was still imagining Kay in London. "Alex, Kay will now be an international journalist and Annaliese is a movie star."

"So?"

"So it's kind of amazing. Our friends from high school."

"What are you implying? You're three intelligent women and they're living up to their potential and you're not?"

"No."

"You want to go to London and write articles and sleep with a married guy like Kay did in Italy, pining away for Mr. Unattainable?"

"No, Alex, and you don't have to sound so angry."

"Angry? Do I sound angry? Maybe you want to be a movie star like Annaliese but mainly a waitress between films. Or be in politics like Sebastian or in law school like Bobby and Marty."

"No."

"No? So what are you complaining about?"

"I'm not complaining. Just commenting."

"Valerie, over a year ago, in December, you were crying and saying 'If the baby is born dead, I don't know how I'll cope. Or if the baby won't be able to ever walk or talk.' Now you have this dear little person that we've created together. Seventeen months old. WHERE'S YOUR GRATITUDE?"

"Alex, please don't scream at me. Marisa and Evalynne are watching TV."

"You know, screaming is really too good for you. How is your wish to have a different life supposed to make me feel? I think I'm giving you everything and I don't mean just the money. I give you encouragement. I give you fidelity. I give you my love. But that's not enough, I guess."

"Oh, Alex, that's not what I meant." I moved forward to hug him and he moved back.

"You don't want me to hug you?"

"Right now, I'm pretty damn disgusted with you. You wanted UCLA, I moved to Los Felix. You wanted a child, I gave you a child. You wanted a house, I gave you a house. You wanted to teach Sunday mornings, I take care of Marisa, which I enjoy, but you dress in a pretty dress and off you go.

"You wanted these social work jobs and every Tuesday and Thursday I come all the way out of my way to pick you up in the slums after I've been working all day."

"But if I could drive and had a car I could drive myself there and back."

"Driving and a car are not open for discussion. You have me and several friends to drive you. You don't need a car. If you have a car, you'll never be home."

"So it's not that I'm so uncoordinated that I can't learn to drive. It's that you want to keep me at home most of the time, like a prisoner. Peter, Peter, Pumpkin Eater. Had a wife and couldn't keep her. Put her in a pumpkin shell…"

"Yes. I treat you just like Otis treats Abigail and if you get out of line I beat you with a hairbrush."

We sat in the living room and glared at each other.

Finally, and I could hear the quiver in my voice, I said, "Alex, I love you."

"Maybe not enough."

"Don't say that. I'll put dinner on the table now."

"Don't bother. I don't want your dinner. I'm too disappointed in you to eat your dinner."

My dinner———my nightly gift to him. My hug. He didn't want either of them.

Alex took off his suit jacket and tie and went into our bedroom to change. I continued to sit in the living room, almost frozen. Then I heard a splintering noise. I ran to the bedroom and Alex had punched the door leading to his closet with his fist——karate chopped it and there was a round hole in the wood.

"Every house, Alex. You've punched a hole now in all three houses we've lived in."

"I'm expressing my anger. Every time. My anger with you. But I don't touch your pretty face."

"Is your hand okay? You're bleeding a little. Please let me hug you."

"No. You're not satisfied with the life I've given you. You not only have a child, another one coming, and a husband but you ARE practicing social work and you ARE teaching. I thought you'd carved out a very balanced life for yourself——wife, mother, social worker, teacher. I never stopped you from doing what you want, from expressing yourself. Do you want to take a full time social work job taking care of disadvantaged kids all day while your own kid is in child care?"

"No, that's not what I want."

"What do you want?"

Right then I wanted him, in his wife beater undershirt, muscles in his arms. I felt desperate to have those arms around me. Why had I felt envy for the supposedly glamorous lives of Kay and Anneliese? And for my friend Arlene who worked for a publishing company in New York City? The path not taken? He'd given up a career in astronomy for me.

I sighed. "What I want is not to have an argument with you. I'm sorry but I do want a little more than just being home with Marisa and I have that. There's a little part of my life where I'm not 'Marisa's mommy' or 'Mrs. Alex Berk'. I'm Valerie Berk, a person in her own right. And you're a wonderful husband and you help me be me. I DO NOT want a full time job at this point. My mother worked full time because she had to, and I hated coming home every single day to an empty house."

"Well, my mother never worked. She did some good things like raising money for immigrant children and that kind of thing with the Sisterhood, but mainly she made sure that my father and I were comfortable and well cared for."

"And look how that worked out for her."

"What do you mean?"

"I mean that after a certain stage in their marriage, your father was spending a lot of time with a woman who worked full time. She worked with him, of course. Maybe your mother could not offer him what Claudia Clemons could."

Alex stared at me as he changed his suit pants into jeans. I knew that this was a very sore point with him."

"Maybe."

"Alex, I'm very happy with my life as it is right now. I don't know why you got so hurt and angry. You usually say something like,' I'll get you a ticket to London, honey' as a joke."

"Well, Valerie, possibly I'm feeling guilty that I captured this bright little butterfly who had all these scholarships for back east and I shut her up in my butterfly net. 'No career in New York City for you, dear'"

"I like your butterfly net. I would have gone to Outer Mongolia to be with you."

"And now?"

"I still would."

Swiftly, I unzipped his jeans and kissed Little Alex. He put his hand on my hair and then caressed my face. I had to be quick because Marisa could be walking in any time now. I was quick but thorough and then Alex kissed my lips.

"This argument can be over if you promise me one thing," he said.

"Anything."

"Promise me that you won't nag me to drive. At least let's give it a year."

So that was the price I had to pay. I could have quite a bit of freedom but had to negotiate it with him. He had to be in control. He could grant me permission to work or to volunteer. It wasn't a matter of my coordination or of money for a car. He needed to know where I was, to be in control. On the other hand, there was Little Alex. He would bring me delight later in the evening. I had such a passion for Alex, a love that Kay, Anneliese and Arlene and so many other girls longed for. He was so loving to me. I had heaven right here on Palos Verde Drive.

"I will not mention the word car for a year," I said, smiling at him. And then we would see.

Alex hugged me and walked me into the kitchen with his arms around me. "What did you make for dinner?"

VALERIE'S REBUTTAL

The next day, I thought about what Alex had said about capturing a butterfly. I thought about how we experienced rapture together and how tenderly he treated me and our little girl. So I put aside the lesson plan I was working on and spent the next hours composing a poem for him.

To Alex,
You said you captured a butterfly.
That is not true.
I was not a being who flew.
You captured a caterpillar, enclosed her above In the warm chrysalis of your love.
You watched me emerge and ,like a painter, drew The outlines of what you knew I would become.
Painted with a light hand
Encouraging, with slight demand
The woman who wanted to do And all because of you. And everything I tried
I needed you by my side.
I go from strength to strength.
You go to any length
To help me gain grit.
Love from the butterfly who won't ever flit.

As soon as Alex came home, I handed it to him. He sat down on our bed to read it.

"Seriously, darling, this is a wonderful poem. May I add to it?"

Will the butterfly who won't flit Come on my lap and sit?

After quite a few kisses he said, "My wife wrote me a poem." Then he got up and removed a photo of us in the snow from its frame and put my poem in the frame and hung it up.

"You really were a butterfly, you know. And in high school you were so oblivious to the guys who admired you and wanted to date you. When you wore that red sweater with the gray skirt, WOW! But you were so serious, concentrating on your grades and your debate tournaments. And you had that 'she won't kiss' reputation."

"Who wanted to date me?"

"You know one, Mike Stein. And Marty Cresig wanted you and so did Bobby Roth. And that captain of the football team. And others."

"You're making this up. Marty was dating my friend Arlene."

"He broke up with Arlene so he could date you. Why do you think he paid $25 for you at the Latin Club Slave Auction when the going price was $5? And when you both acted in JULIUS CAESAR and he was Julius and you were Calpurnia, his wife, remember? He was wearing that laurel crown and I had a part with no lines as Caesar's guard. So when you came out in that skimpy toga, Marty whispered to me. 'Isn't that a tasty dish to set before the King?'"

"Really?"

"Yes. And Mike Stein came up to me and said you and he had been dating on and off for three years and he asked me to leave you alone. I told him we'd both pursue you and you could choose. I'd have been shocked if you'd ever chosen him. And then Marty said I want to ask Valerie out and Marty was a real challenge being your debate mentor and the student body president. So I told him, 'Fuck off, she's mine.' And next Bobby came up to me and said that you and I were wrong for each other because we had nothing in common."

"What did you say to him?"

"Fuck off."

"And I heard you saying to Sebastian that to get me you'd have to intrigue me sexually."

"And I did, didn't I?"

"Oh, yes. My first open mouthed kiss."

"After dating you for three whole months."

"Because by that time I trusted you."

"And after that kiss I knew. I'm going to get this girl and marry her and we'll both be very happy. And one day you would write me a meaningful poem." I hugged him, my Alex.

"Let's go say hello to Little Pooh. What's for dinner? I'm starving."

Part Six

WHAT HAPPENED TEN YEARS LATER, 1970

IT ALL COMES TOGETHER

It was Cletus, Evalynne's son, on the phone. "How are you, Valerie? I thought you'd want to know. My mother had a stroke this morning and she's at Good Samaritan Hospital."

"Oh, no. How bad was it?"

"Pretty bad. She's paralyzed on the right side."

"NO! "

"She can't walk without falling."

"Can she talk?"

"Yes, slightly garbled."

"Can I come see her?"

"Not today but tomorrow. She wants to see you all, she says. There's no set visiting hours, They have a small room we can all stay in and two people at a time can go see her."

"I'll be there. Have you called Audrey?"

"Just called her. She's coming tomorrow, too. And you know, my mother asked me to call Sister Cordelia, too ,because she's hoping those nuns will pray for her. Of course our own minister is coming. We're going to get rid of her discouragement. She said, 'I'll never walk again.' Our job is to tell her, 'Oh yes you will.'"

"I'll try to encourage her. You have such a wonderful mother."

I walked into the small waiting room at Good Samaritan Hospital. Sitting there were Sister Cordelia, Sister Agnes and Mrs. O'Dell. We all hugged. Then in came Barbara Mae, Cletus' wife. Barbara Mae was tall and very thin. She was dressed in a shiny black pantsuit with a red silk blouse. Her long fingernails were painted in a black and red design. She had long straight black hair. Her lips were very red and her eyelashes were so long that they had to be false. Evalynne had described Barbara Mae to me. 'She's not only selfish and lazy but she's the kind of person who is pretty on the outside and ugly on the inside. And she's nosy like you can't imagine.'

"Valerie," said Barbara Mae. "Not twenty five anymore, I see. So how old are you now?" "Thirty two," I said.

"You don't look too bad," she said. Now there was a compliment.

"My goodness, she's a very pretty woman," said Mrs. O'Dell. "We've known her now for seven years and she's still just as lovely as she was then."

"Well, not quite," I protested.

"Ladies, please. We're here for Evalynne. Not to argue," said Sister Cordelia.

"So you've known these nuns for seven years?" asked Barbara Mae. "Aren't there three nuns? Evalynne told me that."

We all looked at Barbara Mae.

"I remember. She was a young Filipino nun, who had two first names, like I do."

"Sister Mary Louise," said Mrs. O'Dell.

"Who we are not going to talk about," said Sister Cordelia firmly.

"Ah, a mystery," said Barbara Mae. "Whatever has happened to Sister Mary Louise? Even nuns have secrets." No one answered.

"I'm going to get soda from the machine," Barbara Mae said.

She left and there was silence in the small room.

"There's a reason why her initials are B.M.," said Mrs. O'Dell softly.

We laughed. "Oh, sometimes you have a wicked mind, Betsy," said Sister Cordelia.

Cletus came in now and with him was his son Tyrique in a navy uniform, holding hands with his pregnant wife.

"Valerie, this is Chun-ja. We met while I was stationed in Korea." Chun-ja and I shook hands.

"Honey, this is the lady I told you about who directed ON -TO- COLLEGE. That organization helped me go to ASU and then I got into ROTC. And Valerie, Clebar is at San Diego State right now."

Barbara Mae was back, drinking her soda, having asked no one if they wanted one. "So you're visiting your maid, Valerie, like a lot of gracious white ladies."

I was surprised at her venom. I hardly knew her.

"Mama, please," said Tyrique.

Cletus looked angry and disgusted. "Barbara Mae! I called Valerie and asked her to come see Mama."

"Oh, don't mind me," said Barbara Mae. "I just tell it like I see it."

Silence in the room.

Sister Agnes always tried to bring peace. "So how did Clebar get his name? I've never heard that name."

"No," said Barbara Mae. "That's because I made it up. Part Cletus and part Barbara. See, Clebar." "That's nice," said Sister Agnes.

I was surprised to see Larry Meade walk into the room. I hadn't seen him in about two years. Working almost full time, I hadn't been attending all the weekly PACE meetings although I still wrote and edited the PACE newsletter every month.

We greeted each other with hugs, still feeling close from having participated in the Woolworth Sit In for a long and sometimes scary day.

"How do you know Evalynne?" I asked him.

"Cletus and I have been friends for a long time. I'm here to support him. And we go to the same church."

"And I heard that your wife had a baby."

"Yes, a little girl. Noreen is still teaching English at Camelback High. And our daughter goes to a nice day care."

"You should send her to Valerie's preschool at the Temple. That's where Tyrique's little boy goes," said Cletus.

"I thought that was just for Jewish people."

"No, it's open to everyone," I said. "We have various religions there and several black families send their kids." "Because the care is excellent and creative," said Tyrique.

Audrey now entered the room, with I.J. and Ruby Lynn.

"Are you talking about the Temple school?" she asked. "Ruby Lynn goes there, in the Kindergarten. Valerie always runs a good school. How is Evalynne?"

"She'll be awfully glad to see you and your kids," said Cletus. "She was so proud to be working for all of you."

Audrey smiled. "My kids love her like their third Grandma."

And now Clebar came into the small room. "Hello, everybody. I just drove in from San Diego. How is Grammy doing?" "You'll see her soon, Son," said Cletus.

Cletus came over to me and shook my hand. "Valerie, I haven't seen you since I was little. I remember coming over to your house one evening and your husband Alex let me look through his telescope. I was amazed. But then something happened to him. Did he die?"

"No. Actually he got well. Not well but better. But I'm not married to Alex now."

The nurse appeared and said two visitors could go to see Evalynne.

"You go, Valerie," said Cletus. "I saw her this morning." "I think Audrey should go. And the kids." "Only two," said the nurse.

"Take I.J., Audrey, and Ruby Lynn can go in next. My mama sure did love I.J. since he was a baby. And still does," said Cletus.

"Yes," said Barbara Mae. "A lot of talk about Isaiah James. My mother in law spent all of Sunday, her day off, talking about Isaiah James and Valerie and Audrey and Jerome. Making us feel like country mouse relatives. You all had so many achievements and she ignored anything I did. 'Yes, I work for a colored lady lawyer. Yes, I work for a school principal. Why, she shook the hand of Martin Luther King! And she'd always say how nice you spoke to your husbands. And look how good your husbands provided for you! Those fancy houses with new appliances!"

So this was where Barbara Mae's antagonism came from. In her bitter speech she'd insulted Audrey and me, but Cletus, her own husband, as well. Cletus looked at her with disdain. Audrey realized that Barbara Mae had also hurt Ruby Lynn by not mentioning her.

"Evalynne loved Ruby Lynn also and took such good care of her," said Audrey, hugging her daughter.

We all took turns visiting Evalynne for five minutes each. Evalynne looked pale and weak and requested everyone to pray for her.

"Jewish prayers like Alex did, Catholic prayers from the nuns and Baptist prayers, they'll all reach God and make me better."

"The doctor wants me to come in every day next week to check my blood pressure," said Mrs. O'Dell.

"Why don't we meet here around noon?" I suggested. "The Temple is only ten minutes away."

We all agreed and Audrey said she'd come whenever possible. The District Attorney's Office was close by as well.

MONDAY AT GOOD SAMARITAN HOSPITAL

I walked into the small waiting room near Evalynne's room. It was noon and there were Sisters Cordelia and Agnes and Mrs. O'Dell.

"Evalynne is downstairs taking a test but we can see her in a half hour," said Sister Cordelia. "She is looking much better and her speech is so improved. And she can walk to the door of her room by herself."

"Remember you said that interesting things happened during your pregnancy with Talia. Why don't you tell us some of those stories?" Mrs. O'Dell suggested.

"No," I said, surprising myself and them. "I think I'd like to tell you what happened yesterday. I'm still a little in shock."

My friends, the three members of the 'Romance Club' who always seemed to enjoy hearing about things that had happened to me, looked at me.

"Well, that got my attention," said Mrs. O'Dell. "What happened?"

THE I CAN'T BELIEVE MY EYES MOMENT

"You know that I teach my Holocaust class on Sunday mornings so at 12:30 I was just getting home to The Lakes. I walked into the kitchen and the whole house was empty. "Everyone, I'm home," I called. "Silence. And then I looked out the window. at the blue green lake with two sailboats sailing by.

"There, on our dock, was Neal and my four girls. And also there was a man and two little blond boys. Were they neighbors?

I went out to our back porch for a closer look and immediately realized that I was looking at Alex's back. Everyone except for Talia and the littlest boy held a fishing rod. Neal and Alex stood together, holding brown bottles of beer and laughing. The line up was the little boy, Josh, holding onto Alex's leg, then after Alex, Saul, a very serious looking three year old, then Neal. then Talia holding onto two year old Emmie's hand, the absolute rule if Emmie was on the dock. Then Shoshana and Marisa. All smiling."

"I walked down the steps to the dock. "Well, hello," I said.

"Alex turned to me. 'I came by to see if Marisa and Talia would like to go to the Zoo with me and the boys. Marisa said they were fishing and Saul said he'd like to fish and then Neal invited us to stay. He had extra rods." Both Alex and Neal smiled at me. Our little table held pretzels and juice cartons and cups."

"Hello, Saul and Josh. It's nice to see you. So what were you laughing about?"

"'You, of course,' said Neal."

"Are you kidding?"

"'He's a lawyer,' said Alex. 'Everyone knows that lawyers always tell the truth.' Now Neal and Alex laughed some more and drank more beer."

"What a scene," said Sister Cordelia. "I can visualize it. Have Alex and Neal ever been together before this?"

"We would all meet for birthday parties and Chanukah and beyond a cordial handshake and 'Hi', they never socialized. Alex would not stay too long. He'd kiss and hug his girls and give them presents and soon after, he'd leave. He'd never brought his boys and Anita had never come either. I'd seen Saul a few times, sitting in his car seat. I'd never seen Josh before. Now Alex and Neal were standing next to each other and I observed them."

"What were your thoughts?" asked Mrs. O'Dell.

"I looked at Alex. Shorter than Neal at 5'10" but very muscular. His face was even more handsome than when I'd married him. His cheeks were more sculptured and his wavy blond hair was now the color of wheat. He was, I thought, a very good looking man of thirty four."

"Neal also looked good. He's 6'3", perhaps twenty pounds overweight but he carries it well. He looked powerful. His hair is black and his thin beard is attractive."

"How old is Neal?"

"Thirty six."

"'This is a really nice place, with the lake and boats passing by. I've only been in the front before,' Alex said."

"'I bought it for Valerie when she fell in love with it. We had already bought a house in central Phoenix but Valerie was so sad, without ever complaining, that I bought it even though we lost $8000 getting out of the contract for the first house.'"

"Both Alex and I understood Neal's subtext. What he wanted to convey was, 'You may have come from money but I earned mine and I bought this woman the home of her dreams on a lake.'"

"After an awkward moment, Alex introduced his boys. 'This is Saul.'"

"Saul! For two pregnancies, for eighteen months, I had carried babies, calling each of them Saul, to be named for Alex's father. But Saul had not come for me. He was a sturdy little boy with blond hair and blue eyes. He had his father's handsome nose but not the defined lips."

"How old are you, Saul?" I asked."

"He held up three fingers, then said, 'I am three.' 'I two' said Emmie, holding up two fingers."

"'And this is Josh,' said Alex. 'He's eighteen months.' Josh was also blonde and blue eyed with a toddler's chubby face. He looked at me shyly and put his thumb in his mouth."

"They are adorable, Alex." I said and they were."

"'This is Marisa and Talia's mommy,' Alex told his boys. I suppose that that was the only way to describe me to them. His former wife? His former lover? The woman who gave him SEFF? His Available Woman? The love of his life on whom he'd played a terrible trick, a far reaching evil trick?" "'So we've all been fishing,' said Alex.

"'Not me,' said Talia. 'I respect living things. I wouldn't catch them and eat them.'"

"How old is Talia now?" asked Sister Agnes.

"She's nine. And then Saul held up a four inch fish. 'I caught it,' he said, very proudly."

"'So as Neal said before,' said Alex with his impish grin, 'he's been telling me all your secrets.'"

"'And Alex reciprocated,' said Neal. 'We both know all there is to know about you now.'"

"They both laughed again, Sisters. The two most important men in my life, teasing me!"

"What a scene," said Mrs. O'Dell.

"'I'm about to get Valerie a new station wagon,' said Neal. 'I think a Pontiac.'"

"'Make sure there's a compartment where she can stash her chicken bones' said Alex, grinning.

"'She ate in her car with you, too?' Neal asked. 'Why didn't you teach her not to?'"

"'I tried,'" said Alex. And both men laughed again .Then both of them looked at my hurt face.

"'Let's change the subject,' said Alex."

"'You're right,' said Neal. 'Only Saul caught a fish. Better catch more fish, everyone, or lunch is going to be very skimpy,'"

"I'll make lunch," I said. "Please stay for lunch," I said to Alex."

"'Are you sure it wouldn't be too much trouble?' he asked me."

"No, not at all," I answered."

"I'd been planning a lunch of leftover roast chicken and leftover baked potatoes with salad. Now I quickly took out two meat loaves and apple pie from the freezer and heated everything while I made a fancy salad with croutons and choices of dressings. I called my girls to come and set the dining room table and called everyone for lunch. Alex asked where the bathroom was and took his boys there to wash up. He asked me where the garbage was to throw away Josh's wet diaper. As always, a very competent father. We all sat down to eat and it seemed surreal, three adults and six children, all related to each other in various ways."

"And all eating together for the first time, right?" said Sister Cordelia.

"Yes. And everyone ate with a wonderful appetite. I'd stuffed a baked potato with cheese for Talia since she'd recently announced that she was now a vegetarian."

"'Do you fish a lot?' Neal asked Alex."

"'No, I like to go hiking.'"

"'When you lived in L.A. did you go fishing with Uncle Ted?'"

"Alex nodded."

"'Well, I went out on that big fishing boat with him several times and when I caught a fish, he made me gut it and clean it. He said you're not a man if you can't prepare your fish. He said you don't bring your wife a fish, you bring her filets that she can fry or broil.' Neal laughed. 'I almost puked.'"

"'He said the same thing to me,' said Alex. 'I guess he was testing us, for manliness.'"

"'Such a good guy,' said Neal."

"'Yes, you have to love him,' said Alex. 'He helped us in a lot of ways. And then, when we were packing up Valerie's things to move to Pasadena, he and I did the unforgivable. We threw out her old teddy bear.'"

"I heard that story,' said Neal."

"'Mommy told all of us that story,' said Marisa."

"'I think she's still upset about it,' said Alex."

"I am still upset."

"Everyone was smiling. Odd, odd, odd, was this charming scene. His. Ours. I shook my head in wonder as I served the apple pie with vanilla ice cream."

'Thank you for an absolutely delicious lunch,' said Alex. Absolutely. That meant, in Alex speak, that it was really good. 'Thank Marisa and Talia's mommy for lunch,' he told Saul, who said 'Thank you.' Neal then said that everything was great. He asked Alex if he wanted to watch the football game in the family room. 'No, but thanks. I have to get these guys down for their naps,' said Alex. He and Neal shook hands and he hugged and kissed all four girls. He thanked me again and headed for his car. He had parked in front of our neighbor's house and I hadn't noticed the car. I followed him. I waited while he put his children into car seats. Both boys fell asleep."

"So?" I asked him."

"'So?'"

"What's happened?"

"'Anita and I are getting a divorce,' he said softly."

"The shock was discernible on my face. "A divorce? Why?"

"'It's been building for some time. We just aren't getting along. It's really better for the kids this way, not to have to hear arguing. And her parents are intrusive and always have their hand out. They need this, they need that. A loan, a new air conditioner, money to pay off the doctor. I don't mind helping out but they think I'm the Union Bank, week after week. But it was mainly me and her.'"

"You initiated it?"

"'I made the decision.'"

"She must be so upset."

"'She'll get over it.'"

"I sighed, beyond surprised."

"You remember Dr. Jouzy? You called him once. So when I went for my six month check up, he said the tumor is growing again.'"

"No!"

"'He said I have two or three years. Like before but this time it's definite.'"

"Do you have pain?"

"'No, not yet. Not until the last months, he said. You know, most people on this planet would like to have that question answered. 'How long will I live?' And I have the answer. So I decided to minimize unpleasantness and have my last two years be as meaningful as possible. Don't cry, Valerie. You asked and I told you.'"

"But the boys. So little."

"'I know. That's the reason I've stayed as long as I have. I've been lucky. It's been seven years of remission. But I need a little happiness. I have the boys three times a week and every other weekend. And I haven't done too badly with the girls on that basis, have I?'"

"No. You've given them what you said you would—-the gift of time."

"'I've certainly been with them a hell of a lot more than my father was with me. No 'hello ,goodbye, I have to attend a meeting now'. Once he explained to me, 'I've got the whole responsibility of the Temple on my shoulders.' And I told him 'Who cares?'"

"When will the divorce be final?"

"'Next week. It goes quickly in Arizona.'"

"Alex, I don't know what to say."

"'I do. But today's not the day.' He nodded towards his sleeping boys. 'Thanks again for feeding the three of us. And you should have seen your face when you saw all of us fishing together.'"

"Oh, Alex." I couldn't control the tears that poured down my face."

"'Don't cry. And thank you. The boys and I had a wonderful time.'"

"He smiled at me, his beautiful smile, and drove off. I watched the car go down my street and I stood on the curb and cried."

"My gracious." said Sister Cordelia. "One can only wonder what will happen next."

"They just wheeled Evalynne back. We can go see her now. Will you tell her about Alex's divorce?" said Sister Agnes.

"I suppose so," I answered.

THE TUESDAY PHONE CALL

"Are you alone in your office?" Alex asked.

"Yes. Anyone could come in anytime though."

"I want to spend time with you."

"Alex, you know that's not possible."

"Listen. I understand that anything permanent can't happen. I told you on Sunday that Dr. Jouzy said I have two to three years. All I'm asking is for a little of your extra time."

"I have no extra time. I'm running the Temple Preschool with 150 children and 18 staff and I still teach Holocaust and I have four children and Neal, and I shop and cook. There is no extra time."

"I know you still care for me."

"How could you know that?"

"The way you look at me."

"How?"

"Hungrily. Don't forget, I know all your looks. The way you linger at the door when I'm picking up, the way your eyes follow me when we're both at school conferences."

"Oh, Alex. Our time together has passed. It's not feasible anymore."

"It has not passed. Tell me you don't think about me. Be honest with me."

"Alex, my secretary is back from her lunch. Bye."

THE WEDNESDAY PHONE CALL

"Are you alone?"

"Yes."

"Take fifteen minutes and think of all the memories you have of me. I'll call you back this afternoon." Click.

The memories? That first kiss on our first date. 'Goodnight, Mrs. Berk. And you ARE going to marry me.' Introducing me to a whole new way of kissing. The magical Senior Prom and the Coconut Grove Nightclub. His engagement speech. 'You won't have to worry about money. I have a trust fund.'

Teaching me how to make love. Making love to" VICTORY AT SEA". The engagement year. Angry words to his mother when she disparaged me. The language we made up to talk to each other secretly. The mountain wedding he'd planned when his mother wouldn't let us get married. The visit to the Rabbi. The visit to our fathers' graves. The wedding, elegant, planned by Jeanette, joyous because we'd finally gotten what we wanted. The honeymoon, sailing in Balboa. And the laughter, always the laughter. Our little cottage in Pasadena, the setting for bliss. Monsieur Pierre. The Ben-Wa Man. New surprises in intimacy. Helping me with labor for the long hours until Marisa was born. The night Talia was born. The trip to Chicago when I became Tatiana, the call girl. Alone together in our pool. Then the afternoon in the dealership.

The Prescott cabin.

Always the clear memories of passion, him making love to me. The fierce love. The gentle love. I sat at my desk with my hand over my eyes, remembering. The phone rang.

"Are you alone?"

"Yes."

"So, being the honest girl that you usually are, do you think of me?"

"Not a day goes by that I don't think of you." I whispered.

"For me as well. I think of you constantly." There was silence on the line.

"Well, then," he said. "I intend to proceed."

"With what?"

"My second pursuit of you." Click.

So why did I shiver?. Because I knew that from this moment on, everything would change.

ON THE ROOF

There had been peace in the home for several weeks. Marisa had not provoked Neal and he had not exploded at her. I tried to reason with her again and again. I told her the way not to anger him. If things had gone well for her at school, she was more likely to follow certain rules. Talia had learned the art of getting along with Neal and her relationship with Neal was pleasant.

Today, a Saturday, Neal came back from a breakfast meeting he'd had with an important client. He held up a paper. "They signed the contract," he said. "Many billable hours." "That's great, Neal," I said.

"Why do they pay you?" Marisa asked him.

"I make sure that in their documents they are following the laws of the federal government and the state government," he explained with pride.

"Oh, you write papers. My Daddy actually makes things. With his hands. He just made something so you can watch TV programs whenever you want."

I took a breath. I didn't think her comment, a little snotty, would cause an explosion. But...

"Your father is an asshole," yelled Neal. "I'm not recognized in my own house!" And he turned around and left, slamming the wooden door.

"My Daddy is NOT an asshole. You're an asshole," Marisa said, shouting and crying. Thank goodness the three younger girls were laughing at a TV program in the family room.

"Marisa," I said "Let's talk," but she ran past me and out to the back porch. Quick as a flash she grabbed the wooden post and shimmied up to catch a branch in the pepper tree and from there jumped onto the steep roof. "Marisa, please come down.

You'll fall. How will we fix things if you break your neck?" She looked at me stonily and said nothing.

Then the phone rang and I opened the window to get the phone from the kitchen counter.

"Are you alone?"

"Oh Alex, I can't talk now. There's been a family fight and Marisa is up on the roof and won't come down."

"On your steep roof? I'll be right over."

"No, please, Alex. That will make matters worse. I'm sure I can reason with her and talk her down."

Click.

I kept talking, begging really and frozen with fear. Marisa was stooped down, holding onto the roof. If she fell two stories she would land on the concrete game court. I talked as calmly as I could. And then there was Alex, running out from the kitchen. He looked around sharply, then grabbed the wooden post, then the tree branch and he jumped onto the roof next to Marisa. He started talking to her softly and I saw her nodding her head. I couldn't hear what they were saying to each other. But I saw that he'd grabbed her wrist. Either she'd be safe or they'd both fall onto the concrete. And in the background was the noise of the silly cartoon.

Now Marisa talked to Alex and he nodded seriously. He answered her. And finally, she carefully stepped down from the roof, caught the tree branch and slid down the post. Alex was right behind her.

"Should I kill her or kiss her?" I asked him. I enveloped her in a huge hug.

"What do you have to say to your mother?" he said gruffly.

"I'm sorry for worrying you, Mom."

"Thank you for rescuing her," I said to Alex. He sat down at the kitchen table, catching his breath.

"Could I trouble you for a glass of water?"

"What about coffee?"

"Water's fine."

"Let me make you lunch. I was just preparing toasted cheese sandwiches."

"I won't say no."

So the four children and Alex and I sat down to a simple meal with green beans with almonds added and just baked cookies. "Do we have to put the dishes in the dishwasher?" Marisa asked.

"No, I'll do it. Go ahead and watch TV." Talia had gone to her room to practice her saxophone. She had asked her dad why he was there and he said he was shopping at Smitty's and just dropped by to say hello. No one questioned this.

Now Alex and I sat facing each other at the table.

"She's eleven," said Alex. "Trying to find herself. Many kids are not hugely content at eleven. I wasn't. But I know she's going to be all right. She's basically a good kid."

"I know."

"How often does this happen, this fighting with Neal?"

"Too often."

"Maybe we should get some help."

"I tried. She won't go."

"Not for her. I meant for Neal."

"I'm taking this very seriously, Alex. My child could have broken her neck. I'll try to get Neal to see someone. Maybe Dr. Shellenberger, a psychiatrist who helped us in the past." "Okay, Valerie. Do it soon."

I got up to put food back into the refrigerator. Alex stepped behind me, the refrigerator door blocking us from view. He put the block of cheddar cheese on the shelf and grabbed my hand. He put it up to his lips and placed a kiss onto my palm.

"Don't look so alarmed. I know we haven't touched since my Mother's funeral. And I'm thirty four, finding myself. I'm basically a good kid, too." He smiled. I looked at him. And smiled back. Now he smiled his lips up. "We haven't crossed into the inappropriate. Yet. But we will, Valerie." He grabbed my hand again and squeezed it. "Bye, girls," he called into the family room.

"Bye, Daddy." They rushed out and hugged him. He smiled at me, his assured, confident smile, gave me a salute and left.

Seduction, I thought. Welcome to the Land of the Confused.

DR. SCHELLENBERGER AGAIN

Now I was at the psychiatrist's office and the reception room had barely changed in the seven years since I'd been there. The magazines were dated 1970, of course, not 1963. And here was Dr. Schellenberger, standing smiling at the door to his office.

His hair was all gray now and his body a little more corpulent. As before, he wore a somewhat rumpled brown corduroy suit with a woolen tie over his white shirt.

"Valerie Caplan! So very nice to see you, my dear," he said in his strong Viennese accent. "Please, come in. Sit down. Can I offer you coffee or tea? Cookies?" He was the only medical professional I'd ever visited who offered food.

On an electrical burner he had a large glass pot with which he could make instant coffee or tea. When Neal and I had spent three hours with him on that tortured August afternoon, we'd not only accepted his coffee but also his wife's cookies.

"Is your family well?" he asked. "I received the birth announcement of your third little daughter. Isn't she about six now?"

"Yes and I've had a fourth daughter since then. She's two."

"Wonderful. So what brings you here today, Valerie?"

"I have a very deep problem. And you were so wise about helping Neal and me come to a decision seven years ago, that I hoped....Well, it's Marisa. She's eleven now. And she and Neal fight almost all the time. We'll sit down to dinner and she'll do something like knock over her glass or she'll say something to Neal and he'll take it the wrong way. Then he either makes a disparaging or a sarcastic remark. And then Marisa bursts into tears and runs from the table to her room. So I get up to follow her and comfort her in her room. And there's our dinnertime, shot to hell. Excuse me, Doctor."

"Don't apologize. You've described a very upsetting situation. How often does this happen?"

"Every few days, it seems. Neal is very good with the other three children. He has genuine feelings for Talia who is sweet and a very easy child. And of course he's delighted with his own two, Shoshana and Emmie. We hardly ever have a problem with the younger three. But Marisa struggles in school and he tries to help her and then he has no patience when she can't remember math facts."

"You told me years ago that her father was a math genius and yet she struggles?"

"Yes, she does. And it's not all Neal's fault. Some-times she seems to provoke him on purpose. I went to a family counselor for suggestions and she was no help at all. So what I thought, what I was hoping, was that you could talk to Neal. The way you talked to him and clarified things before."

"My first question is, have you talked to him, explained your feelings?"

"He knows my feelings. I'm very clear on my feelings. I've talked and talked. And I've talked to Marisa. I'll say,' Think before you just blurt something out. If he says something to you, can you just ignore it so we can have a peaceful meal?' But she has to retaliate."

"I see."

"But Doctor, that's not the complete Marisa. With Alex she's polite and considerate and if he corrects her, she'll say, 'Okay, Daddy.'"

"So Alex is still part of the picture? The last time I saw you, you told me he had two or three years to live."

"He did but he lived on. The doctors were wrong. He eats correctly and exercises. And he sees his girls very regularly. In the seven years that have passed, he remarried and has two little boys. (And now he's divorced and wants my attention.) But I didn't share that.

"And he is cured of his brain tumor?"

"No, he's in remission. The latest his doctor said was another two or three years."

"But, as I recall, you didn't go to Israel with Alex, your mother became seriously ill and Alex arranged for a divorce and went alone to Israel."

"Yes, that's what happened. And Alex and I were married to other people and we remained cordial with one another but only saw each other for more than hello on Chanukah and the girls' birthdays. We talked on the phone and made arrangements. But this is my main problem with Neal—Marisa. It's harming our family life. "

"Is Neal willing to come in and talk to me?"

"No. He says 'Take Marisa to a psychiatrist. She's the one who needs a psychiatrist.'"

"So he's negative about coming in?"

"Well, I thought you could phone him and persuade him."

"Oh Valerie, you know I can't do that. Therapy can only be effective if the patient wants to change or wants some guidance."

"So you can't call him?"

"It wouldn't work, Valerie. I'm sorry to disappoint you. You try to get him to call me and then perhaps we can make some progress."

"Thank you, Dr.Schellenberger."

I had thought that this might solve my problem and my disappointment was visible as I walked out of his office.

THE FAVOR

Alex called. "Valerie, I have a tremendous favor to ask of you. Anita is suing me in Family Court over my visitation rights."

"No! Why would she do that?"

"Just to make trouble. So I've hired Brad to represent me."

"Eugene Silver, I think, does more divorce work."

"I WOULD NEVER HIRE EUGENE SILVER, AND YOU KNOW WHY!"

"Okay, Alex."

"Anyway, Brad said that your testimony, that I took good care of our girls when they were that little, would help enormously. Would you be willing to come to court on my behalf?"

"Yes. I'll do it."

GOING TO COURT

As a debater, I was comfortable speaking to a crowd. Also as a debater, I loved the aspects of trials, opening statements, presenting your case, testimony, witnesses, cross examination, rebuttal and closing statements. Brad had prepared me, using potential questions. He said I was ready.

In this case, in Family Court, there was no prosecutor, just the two attorneys, arguing before the Judge who would decide. Anita's attorney was tall and suave, in what looked like a very expensive gray suit. Although, through Neal and PACE, I knew many attorneys, I did not know him.

He began. "Your Honor, Mrs. Anita Berk is not asking to separate her sons from their father. He is welcome to come to her house in Scottsdale for supervised visits. On a decided upon schedule, of course. Mrs. Berk is primarily concerned with the safety of her little boys. She feels it is NOT safe for Mr. Berk to take the children to his home or on outings. We will now present the many reasons why she justifiably has these fears."

Judge Martinez—-I want to hear those reasons.

Mr. Montrose, Anita's attorney—As an overview, Your Honor, which we will soon prove, Mr. Alex Berk has grave health problems and at any time could have a possibly fatal attack, leaving these very young children uncared for, unsupervised and in danger. Mrs. Berk does not want to take that chance with her two preschool children.

Judge Martinez—-I see. We'll proceed with the evidence.

Mr. Montrose, —For our first witness we call Mrs. Valerie Caplan.

I was sworn in, promised to tell the truth.

Mr. Montrose—-Is it true, Mrs. Caplan, that you were married to Mr. Alex Berk?

Me—-Yes.

Mr. Montrose—-Please tell us the dates of that marriage.

Me—-August 4th, 1956 to October, 1963.

Mr .Montrose—-And please tell the Court what caused you to dissolve that marriage after seven years of marriage.

Brad was up in a flash—-This is not pertinent to the reasons of this hearing, Your Honor.

Judge Martinez—-Sustained. The witness does not have to answer this question.

Mr. Montrose—-Mrs. Caplan, would you like to voluntarily share some details pertinent to your divorce.?

Brad—-Just ruled upon!

Me—-No.

Mr. Montrose—-What were the ages of your two children at the time of your divorce?

Me—-Three and five.

Mr. Montrose—-Did their father, Alex Berk, take your children on outings and to his home?

Me—-Yes.

Mr. Montrose—-How frequently did he take them?

Me—-Usually two evenings a week and every other weekend for the entire weekend.

Mr. Montrose—-By that you mean Friday evening to Sunday evening?

Me—-Yes.

Mr. Montrose—-And please tell the Court what fears you had when Mr. Berk, who had recently had brain surgery and seven months of treatment for a brain tumor, when Mr. Berk took your young children on outings.

Me—-(I recognized how tricky this guy was.) I did not have fears.

Mr. Montrose—-What were your concerns when he left with your children?

Brad—-Asked and answered!

Judge Martinez—-Sustained.

Mr. Montrose—-Did Mr. Berk ask for extra time?

Me—-I wanted to let the girls see their father whenever he asked. Aside from their regular times.

Mr. Montrose—-Mrs. Caplan, did you ever witness any carelessness on the part of Mr. Berk towards your children?

Me—-No, I did not.

Mr. Montrose—-Mrs. Caplan, do you recall a time when Mr. Berk was hiking with both your daughters on Camelback Mountain and he left the younger daughter alone on this mountain to catch up with the older daughter?

Me—-No, I don't know about that.

Mr. Montrose—-You don't know because Mr. Berk never told you? Did he tell you?

Me—-No.

Mr. Montrose—-And neither of your children told you?

Me—-No.

Mr. Montrose—-And do you recall a time when the three of them were hiking and a rattlesnake threatened your three year old child and Mr. Berk took out a loaded pistol and killed the snake? Didn't it alarm you that he might have misfired and killed your child?

Me—-No, he is an excellent shot and he was protecting my child from being bitten by a poisonous snake.

Mr. Montrose—-Is it true that Mr. Berk would sometimes get headaches so severe that he could not do other tasks?

Me—-Yes.

Mr. Montrose—-And yet you allowed your children to be alone with this impaired man? No further questions.

Me—-But that's not....

Brad now took over.

Brad—-Mrs. Caplan, in conclusion, what was your level of confidence in the care that Mr. Berk exhibited toward your young children?

Me—-Very confident.

Brad—-Thank you, Mrs. Caplan. You may step down.

I felt terrible. Had I not explained well enough? Had I ruined Alex's case?

Mr. Montrose then called a variety of other witnesses: Anita's father, her mother, her sister, and a girlfriend. All of them related incidents that would be detrimental to Alex's case. He then called Anita Berk. She had slimmed down since the last time I saw her. Her blonde hair was in a French twist and she was very attractive in a black suit with a white blouse. She testified, repeating herself over and over that Alex was reckless and possibly suicidal and could endanger or kill her children.

Brad did a great job with the father and mother and demonstrated inconsistencies in their testimony. He also shredded Anita's testimony, getting her to admit that she now hated Alex because he'd left her. Brad got her to admit that Alex had left the Scottsdale house to her, that he paid regular child support and that she had enough funds from Alex that she did not have to work outside the home.

For Brad's case, he called upon Alex who testified very sincerely that he loved his boys and was able to protect them and bring them home safely. Brad then introduced Exhibit A which was a cloth satchel. He asked Alex to unpack it and they discussed the contents.

Brad—-Mr. Berk, is this the bag you take with you, both in your car and on all outings?

Alex—-Yes, it is.

After Brad asked him, Alex took out the items and held them up.

Alex—-This is a complete and up to date first aid kit. I have recently renewed my first aid certificate. These are walkietalkies which my three year old knows how to activate by pressing one button. The Fire Department will answer. Here we have extra diapers and clothes and nutritional snacks if we need them. These are flares for the car. These are medical insurance cards for me and the children. This is my Merck Manual so I can look up possible health concerns.

Brad—-So you are well prepared for most emergencies that can be foreseen?

Alex—-I think so.

Brad—-Finally, Your Honor, we have a short video that my colleague in Houston has prepared, having deposed Mr. Berk's doctor, Dr. Jouzy.

A large screen was set up.

Dr. Jouzy—-Yes, Mr. Berk is currently in remission having had surgery for a tumor with a smaller brain tumor inoperable. However, should Mr. Berk's condition get to a critical point, there will be ample warning, months of warning. In my opinion , it would be extremely unlikely that there would be a sudden emergency while Mr. Berk is with his children.

Mr. Montrose—-This is extremely unfair since I cannot have cross with a doctor from Houston who is on video.

Judge Martinez—-Your concern is noted, Mr. Montrose.

We will now have a twenty minute recess while I consider the facts in this case. Let's reconvene at 10:40.

Outside, in the hall, I approached Alex. "I hope I didn't damage your case. I tried to be very positive."

"You did fine, Valerie," said Alex. "You were very helpful."

"Yes, you did a good job," said Brad.

Anita's father came up to me. "You're a liar and a cheat!" he said, practically spitting on me in his anger. Quickly, Brad and Alex steered me down the hall. But I noticed Anita and all her family giving me hateful looks.

We went back into the courtroom.

Judge Martinez—-In my judgment, Mrs. Anita Berk has not proved her claim of endangerment to her children. The custody arrangements and visitation will remain in place. The request for supervised visitation is denied. However, Mrs. Berk has requested that the children be with her on both Thanksgiving and Christmas and Mr. Berk has voluntarily agreed to that request. This case will be revisited in twelve months if Mrs. Berk chooses to do that. Thank you all. (The gavel banged.)

In the hall, Brad and Alex hugged each other. Anita and her family passed us with their furious looks. "IF MY CHILDREN ARE EVER HURT, IT WILL BE YOUR FAULT, VALERIE," she screamed at me.

"Let me take both of you to lunch," said Alex.

"Thanks, Buddy, but I have to run for a deposition. Glad we won! See you, Valerie." And Brad headed for the elevator.

"Valerie, come on. Let's celebrate with lunch. I want to thank you for your help."

"All I did was tell the truth. But I have to get back also. I have a 2:30 meeting."

"It's 11:00 now. You'll be back by 2:30. Come on, Valerie. Let me take you to your favorite restaurant, Lunt Avenue. You can get that blue pina colada and you love their salads."

"I really can't. And I certainly can't drink on a work day."

"Come on, Valerie. Just forty five minutes. It's so close to here." When had I heard those 'come on, Valerie' appeals? Often.

"Okay, Alex. I'd like to talk to you about something anyway."

"My car?"

"No. we'll take both cars."

This is not a date, I told myself. I was not being unfair to Neal. This was merely a meeting.

THE LUNT AVENUE MARBLE CLUB RESTAURANT

Alex stood up from his table when I arrived.

"You look very pretty in that blue suit, Valerie." he said, pulling out a chair for me. We ordered and soon a delicious lunch appeared. Alex, as always, ate with great appetite.

"Alex, I want to talk to you. I've thought about what you said on the phone and I realized the kind of relationship we have to have. We have to have a friendship. We do have years of history and two children, but friendship is the only course possible."

"Friendship, huh?"

"Friendship with rules."

Alex's mouth curled up with amusement, which really annoyed me.

"With rules? What rules?"

"No touching. No kissing the palm of my hand. No going out unless our children are with us. No inviting me to places."

"How about phone calls?"

"Phone calls are fine. I like to talk to you. And we often have to make plans."

"So, no touching, no unsupervised outings, no kisses on your hand. But phone calls are okay?"

"Yes." I said. "And by your tone, I think you're making fun of me. You're not hearing me."

"I heard every word you said."

"So those are the rules for our friendship."

"Valerie, do you think I would ever allow you alone to define our rules? Don't you know me by now?" I looked at him.

"That was before, Alex. I make some rules now. Thank you for a delicious lunch." And I was walking quickly, out the door of the restaurant. I saw Alex signaling the waiter for the check.

Alex caught up with me as I was entering my car and he forcefully sat down in the passenger seat.

"Valerie, you don't understand. We have to be together. A love such as ours is very rare. You're right, we'll be friends. But also soulmates and also lovers. We have to take this moment in time and be together."

"I don't think we can. And it's not fair to Neal."

Alex responded by grabbing my head with two hands and kissing me, insistently and intimately. And the pattern from the past continued. I was unable to resist his kiss or being in each other's arms. My body responded, almost healing the years-long ache in my heart.

"We have to be together, Valerie," he repeated softly.

"We can't. It's impossible."

"It begins. Us. NOW." And he ran to his car.

THE HAVDALAH CANDLE

Alex called.

"Are you alone?"

"Yes."

"I thought of something. Remember at our wedding what Rabbi Nussbaum said at the Havdalah Ceremony?"

"What did he say?"

"He said, 'As this candle is braided together with three candles, so are your souls, Alex and Valerie, now braided together.' Valerie, my soul is braided to yours and I can't let you go."

"That was a long time ago, Alex."

"But during our marriage, it was always rebraided. We got closer and closer. Those were such happy years."

"So what happened?"

"Life. The 20% bad happened. That last year that I was so sick was such a bad year that we each made bad decisions. But our souls didn't unbraid."

"I have to go to a meeting now, Alex. I'm sorry but I have to go." I realized that this was another campaign. Alex was going after me much the way he had when we were in high school. Then he'd campaigned for me to open my mouth and kiss him and then go to his Senior Prom with him .When I'd already promised Mike Stein. Now he wanted me to go away for several days. I told him I didn't see how it could be possible.

LOVE STORY

The following weekend, the girls were with Alex. He brought them back after dinner on Sunday night.

"So what did you do with Daddy?" I asked.

"On Saturday we went hiking and went to a llama farm and today we went to a movie," said Marisa.

"What movie?"

"It was *Love Story* and Daddy said, 'This is like the story of your Mom and me. They met in college but we met in high school. And my family had money, like Oliver Barrett's, and her family did not. And my mother, I'm ashamed to say, did not accept her for that reason. Just like in the movie. And just like in the movie, we were tremendously in love. The things they did on the beach, we did those things. And our marriage was very happy."

"Daddy said that?" I asked Talia.

"Yes," she said. "And I asked Daddy, was Mom as pretty as Ali McGraw? And he said, 'Your mother was, and is, much more beautiful than Ali McGraw.'" "He said that?" I asked my girls.

"Yes. I think he still likes you, Mom." said Talia.

"No. we're just friends." So why did I feel such a glow?

TALIA CAUSES AN ARGUMENT

The following weekend, Alex had had the girls and now was dropping them off. I was clipping roses in the side of the house and I don't think the girls or Alex saw me.

"I'm really sorry, Daddy." said Talia.

"No more, Talia. From now on, you pay for your carelessness."

"I know, Daddy."

"And I'm going to talk to your mother about this, also."

Talia and Alex hugged and she ran inside. I came around the corner of the house.

"What happened, Alex?"

"Oh. I was going to look for you. What happened is we just went out to dinner and I was driving the girls home. When we were at the gate to The Lakes, Talia said, 'Oh no. I left my retainer on the table.' So I turned the car around and we went back to Wings and Things. And the waiter told us he'd thrown out everything that was on the table."

"Talia started to cry so I said, "It's okay. Everyone is allowed one lost retainer. I think the orthodontist will replace it for free." Her face crumpled up and I said, "You've had your braces off for three months. Isn't this the first one you've lost?"

'No.'

"Your second one?"

'No.'

"Your third?"

'No.'

"Your fourth retainer? In three months? Who paid for the second and third retainers?"

'Mommy.'

"Now I exploded," said Alex.

"Don't be mad at her, Alex. She's such a good girl."

"I am mad at her. And I'm mad at you."

"Me?"

"Am I not her father, Valerie?"

"Of course you are."

"And didn't we agree that we would co parent?"

"Yes."

"So you go behind my back and don't tell me important things and you conspire with her to leave me in the dark."

"I didn't think it was that big a deal."

"'You didn't think' is the operative phrase," he said caustically. "And it is a big deal. So far it's $180 that we didn't need to spend and you're allowing her to lie to her father. Besides, you had a retainer when we were first dating. Did you ever lose it?"

"No, I didn't. I'm sorry, Alex."

"You should be," he growled. "If we were still married, you know what would happen."

"You'd spank me?" I felt a combination of thrill and confusion simultaneously.

"You're goddamn right I would. You know I hate deception and carelessness."

"It won't happen again, Alex."

"All right. What are you going to do from now on?"

"Tell you whenever there is misbehavior. Keep you informed."

"And here's what I'm going to do, Valerie. When I pick her up on Tuesday, she's going to clean my car. She's going to work off every penny of that $59. Just because we have some money doesn't mean that we throw it away. I want her to learn to be responsible. Fashtesht?"

"Ich fashtain."

"Okay. And I still love you, Valerie." He got into his car and I watched him drive down the street.

THE RECORD

And then it was Tuesday and when Alex picked up the girls he handed me a record. "Play it," he said.

It was the *Unchained Melody*.

Whoa, my love, my darling, I've hungered for your touch A long, lonely time. And time goes by so slowly And time can do so much.

Are you still mine?

I need your love. I need your love. God speed your love To me.

"Thank you for the record," I said when he brought the girls home.

"I let the Righteous Brothers say it for me. *I hunger for your touch*. What do you say to that?"

"No touching. Friends."

"There will be touching," he said and left.

WHAT DID YOU DO WITH THE LAST $40, VALERIE?

I was in the bank, "I'd like to withdraw $40, please," I told the teller.

A voice behind me said, "What did you do vit the last $40?"

I turned and two people behind me stood Alex. I collected my money and stood by him as he cashed a paycheck. We walked to the lobby.

"Is that your Hungarian accent?"

"My false Hungarian accent. But I know what you did with the forty dollars."

"What?"

"You spent it on your usual 'this and that.'"

"Yes, I did."

"Do you want to come to my place? It's seven minutes away."

"I just dropped Talia off at her music lesson and then I have to pick her up."

"Coffee, then. Next door. For twenty minutes."

"All right."

Alex went to the counter and bought me the pecan muffin I liked and black coffee.

"So, Valerie, when will you go away with me? For just a few days?"

"Alex, let's just talk about our work. Or our daughters."

"Oh, you decide our topics of conversation now?"

"Alex, please."

"How is Marisa doing? What's going on with Neal?" "A little better. I'm still trying to get Neal to go see Dr. Schellenberger."

"He won't go?"

"I think he will, eventually."

"And has Talia lost any more retainers?"

"No. And I think you were completely justified in your approach to that."

"Thank you. Well, we seem to have five more minutes. So no more awkward conversation. I will now tell you five things. You look very beautiful today and I like your hair that way. You love me and you miss me. And we will soon go away together for a short but wonderful time."

He grabbed my hand and shook it formally. "So nice to have seen you at the bank today. Don't forget the five things I just told you." And he left me sitting at the table.

THE PSALM

On Thursday, he handed me a note as he collected the girls. In his loopy handwriting, he'd written:

Songs of Solomon

For now, the winter is past, the rain is over and gone. The flowers appear on the earth, the time of the singing of birds has come and the voice of the turtledove is heard in our land. Arise, come away, my beloved, come away with me. my beautiful one.

My reaction to all of this? I felt that I could not share it with anyone, not my girlfriends, the dear girls from high school or the friends I'd made in Phoenix. And I could not share it with the nuns. Early every morning I went to a half hour exercise class at a small gym. As I rode the exercise bike, I reflected. I am being pursued. And I thought about my friend Arlene, talking to me in high school. "Alex wants me to give him what he calls 'a proper kiss,'" I'd told her. "And you don't want to?" she'd asked. "No, it feels too invasive to me." "So why is this good looking guy chasing after you, Valerie? Because he knows that soon you're going to do what he wants. He just doesn't know when. All his other girlfriends did what he said. He's enjoying this. It's fun for him."

Arlene was right. Alex was playing with me. It was fun for him. I put the King Solomon psalm in my underwear drawer and the Righteous Brothers record in a different record jacket.

But this time Alex was not going to get me to do what he wanted. I was not seventeen and insecure and naïve. Not anymore.

COMPANY

"The musical *Company* is now at the Carousel Theater and you love Stephen Sondheim musicals. Would you go to a matinee with me?"

"You're crazy, Alex. We can't be seen out in public like that."

"We're friends. Friends go places together."

"No. Absolutely not."

"We could take the girls with us."

"No."

"Well, I'll go by myself then. You have no heart."

The following day he did not call me at 11. I was able to admit to myself that I'd been waiting for his call. Then the next morning, without any hello. he sang:

"Verse One"
Somebody hold me too close.
Somebody hurt me too deep.
Somebody sit in my chair and ruin my sleep
And make me aware of being alive
Being alive.

Click and the line was dead. He repeated his performance the next morning with another meaningful verse. "Wonderful Stephen Sondheim lyrics!" he said.

"Verse Two."
Somebody need me too much.
Somebody know me too well.

Somebody pull me up short and put me through hell And give me support for being alive. Make me alive. Make me alive.

Click.

Yes, I suppose I'd put him through hell. But he'd put me through hell first.

I delivered my payroll sheets to the Temple office and on sudden impulse, walked into the Sanctuary. I sat in the front row and prayed. "Dear God, give me the strength to resist him. I do not want to ruin my marriage. I do not want to hurt my children. I do not want to be selfish. Dear God, help me to be strong,"

The senior Rabbi walked by me. "Valerie! You're praying? Is something wrong? Is somebody ill?"

"No, Rabbi. Thanks for asking. I was just trying to think some things through."

"Remember, my door is always open. If I can help you, just come in and tell me your concerns."

"Thank you, Rabbi, that's so kind of you."

"You can trust me to be discreet."

I trusted the Junior Rabbi but not this man, the Senior Rabbi. He would come out of a private conference in his office and say to us, the staff, "Wait until you hear what she just told me." He'd share the dirt. I would trust him NEVER.

I was very conflicted. And who could I talk to? And I thought back to January, four months ago, when Sister Mary Louise had called me at my office.

SISTER MARY LOUISE

"Valerie, would it be possible for me to see you? Alone. Just me."

"Yes. Do you want to go to lunch?"

"What I have to say is very confidential."

"We can go to that quiet alcove in the Chinese restaurant."

We settled there and ordered. Seven years had passed since I'd first met Sister Mary Louise, the year that Alex had been so sick.

She would now be thirty seven. Her acne was gone and her face was now thinner. I admitted to myself that I was very curious. But she wrung her hands and tapped on the table and changed her order twice. "I don't know if I can say it," she said.

"Sister, for years I've been telling you the stories of my life, some very private things. I think you can trust me by now."

"I do. But this is very difficult to say."

She was silent for a few minutes while I sat and wondered.

The soup was brought and she sipped on it.

Finally, I said, "Does it have to do with Sister Agnes or Sister Cordelia?" She shook her head, No. "With Mrs. O'Dell?"

"Oh, no."

We were playing Twenty Questions. "Does it have to do with your family in Manila?"

"In a roundabout way," she said. "But no."

"Is it some impropriety that you've discovered?" Now I was really curious.

"Would it be all right if I give you the background, Valerie?"

"Fine."

"Do you remember about four years ago, Mother Superior asked me to take on a new assignment and I moved from teaching social studies in junior high to working at our Mother of Peace home. You know, that's the blue building on the west side of the Good Shepherd property. So we have twenty beds there and the pregnant girls range from thirteen to twenty one." She paused, looking at me.

"Do you like working there? I remember you said you did."

"Oh yes. It's God's work, seeing to these girls in their time of confusion and need. Each girl has her own story and many of them are sad. Of course, I loved the teaching also."

"So what is it, Sister?"

"Three months ago, a girl named Margarita was enrolled by her father, three months pregnant. She had just turned sixteen. She couldn't stop crying, and didn't want to be there. Her father asked me if I could help her adjust, keep an eye on her. Of course I said I would.

"So the father's name is Jorge Guzman and he can't walk, he's in a wheelchair. He was in Viet Nam, injured there. He came back to Phoenix and had rehab here and he married a Nurse's Assistant. Soon after, she got pregnant, yes, he can still have children, but when the baby, Margarita, was four months old, her mother left them."

"So sad."

"Yes, and Jorge told me that his wife told him she only married him out of pity and because he'd inherited his grandmother's house and she wanted her own house. And she hated taking care of a baby."

"Terrible."

"Yes, he was very hurt by that. But he loved his little daughter and he raised her all by himself. He's a baker and he has a little shop. He bakes breads and cakes and pies. So he goes into his shop at 3:30 am and opens at 6 and he just took the baby with him. He said customers would hold her for him when he got really busy.

"So, the problem was that the doctor told him to watch Margarita because she's having a high risk pregnancy and here he has to go to work at 3:30. What if something happened during the night? She did faint once. So he brought her to the Home.

"His store is just a breakfast place and he closes at noon. So he visits Margarita every afternoon and when she wants to go off with two friends she's made here, then he and I have been talking. And every day, he brings us baked goods, for all the girls and for the other four nuns and me. And after a week, he asked me to tell him my favorite cake or pie, so he could make it for me."

A lot about Jorge, I thought.

"Margarita is a nice girl, maybe too innocent. She was in love with a boy named Armando who told her they would be married and he was going to be a national baseball player and they'd be rich and live in a huge Scottsdale house with a pool. When she told him she was expecting, he said it couldn't be his, he'd taken such perfect precautions. When she wouldn't stop crying, he offered her $400 for an abortion. She finally confided in her father who told her, as devoted Catholics, abortion was not to be considered. He told her he was by her side. She could have the baby and give it to a nice family for adoption or she could keep the baby at their home and he would help her. 'Who cares what neighbors or other people think.' he told Margarita.

"So she came to the Home and Sister Cordelia counseled her and took her through various scenarios. After two weeks, and after seeing the baby in the ultrasound, Margarita decided she wanted to be a mother and would keep the baby. Jorge told me that he was fine with that. He told me that he felt guilty about it all. His little bakery was doing well and the shop next door became available. So he rented it to become a sit down place where customers could not just take out the baked goods but could sit and have coffee and also quiche or ham and cheese buns. And he was very busy renovating this shop and painting it. Before that, he'd kept a close eye on Margarita. Now he thought she was fifteen and very responsible and as long as he was home by 6 and made dinner, she would be all right. She had told him that after school she watched her boyfriend Armando practice baseball. Now he knew it was more than watching.

"I tried to reassure him that he was a good father and wonderful to be accepting the baby into his home. And he visits Margarita every single day and we have a little conversation. Sometimes, Valerie, we have a big conversation and we tell each other our stories, my poor childhood in Manila, his upbringing by his grandmother and many horrible experiences in Viet Nam."

Now Sister Mary Louise was silent, lost in thought or having lost the courage to continue. I waited.

"Valerie, he kept bringing me these delicious lemon pies with whipped cream and then last week he told me that I had beautiful, kind eyes. And I said, "We're friends, Jorge. Please don't say things that are personal." And he said, 'I can't help it. I am beginning to have such feelings for you and I think of you all day and all night, as I am baking and as I cook and clean my house and try to sleep at night.'"

He is wooing her. I thought. And how well do I understand this scene.

"You've told me Jorge's feelings. What are your feelings?"

"I am so confused, Valerie. I've been a nun since I was twenty two. The convent in Manila put me through Teacher's College, gave me a home. I've been a nun for fifteen years. This is my vocation. This is my life. Everything is set."

"But?"

"Yes, but. Sometimes, especially at night in my room I think, could there be a different path for me? Could I be a wife? Or even, if it isn't too late, a mother? "

"What are your feelings towards Jorge?" Silence again.

Now a whisper. "I like him, Valerie. At first I liked him because he has such fine character, faithful to his child and hardworking. But recently I have felt that I like him in another way, a personal way. When I see him, something in my chest bubbles with gladness and something else. And yesterday, he put his hand over mine and squeezed it and said, 'Amor'. He called me, 'Amor.' And I knew I needed serious advice and that's when I decided to call you."

"Well, Sister, I'm afraid we both have to go back to work now. I'm here for you. We can have lunch in a few days. You don't have to decide anything today. You'll keep thinking and things will unfold."

"Thank you, Valerie. But this is so serious. What I decide, to encourage him or firmly cut it off, maybe transfer somewhere else, what I decide will affect the rest of my life."

And I thought, what I decide, with Alex sending me notes and a record and his little messages and songs, what I decide will affect the rest of MY life.

Sister Mary Louise and I decided to meet for lunch every Wednesday. I understood that I was the only person she thought she could talk to.

BEING ALIVE

The next morning I had a very concerned parent in my office.

"Mr. Berk on Line Two," sang my secretary.

"I told him you were with someone but he insisted."

"Verse Three." said Alex.

Somebody.......

"Alex, I'm sorry. I'm with a parent. Could you call me later?"

"Sorry to have disturbed you."

Click. And I knew he was hurt.

No call that afternoon and no call the next day.

The following day he called. "Don't forget, I'm taking the girls to Flagstaff this weekend. Could you just check their warm clothes?"

I was alone in my office. "Alex, would you sing me the rest of the song?"

"What song?"

"You know. The being alive song."

"No."

"Why not?"

"Because it isn't just a song. Momentarily it expressed my deepest feelings of longing for you. For the old you."

"Alex, sing me the damn song."

"Don't swear. It doesn't become you."

"Please."

"Are you sure you're not too busy?"

"Alex! Sing!"

"All right. Verse Three.

Somebody crowd me with love.
Somebody force me to care.
Somebody make me come through.

I'll always be there, as frightened as you Of being alive. Being alive. Being alive.

"You're right. I am frightened. Oh Alex, where are we going with this?"

"We're starting."

"No. We're not starting. And please don't feel hurt but I have to do the school newsletter now because they need it by 3."

"Put in a small article on the last page. Boy wants girl. Boy needs girl. He gets girl. Because she wants to be alive with him, too." Click.

Two days before I had called the Broadway office for show albums and ordered the album for *Company*. They wanted to know if I also wanted the T-shirt that said, from the song by that name, 'You could drive a person crazy.' I ordered that, too. It came, a black T-shirt with white letters. I wore it when Alex came to pick up the girls.

"YOU COULD DRIVE A PERSON CRAZY." he read.

"You've got that right."

I had told Alex, "I want to be a good wife."

"Is Neal a good husband?" he'd said.

Why had he said that? Did he know something?

A GOOD HUSBAND

The next day when Alex called he said, "Remember a few months ago I asked you if Neal makes you happy and you answered 'Most of the time.' Why most of the time?"

"I probably shouldn't have said that. You know, no situation is perfect."

"We were perfect. 97% of the time."

"Mathematical terms."

"Well, we were. You were what I wanted, a beauty with brains. Jewish. The bonus of your cooking."

"Oh."

"I told you that so many times. And after some suggestions from me, you became a lot of fun."

"But Anita did things that scare me. She went mountain climbing with you, scuba diving. Your mother told me all that. Anita must have been fun."

"Anita Is No Goddam Fun!" he said. Click. He'd hung up.

Why had he married Anita? Their relationship had been a puzzle and here was a piece of the puzzle. She was no fun. The next morning he said, "So tell me the story."

"There is no story."

"Is he unfaithful?"

"Why would you ask that?"

"Last year I was having lunch at Bruno's in Scottsdale and he was there with a girl with long straight brown hair."

"It may have been a client. Or another lawyer. People eat lunch. We ate lunch at Lunt Avenue."

"Right. Probably nothing."

"What was their demeanor?"

"Very friendly. And laughing."

"Was he holding her hand or anything?"

"No."

"I'm sure it was nothing." We chatted then hung up. But I wasn't so sure it was nothing. Because of what had happened when I was six months pregnant with Emmie, two years ago.

Sandi was a special needs teacher who worked part time for our Temple school. She was very beautiful with long strawberry blonde hair. She was married to a policeman and they had a three year old son, Charlie, who was enrolled in my school.

One Sunday night in October, our phone rang at 1 am. Sandi was crying and said she was at a liquor store. Her husband had beaten her up after a fight and she'd grabbed Charlie and run. She wanted to know if she could stay at our house for a day or two because her husband would be trying to find her at the homes of her friends. Her husband didn't know us at all. So of course I told her to come.

Soon she arrived, carrying her sleeping son. We put him in the crib we'd set up for the new baby. Sandi's lip was swollen and she had a black eye. There was a large bruise on her arm and her cheek. She was wearing pajamas and a silk robe. I gave her two outfits from my closet for the morning and asked if she wanted to eat something. No, she said and she went to sleep in the extra bed next to Charlie's crib.

In the morning I made breakfast and sent the three girls off to school. I gave Charlie a shirt and shorts from Shoshana. Sandi called in sick to her public school job and sat at the table in her pajamas and robe. Neal, dressed for work, joined her at the table. While they ate, Sandi asked him questions about divorce law and custody and alimony.

Then I put Charlie in my car and drove him to my school. "Why did my daddy hit my mommy?" he asked me.

"Sometimes people make mistakes," I told him. "A daddy should never hit a mommy."

"I know," he said.

At the school I conferred with Naomi, Charlie's teacher, so she'd be aware of his anxieties. She said she'd give him lots of extra love and keep him busy.

I went into my office feeling unsettled. And I soon made up my mind. "I left the Budget for the Board Meeting home." I told my secretary. "I'll run home and get it and be back in an hour."

Sure enough, Neal's car was still in the garage. I walked in and they were not in the kitchen. Then I heard them in Neal's den, Neal at his desk and Sandi facing him. I walked in and Sandi was still in her pajamas. Her robe was draped around her chair. Neal's suit jacket and tie were off and his shirt was unbuttoned at the top. Two half filled glasses of liquor were on his desk. So he had offered Sandi a drink. What was wrong with that? But both of them looked at me with guilty faces.

"Neal is going over some of my options," said Sandi.

"I'm referring her to Eugene Silver. He does divorce work." I saw Sandi's nice bare breast poking out of her pajama top. Why had she taken off her robe? Why hadn't she changed into one of the outfits I'd given her?

And I knew the answer. She was feeling betrayal. And she was needy. She had arrived in the middle of the night with her hair in a ponytail. Now her strawberry blond hair was loose around her face, partially hiding the bruise on her cheek. Her body was trim and athletic. And my body was, well, six months pregnant.

So had anything happened? No, I didn't think so. But possibly it was about to. And why hadn't Neal left for his office at 8:30 as he usually did?

Neal left for his office and Sandi, dressed in one of my outfits, left to see Eugene. That evening she asked me if she could stay until the end of the week and I'd said No, that my mother in law was coming and we needed the room. Sandi moved to a friend's house.

And my mind moved to the mistletoe story. I was in my 9th month of pregnancy with Talia and Alex and I were invited to his supervisor's house for a Christmas party.

We walked into the large and lovely home and were greeted by the supervisor and his wife. They gave me a drink of ginger ale. Then the supervisor said, "Alex, could you help us out? Something is wrong with the stereo and we want to play Christmas music."

"Will you be okay?" Alex asked me.

"Sure. Go ahead." Alex and his supervisor went to their den.

I didn't know anyone at the party and, of the perhaps thirty guests, no one talked to me. How could I be invisible in a large red maternity dress? But I was. Then I spotted something good. I sat in a wing chair next to a bowl of warm chili con queso. Next to it was a platter of carrot sticks, celery sticks and jicama.

I was quite content, munching away. No one said a word to me. The night before we'd been at a Chanukah party at Erica and Steve's house. People that I knew and new people clustered around me. When was I due? How did I feel? How many children did I already have? Various people brought me plates of food and glasses of soda. The correct way to treat a very pregnant woman.

Then I looked up to see Alex approaching. As he walked towards me, a cute girl with short red hair and a sparkly silver dress grabbed Alex and moved him two steps so they were under a bunch of hanging mistletoe. I watched with great interest.

Redheaded, sparkly girl now put her arms around Alex's neck and leaned her head up for a kiss. Alex smiled at her and reached his hands up, removing her arms. He smiled at her very pleasantly and said something to her. She shrugged and very loudly said, 'Your loss!' and walked away and then he walked up to me.

"Do you want to go, darling?"

"Don't we have to stay one hour?"

"I'll say you were feeling contractions."

In the car I asked him who the red haired woman was.

"Oh, Rhona. She's an engineer."

"Did you think she was pretty?"

"A little cheap in that very short, glittery dress. Like Vipka the Vampka. But she's a good engineer. Not on my team. On Paul's team."

"Oh."

"Let me rephrase my answer. She's a little pretty but not nearly as pretty as you. And not nearly as clever. You're my vibila and the mother of my daughter. You're the one I love."

"Thank you, Alex."

"Don't thank me. My bun, as they say, is in your oven. And that makes you very, very special." Two pregnancies, two men.

SISTER MARY LOUISE IS WAVERING

"Margarita is in her seventh month. Jorge and I have been friends, or whatever we are, for four months now. And I have such disturbing thoughts. Another nun could fill my place as an encouraging counselor. But who could take my place as the encourager of Jorge? He says such wonderful things to me.

He says he lives for the afternoons when he will come to see Margarita and me. He says he has abiding love for his daughter but thinks of me in an entirely different way. Last week he got very hurt because he said he realized that I wouldn't consider him because he is crippled, confined to a wheelchair."

"And what did you say?"

"No, no, that never bothered me. So since Sunday, we've been walking for a little bit in the rose garden now that it stopped raining. And yesterday, he stopped his wheelchair and reached up and kissed my cheek."

"So what did you do?"

"I realized that I wanted him to continue. I yearned for him to continue. And so I said to him, "Jorge, I am giving our relationship very much thought. I am trying to figure out what to do." And he was so happy, I had never made anyone happy before in that way, that I would be with him. No one before had said they wanted me."

That I would be with him. I would make Alex happy if I said I would be with him. Again. After all these years. Both Sister Mary Louise and I had to have serious thoughts about what to do. And I wished that I could confide in her and tell her that I too was inhabiting the limbo land of indecision.

SISTER MARY LOUISE DECIDES

Sister Mary Louise called me. "Valerie, I did as you suggested and I told Mrs. O'Dell. And she was lovely, and didn't judge me at all. She went with me to tell Sisters Cordelia and Agnes. They were very quiet. Sister Cordelia shook her head and sighed in disappointment. Sister Agnes cried. Maybe they were angry with me or maybe they envied me. Anyway, they both told me I must tell Mother Superior about my confusion and thoughts.

I went to see her. She was composed and didn't try to argue with me. She said, "Sister, you must take a four week break. I am going to send you to our convent near Flagstaff, next to the Navajo Reservation. There you will help the Sisters in the preschool, all Navajo children. And you must do two other things. You must pray and ask God and the Holy Mother to guide you in your decision. And you must walk at least an hour every day, to help you in your thinking. This is a huge decision. After four weeks, we shall see. So I'm leaving in the morning and I promised her that I would not contact ANYONE, by phone or by letter."

"I sincerely wish you good luck. Whatever you decide, we're close friends."

"Thank you. May I ask you your opinion on a related matter? One of the things that's been bothering me is my family in Manila. They will be so disappointed. They are proud to have a nun in the family, a college graduate. Am I silly to be so concerned about them?"

"You'll still be a college graduate."

"But they thought that I brought honor to the family. They have plenty of grandchildren already. What do you think?"

"When was the last time you saw them?"

"Twelve years ago, when I left Manila."

"This is just my opinion. You have a lot to think about; your work for the next twenty five years, your deep friendship with fellow nuns. And then your feelings for this man, how it would be to live in his house with him. Marital relations. Your relationship with Margarita. Her new baby."

"You are helping me very much, Valerie. So my family's feelings should not be crucial to my decision?"

"Only my opinion, Sister. But I'll tell you what Alex always says. 'The heart wants what the heart wants.'"

"Thank you, Valerie. A lot to think about. I'll call you when I return in four weeks."

CLAUDIA CLEMONS

When I returned from work the next day, boxes were disrupted in the garage and Talia was dragging the small antique desk with the marble top into the house.

"Mom, you said I could keep this in my room, the desk from Grandma's house. I want it."

"Just help me put all these boxes back and then we'll polish the desk and bring it to your room."

Two years ago, the week after we'd returned from Jeanette's funeral, Claudia Clemons had called me.

"It was so good to see you and your daughters last week. You all looked lovely. I'm calling you because this morning Mrs. Trusty phoned me. You know they're selling the house?"

"That beautiful house.?"

"Yes. So Mrs. Trusty said, 'Miss Clemons, you'd better get over here. Anita is acting like the Queen of the Manor and ordering Ida Mae and me around. She's having us pack everything and I mean everything. I asked Anita, don't you think Mrs. Berk would want some things to go to her granddaughters? 'I'll decide who gets what', said Anita. And nothing for the girls. So come as quick as you can while she's gone shopping.'"

"When I got there, Mrs. Trusty said that Alex was at the lawyer's office, Anita was shopping and the baby was sleeping. She took me up to the guest bedroom and there was your wedding gown, that beautiful gown that your designer designed just for you, all cut up into a million pieces!"

"No! We were saving it for Marisa and Talia. It was in a special case. A million pieces?"

"Yes."

"And the long veil?"

"All cut up. Who does such an evil thing? Yesterday afternoon, Mrs. Trusty discovered it and showed Alex, who is already depressed. He went into their bedroom and shouted at Anita and she was shouting back. Mrs. Trusty couldn't make out what they were saying but heard the words ' wedding gown'. Last night Alex slept in his old bedroom and she slept in Jeanette's room. And Valerie, there's more."

"More?"

"Yes. Down in the living room, you know that oil painting that you painted of Alex? That she had on the fireplace mantel? Anita cut that up, too. Took the canvas out of the frame your uncle made and stabbed it with a knife and then cut it into pieces."

"No part of it could be saved?"

"Oh, no. I never knew that you were an artist."

"I'm not. Alex and I were at a jazz club and a photographer took our picture. He was so handsome that I sent in the photo to this company. For $49 they made it into a paint by numbers kit. I painted a little every day and when it was done, I wanted to keep it. But I felt sorry for Jeanette so I gave it to her for her birthday."

"She loved that picture, showed it to everyone. Well, there were boxes everywhere and since Alex and Anita were out of the house, Mrs. Trusty and Ida Mae and I peeked inside them and brought six boxes out to my car. We also took that little antique desk that stood in the entry hall."

"The one with the marble top? Talia loves antiques."

"Yes. So everything is in my car and my brother Will said he'd drive us to Phoenix with it all. Will calls it 'the loot' but I don't feel bad because it should go to your girls. I'm sure that Saul, who probably bought all of it, mostly from England, would want the girls to have it. Do you have room in your garage?"

"Yes, we do."

Claudia and Will were tired after driving eight hours so they came over the next morning and I made breakfast. Then Will went to explore Phoenix record shops and Claudia and I unpacked the boxes.

"Saul had a fine eye for lovely things," she said and then she blushed.

One box had beautiful dishes, blue with gold rims, service for eight. Another box was filled with silver, soup tureens, candlesticks, and serving platters. There was a box of figurines, shepherdesses, hunting dogs, and horses. Another box held a colorful large ceramic coffee server with matching cups and saucers. Another box was filled with baby books of Alex. The last box had fine tablecloths with matching napkins.

The small desk was charming and perfect.

"Did you want some of these things for yourself since Saul picked them out?"

"I have an entire house of special items that Saul picked out." She smiled a smile of reflection and sadness. "Mrs. Trusty said that she has never liked Anita, she isn't a nice person. And Ida Mae agreed. Now Valerie, they said. She is a nice person. Saul would have liked you."

"You still think of Saul?"

"All the time."

"How about another muffin and more coffee?" I poured it.

"Claudia, a few years ago when we talked about working for Saul and the Nazi party trying to influence Los Angeles, you said you'd tell me how you and Saul finally got together. If you'd like to, I mean."

"I remember. I told you how he kissed me, after driving me home when it was raining and we'd gotten all wet. And then he was sorry and ashamed and told me that for us to be together was impossible. Alex was only three, Jeanette depended on him so much. And I understood. It was part of why I admired him, loved him, that he was responsible and caring, and had such a good character. So I kept working for him, loving him from afar. I couldn't seem to do anything else and I loved being with him in the business. Then it was early 1942 and we were now at war. Saul was busy saving Jews who'd escaped from Germany. He was building the business and he was the President of his large Temple."

"But you saw him every day."

"Not on weekends but yes. We went on day by day, working together, attracted to each other but never touching, always polite with one another. And Saul kept giving me more responsibility, writing letters to sponsor Jews who needed to escape from Europe, helping Jewish servicemen, fundraising for the war effort at his Temple. And even with the war, the business was growing, people wanted nice fireplace fixtures in their homes. Sometimes I would stay an hour later, to get everything done. And to see this handsome man with abundant brown hair, working at his desk, his shirt sleeves rolled up, his tie off, just to see him gave me joy. And he was very generous and gave me large raises and bonuses if I helped make a sale.

"And Pearl Harbor, on December 7th, 1941, that was horrible for me personally. My father was in the Navy and was on the SS Arizona. When the Japanese bombed the ship my father got burns all over his legs. More than a thousand men died. My father received treatment in a hospital in Hawaii, then they flew him home to the Veteran's Hospital. And Saul said he wanted to drive me to the hospital after work so I wouldn't have to take the bus. And he wanted to meet my Dad. They met and Saul would sit by his bed and ask him questions and call him Petty Officer Clemons. So they'd talk and my father told Saul more than he'd told me. And my father, I'd told you, mistrusted Jewish people. But he said that Saul was entirely different, a fine gentleman.

"And then Saul made some phone calls about getting a special car that my father could drive with his impaired legs. I still don't know who paid for that car but it was delivered to our apartment. After that, two or three times a week we'd go to the Veteran's Hospital and then Saul would ask me if I wanted some dinner. But I knew we had no future beyond my further broken heart, so I said No.

"Then it was April, 1942. Saul had asked me to book him two plane tickets for Tulsa, Oklahoma for the following Friday. The Rabbi at his Temple was retiring. In 1940. Saul and other Jews had sponsored Rabbi Nussbaum and his wife to get out of Germany on almost the last ship to leave. Rabbi Nussbaum learned English, helped by his wife, and got a job as Rabbi at the synagogue in Muskogee, Oklahoma. Saul and a member of his Board of Directors, Mason, were flying out to interview Rabbi Nussbaum for the position at Temple Israel, to start in July.

"I was sitting in his office, taking dictation, when Saul got a call. 'You broke your leg playing handball, Mason? Alright. Don't worry about it. I'll take care of it. Rest and feel better.'"

"Saul looked at me for a long moment. 'Have you ever been to Oklahoma, Claudia?'"

"No, I never have."

"'Would you like to go? I have an extra plane ticket. I mean, would you like to go WITH ME? And instead of flying back we could take a week and drive back together. Do you understand what I'm asking you?'"

"I sat in my chair, restraining myself from doing cartwheels in his office. I said, 'I think I do.'"

"'We've been saying No to ourselves for a long time. But who knows how this war will end, whether now our entire world will turn upside down? You're such a lovely girl, such a remarkable person. As long as we don't hurt anyone, why shouldn't we be together? And of all places, in Muskogee, Oklahoma. What do you say, Claudia?'"

"The musical *Oklahoma,* by Rodgers and Hammerstein, was going to open on Broadway and a few songs were being played on the radio. So I stood up and sang:

Oklahoma, where the wind comes sweeping down the plain. You're doing fine, Oklahoma. Oklahoma, okay. And both of us laughed. He kissed me softly and told me to go home then and pack and he'd pick me up at 7 am."

"When I got into his car that morning, Saul spoke to me as he drove. I knew him well enough to know that he had thought about and rehearsed what he would say. 'Claudia,' he began, 'Not only do I want to be fair to my little Alex, but also to you.

I want us to pledge to always be honest with each other. I have been thinking about you seriously for two years now.'"

"I listened quietly. 'I need you to understand that I will not be divorcing Jeanette. Alex is only six. So if we have a relationship, which will be up to you, there are things I can't give you, things that you deserve. Like respectability, recognition as my wife. A child. You need to think about these things. I've been invited to the Rabbi's house for Shabbas dinner tonight and I'd want to take you with me. But I can't. When we get to the hotel, perhaps you'll want us to get two rooms. It's up to you. We can be lovers or we can be fond companions. It's up to you, Claudia.'"

"So how did you answer him?"

"I said 'I want to be with you. One room, double bed. I'm very happy, Saul.'"

"And then he said an endearment for the very first time. 'Sweetheart,' he said. And we held hands on the plane for hours, looking at each other and smiling. The room at the hotel was very nice. A big king size bed. I said,' Saul, we left so quickly that I didn't buy a new nightgown or robe.'"

"He hugged me.' Do you think you will be wearing a nightgown? That's not my plan. But on this trip I will be buying you nightgowns and negligees.'"

"Saul explained our itinerary. It was then 1 pm. At 6, he would go to the Rabbi's house for dinner. Then he'd go to Sabbath services at the synagogue and be back to the hotel by 10. I could order dinner and would I be all right for the evening? Of course, I said."

"Then in the morning, he would attend a Bar Mitzvah and see how Rabbi Nussbaum conducted it. He'd be back by 1. Then Sunday morning he would visit the Religious School and talk to Rabbi Nussbaum about his thoughts concerning Jewish education. He'd be back by 1."

"I assured him that I could listen to the radio and I'd brought two books to read. I would be fine. On Monday morning, he said, we would begin our trip. It had been raining with extreme wind since we'd arrived. Saul used this as his excuse. He called his brother and his wife to say that his flight home was delayed. Rather than wait around Muskogee, he wanted to rent a car and drive back to California. He loved road trips and needed a chance to relax from so many problems and pressures. It was getting almost impossible to import fireplace fixtures from Scotland and France. So he felt it was important to visit an andiron factory in New Mexico and order from them. His brother and his wife agreed. Saul told them that he would also visit synagogues in Texas and Arizona and talk to their Rabbis and Presidents about important issues facing the Jewish community. Saul had already hired our part time salesman Raymond to run the store all week."

"He embraced me and led me to the bed. I felt that I had to be honest with him.' Saul,' I said,' I have never been with anyone before. You'll have to show me what to do.'"

"He was very surprised. 'But aren't you twenty nine? And I've seen men who came to the store to take you to dinner. Your Youth Minister, salesmen, that man from the bank, even customers wanted you. You just ate dinner?'"

"No one compared with you," I told him." I tried to fall in love, really. But all the other men fell short of you."

"'Oh, sweetheart,' said Saul. And it began. And it was more fulfilling than I'd imagined in my dreaming of him. He took care of me in every way."

"I was a virgin with Alex also," I said.

"Yes, but you were seventeen. I was an old virgin at twenty nine. But we both did what my mother told me was proper, saved ourselves for the men we loved."

"After he left for his dinner, I slept then took a bubble bath. This is my honeymoon, I thought, and I don't care if it has to be secret. A housemaid knocked and asked if I needed anything.

"I have everything I need," I told her. "I have everything."

"Then Saul came back and told me about the dinner. I loved it when he told me about meetings he'd had or appointments at the homes of customers. He told me that the Rabbi's wife, Ruth, was beautiful and it was evident that the Rabbi loved her very much. Almost with adoration, the Rabbi recited the special Sabbath blessing for one's wife, A Woman of Valor. And then he blessed his children, their daughter who was seven and their son who was one. As his wife served the dinner, the Rabbi said, 'I turned my life around so I could marry her. We have a lifelong love affair.' Isn't that so lovely, Claudia? A lifelong love affair! His wife is very accomplished and taught him English on the boat coming to America in 1940. She also drives him everywhere since he doesn't drive.

"So she drove us to the Synagogue where the Rabbi delivered a magnificent, rousing sermon about the life of the Jews as slaves in ancient Egypt and relating this to our present day war with Germany. As I heard him I knew that we must hire him and he would make an excellent Rabbi for Temple Israel."

"Then, Valerie, more romance and I could not stop smiling with the joy of it all."

"In the morning, we ate breakfast and had more romance. And Saul kissed me and he said, 'Here I am, forty one, and I feel like a young man again. You are very, very beautiful, Claudia.' Then Saul went to the Bar Mitzvah and luncheon. When he came back, it was raining fiercely so we stayed in the room. We turned on the radio and danced to Benny Goodman's Dance Band. Saul told me that he and Jeanette had taken dance lessons at Art Linkletter's Studio and he held me close, a really good dancer."

"In the morning, Saul went to visit the Religious School. He liked Rabbi Nussbaum's views on making Judaism relevant to children and teenagers. He told the Rabbi that he was very impressed with everything and invited him to fly out to Hollywood and meet the congregation of Temple Israel and the Board, as soon as possible. The Rabbi would be able to see the Temple, see the plans for expansion in the future and see the Rabbi's home on Ivar and Hollywood Boulevard. Rabbi

Nussbaum said he would come in a few weeks. He was very interested.

"By Monday morning, Saul had rented a nice car and we began our trip. Every morning of the trip, he called Jeanette and was kind and gentle with her. He called her 'dear' and I tried not to have it bother me. I reasoned that half of him was better than the five years of yearning for him from afar. And the physical part of our relationship was amazing to me. I could not get enough of him and he wanted me too. 'You are so easy to be with,' he told me. 'I don't want to speak ill of the mother of my son, but sixteen years of drama and negativity is very exhausting.' Another clue about his life with Jeanette and my blueprint for our future together. So, many times during that trip, I thanked God for this time alone with him. And we drove in the car with his arm around me."

"Did you feel guilty?"

"I had stayed away from Saul for five years, due to my guilt and his guilt. But when he told me that he needed me, that my comfort kept him going, I realized that if I could help him, I should. I would never break up his family. But it was evident that Jeanette upset him and that I calmed him. And taking care of him, helping him in every way that I could, became my mission in life."

"I understand what you're saying," I told her.

Saul said, "I mapped out the whole trip. This is our respite from responsibility, our brief moment in time," I remember every word he said to me on that trip and his every action. Sometimes we talked and sometimes we played the radio. And when *As Time Goes By*, sung by Dooley Wilson, was played, Saul said, 'This will be our song.' Do you know that song, Valerie?"

"I do. But would you sing it?"

You must remember this. A kiss is just a kiss. A sigh is just a sigh. The fundamental things apply As time goes by.

And when two lovers woo, they still say I love you.

On that you can rely.

No matter what the future brings
As time goes by.
It's still the same *old story, A fight for love and glory A case of do or die.*
The world will always welcome lovers As time goes by.

"That's lovely," I told Claudia.

"*No matter what the future brings,*" Saul sang in a nice voice. And that song came on the radio at least every day during that trip and we always laughed and hugged. So that Monday we just drove two hours to Oklahoma City in the rain. We went to a hotel and danced and continued our honeymoon. Valerie, is this all too much information? I don't want to bore you."

"I'm fascinated. Saul, after all, was my father in law and for years I've been wondering about your relationship with him." And how to compare Saul with Alex, I thought to myself.

"Well, tell me if it gets boring. So on Tuesday, we drove four hours from Oklahoma City to Amarillo, Texas. And it had stopped raining. In Amarillo, Saul spotted a fancy lingerie shop and stopped the car. He bought me four nightgowns and negligees in red, black, white and purple. I protested because they cost so much money. One or two would have been enough, I told him. 'We'll be needing these,' he answered, 'As time goes by.' So that was the answer to what I'd been wondering. Was this it? Or would it continue once we got back to Los Angeles? It appeared that he wanted us to continue. Then he bought a lavender gown and negligee for Jeanette and had it mailed to her. I tried not to let it bother me. It seemed that he was going to be adept at keeping both of us happy.

"On Wednesday, we drove four hours from Amarillo to Albuquerque. As we drove on Tuesday and Wednesday, Saul told me what he'd learned talking to Rabbi Nussbaum. The Rabbi was about thirty two, younger than Saul, and Saul was fascinated with his story. Did you know that he was born in a part of eastern Europe that was changing from Romania to Austria and back?"

"Yes, the Rabbi told me that. I don't know if you knew this but Jeanette told me I had to go see Rabbi Nussbaum to see if he would approve of me marrying Alex. He told me then that most people thought he was born in Germany but he was born in the Bukovina area, a part of Romania. Like my father. So anyway, he approved of me. And the wedding was nine weeks later."

"A beautiful wedding. You were so pretty and Alex was handsome. The smile never left either of your faces."

"It was a great memory. Such a joyous time. And I'm so sad about that wedding dress. But, oh well. Tell me more about Rabbi Nussbaum."

"So, Saul said, the Rabbi received a PhD from the University of Wurzburg and was the author of several philosophical books. He was ordained as a Rabbi and he met Ruth who was a young and beautiful divorced mother. She was a year younger than the Rabbi, She was from a very cultured German Jewish family, well educated and spoke French and English as well as German. She was lovely and gracious, five feet tall. The Rabbi was not a tall person either but was handsome and well built. Ruth told Saul that after she met Max she was passionately in love with him and still was. Their young daughter Hannah was from her first marriage. Ruth had escaped Germany when the anti semitic laws came and she went to Amsterdam. She lived around the corner from Anne Frank and her daughter played with Anne. Rabbi Nussbaum pursued her and they were married in a civil ceremony in Amsterdam and Ruth joined him in Berlin. At that time he was the Rabbi of one of the largest Reform synagogues in Berlin. A Jewish wedding was planned at the Rabbi's Berlin synagogue."

"The Rabbi was also the Director of the League for Jewish Culture and the Gestapo arrested him. He was detained but a Nazi commander enjoyed talking to him about philosophy. The Nazi commander released the Rabbi 'as a wedding present' so the Rabbi could marry Ruth at the Jewish wedding.

"Saul and Ruth sat together at the Bar Mitzvah and she told him what happened at Kristallnacht, November 9th and 10th, 1938. They were eating dinner when the Shammas, like the Temple custodian, came to tell them that their synagogue had been set on fire by the Nazis. They grabbed coats and ran to the synagogue, blocks away. Firemen were standing on the sidewalk watching the flames. The police were under orders NOT to put out the fire. Ruth told Saul, 'I knew what was in his mind. I said,' Max, don't do it! 'But he didn't listen to me. He ran into a side door and moments later, came out carrying one of the Torahs. His eyebrows and some of his hair had burned and his coat was singed and the outer covering and some of the parchment of the Torah was burned. But in an act of defiance of the Nazis, he brought out the Torah. I had on a fur coat so I carried the Torah under my coat as if I was pregnant. Quickly we walked back to our apartment and hid it."

"And that Torah was at my wedding. We called it the Nussbaum Torah." I told Claudia.

"And then Saul told me how Ruth and the Rabbi escaped from Germany After Kristallnacht they realized that there was no hope for Jews in Germany. The Rabbi wrote to every contact they could think of to help them escape.

"Rabbi Stephen Wise of New York sent notices out across the country to help this young couple and Saul, then the President of Temple Israel, responded, as did others. To get into the United States in 1938 one needed a definite job and a sponsorship by putting up $1200, a year's wages in Germany. Rabbi Wise secured him the job at the small synagogue in Muskogee and Saul and others guaranteed the $1200. Still, to get the visas and all the required paperwork took fifteen months and conditions worsened for the Rabbi and Ruth every day.

"One day in early 1940, the Gestapo came to their apartment to arrest the Rabbi again. Ruth had him go into the bathroom and she graciously welcomed the two Gestapo men. She told them that her husband was away at a meeting and had them sit in her living room. She served them snacks and drinks, one drink after another and finally they became drunk and left without searching the apartment. Then their paperwork came through but to their dismay, it did not include five year old Hannah because she was not the Rabbi's biological daughter. After agonizing discussion, they decided that the only hope for all of them was to leave Hannah temporarily with Ruth's parents. They sailed to New York and Ruth taught the Rabbi English on the boat. They were met by Rabbi Wise who had gotten them an appointment with Henry Morgenthau, the Secretary of the Treasury. They immediately got on a train to Washington D.C. and begged Secretary Morgenthau to rescue their little daughter and Ruth's parents. He did and the parents and little girl were able to leave Germany but they traveled to country after country for five months until they were able to enter the United States."

"Imagine what that mother went through," I said.

"I know. Some story. Anyway, back to our trip. After a barbeque lunch, we went to the andiron factory and Saul spent three hours ordering fireplace screens and andirons that were very unique. And as before, he often asked my opinion and said that I had very good taste. Driving away, he said, now we can certainly claim this trip as a legitimate business expense. Since I can't import them, I had to get fireplace fixtures. Right?"

"Then it was Thursday, one week from the magical moment that he'd said, 'Have you ever been to Oklahoma, Claudia?' We drove from Albuquerque to Flagstaff, stopping at the Zuni Indian Reservation and the Hopi Indian Reservation. There he bought me turquoise jewelry and also bought some for Jeanette. I realized that it would be best for us if he kept her happy. As I told you, he called her every day. But on Friday morning she exploded.

"We had arrived in Flagstaff and after breakfast we were going to the Grand Canyon. He called Jeanette and she spoke so loudly that I could hear her on the phone. 'You're only in Flagstaff? I thought you'd be home today. It's been a whole week, Saul!'

Saul started to placate her in a moderate tone. He spoke about a delay due to car trouble and how necessary it was for him to purchase the fireplace fixtures from the Albuquerque factory and how long that had taken. I realized for the first time that he could lie quickly and easily. Then she was yelling and his voice got less pleasant and finally he said,' I'll see you when I see you' and 'Good Shabbas' and he hung up."

"And I said, 'I never realized that you could make excuses in two seconds' and he said,' You, too?' So then I realized that I should not be criticizing him when he was trying to create joy for us but not hurt her.

"'I'm sorry. I'm sorry. That was a silly thing for me to say.' And I held him. And he said, 'Good rules for relationships is to ask oneself, Is this what I want to say? And do I want to say it NOW?'"

"That's exactly what Alex told me, in the early days of our marriage."

"Saul must have taught him. And Saul said, 'I'm going to teach my son to pick a calm, pleasant woman. Otherwise she'll drive you nuts.'"

'Claudia, that is so interesting. Calm and pleasant."

"Yes, calm and pleasant. And that's how I determined I would be from then on."

"I was pleasant in my marriage to Alex because I was so happy, almost all the time. And I sensed that he did not like a lot of drama."

"Saul didn't either."

"But if it happened, Alex knew how to calm me, to hug me and reassure me."

"Saul also, with me."

"So you were in Flagstaff."

"Yes. We went to the Grand Canyon and were awed by it and then we went to Sedona and walked around and had lunch. Then we drove to Phoenix and Saul went to Shabbas services at the very Temple where you now work. The Rabbi arranged for Saul to speak to the Temple Board about some briefings he had received on concentration camps in Germany and Poland. He spoke to the Board on Sunday morning but on Saturday he said, 'We must be shomer Shabbas which means we'll rest all day Saturday.' So we did. On Sunday afternoon we drove to Blythe and spent the night and the next day, Monday, we arrived back in Los Angeles."

"Some trip!"

"As you can see, I remember every minute of it. The trip that changed my life."

"I don't want it to end," Saul said. And I felt the same way.

"When you were back in L.A., did you only see him during the week?"

"No. We got into the habit of eating lunch in the shop together, ordering from one of the nearby seven restaurants. And sometimes we'd put a sign on the door, Closed for lunch, back at 1. Definitely, Saul reserved Friday night and Saturday night for his family. And he went to services on Saturday morning. But sometimes on Saturday afternoon, he would come to my apartment for an hour or two. Even after my father was released from the hospital. My father said, 'You're thirty years old and you know what you're doing.' 'I love him, Dad,' I told him and he said, 'I know. And he's a first class gentleman.'"

MISSIONS TO ISRAEL

Neal was the Chairman of the Community Relations Committee, a voluntary position for the Jewish Federation. In that capacity, he led thought leaders on trips to Israel, fully paid for by the Federation. The leaders were often political figures or journalists or TV or radio personalities or high school or college professors. Neal organized and led two Missions every year.

Before the trips, we would host a party at our home so the people could get to know each other. Two weeks after they returned, we'd host another party to talk about their impressions.

Their impressions were usually very positive towards Israel. They had seen with their own eyes the struggles of Israel which, not a perfect country, was still filled with many hard working people resettling thousands of Holocaust survivors and thousands of Jews who'd been expelled from Arab countries. And they'd been able to explore the many sites and buildings central to Christianity. They'd seen the care that Israeli officials accorded to every religion and their sacred places.

So now, in six weeks, Neal was leading another mission, this time all ministers and priests and nuns. I had asked him if he could include one or more of my nun friends but he said he had to invite Mother Superiors or college professors who were nuns and taught religion or history.

Neal had almost finished his list of religious leaders who would be invited on the trip and asked my opinion on two choices. They would be going the last two weeks of June.

Meanwhile, I was very busy with the ongoing needs of my four children and the daily problems of running a large preschool. The school had grown to 125 children, including three Kindergartens. I had a wonderful staff, including my friend Erica who taught one of the Kindergarten classes. All the teachers were lovely with the children and highly experienced. Several of them were Israelis.

Now Orna, the Israeli music and dance teacher, came into my office. She had a few questions about our schedule but then asked me if I was going with Neal on the minister's Israel Mission.

"No, I went three years ago."

"You should go on this one."

"Why?"

"Just make sure that you go. Talk to Neal."

That night I asked Neal if I could go. My preschool semester was over June 11th and then we ran a summer day camp. I could be gone for twelve days in June. Emmie was two and Evalynne would be available to stay at our home. The older children would be going to camp.

"No," said Neal. "The group list is all filled and there's no room."

The next day when Orna asked I told her that the group list was all filled.

"What's full?" she said. "Israel? So you take another plane. Meet up at Lod airport. You can stay in Neal's hotel room at no extra charge."

Why was Orna being so persistent?

"Besides," said Orna, "did you know that Shulamit is going on this trip?"

Shulamit. Our new Hebrew teacher, having worked at our school for just seven months. Last September I'd received a phone call at home from Judge Saltman, one of Neal's friends. "I'll get Neal " I'd said. "No, I want to speak to you," said Judge Saltman. The Judge was a widower with grown children, who was active in the Jewish community and contributed to many causes, including my pre-school's scholarship fund.

"Valerie," he said. "I want to ask you for a favor. On my trip to Israel last week, I met a very worthy young lady who wanted to come to the United States. She was one of my tour guides and is a very delightful girl. So she and I went on a side trip to Eilat and I decided to help her. So she came back to Phoenix with me on a visitor's visa. She might be able to get a resident visa if she's teaching here. I wondered if you possibly might have a teaching job for her."

"My staff is all hired since it's October," I said.

"Is there any way you can help her? Her name is Shulamit. She doesn't know anyone in Phoenix other than me."

"I'll try," I said. "Meanwhile, tomorrow is Shabbat. Why don't you and Shulamit come to dinner and I'll get to know her."

They walked into our house, the tall Judge with abundant brown and gray hair and the fabulously gorgeous young Israeli woman. She had movie star looks, long black very curly hair and a lovely figure. Neal appeared to be as charmed by her as the Judge was. She had been a tour guide and spoke English well, with a charming accent. She said she had come to Israel from Hungary as a young girl, saved by Kastner on the Kastner train which saved hundreds of Hungarian Jews in 1944.

Neal had always been very fascinated by the facts of the Kastner train. Rudolf Kastner was a Hungarian Jew who was a lawyer and a journalist. He was one of the founders of the Budapest Aid and Rescue Committee and was able to bring many European Jews to the relative safety of Hungary during the early war years. Then in 1944 the Nazis invaded Hungary and Kastner and his committee realized that Hungarian Jews were also going to be murdered in the death camps.

"Shulamit, do you know about the Kastner train?" Neal asked her.

"Of course. I was on the train with my parents although I was only five. My mother died in Bergen Belsen. I wrote a paper about the Kastner train when I was in college."

"About how many Hungarian Jews were there?" Neal asked her.

"437,000 Hungarian Jews and the Nazis murdered three fourths of them."

"How many were on the train?"

"Over 1600 Jews. We were in 35 cattle wagons."

"And from what I've read, Kastner negotiated with Adolf Eichman and Kurt Becher, who were German S.S. officers, to give them great amounts of money to save a group of Jews."

"You're correct, Neal. My father had money so he gave $1000 each for me and my mother and himself so we could be on the train. Other wealthy Jews paid that also. But Yitzchak Sternbuch was a Swiss Orthodox Jew and he paid an enormous amount of money so poor Jews could also be saved. Of course, Kastner saved all the members of his large family, but who could blame him for that?"

"Apparently a lot of people did blame him. What do you think?"

"I think he was a man in a frightful situation and he knew he couldn't save all of the 400,000. So he did what he could, negotiated with devils and saved 1600. He was able to give Eichman and Becher suitcases filled with gold, diamonds, cash and shares in companies."

"Were there many children on the train?" asked Marisa.

"There were 273 and I was one of them. We were told to pack two changes of clothing, six sets of underwear and food for ten days."

"Where did the train go?" Talia asked.

"We were told that we were going to Switzerland but the train took us to Bergen Belsen. When we got to Linz in Austria we had to get off the train at a military station for medical inspections. My mother and father and I and all the others were forced to take off our clothes and stand naked for hours waiting for the doctors to examine us. Finally I went with my mother to a room and doctors examined her so roughly and intimately, if you know what I mean, that my mother was screaming. Then they shaved off all her long hair and shaved mine also. My mother could not stop crying but when we met up with my father, he said, 'Shhhh, your hair will grow back.' We arrived in Bergen Belsen in July. The food was mainly bad bread and turnips but all the children and I got a glass of milk every day. Some Jewish person, I don't know who, paid thousands of dollars to the Nazis so the children could get the milk. That milk may have saved me. But my mother got sick and died in Bergen Belsen. A group of about 300 people were able to leave and go to Switzerland in August but not my father and me. Then in December a train arrived and took all the rest of us to Switzerland. We stayed in the Hotel Esplanade. The Orthodox Jews stayed in another hotel. Then finally, after Israel gained independence, in 1948, my father and I were able to leave and we went to Tel Aviv. By that time, I was nine. And that's my story of being saved by the Kastner train."

With this information, I calculated that Shulamit was about my age, thirty two.

She was an interesting guest, told amusing stories about her life as a tour guide, drank repeated glasses of Shabbat wine and also paid attention to my children who were at the table.

"Have you ever been a teacher?" I asked her.

"No, but I worked with young children on my kibbutz. I know all about the entire country of Israel and could teach geography and history."

She also told me quietly that she'd been married twice and divorced twice and that her dearest hope was to have a child like my Emmie. "She's adorable," she said.

"Sadly, I don't have a job available but I can ask other directors," I told her.

The next week, fate had intervened. My excellent Hebrew teacher, Miriam, who had worked for me for four years, was diagnosed with cancer. Her family was taking her to Los Angeles for treatment. I called Shulamit.

"Could you teach Hebrew? The curriculum is all done, the games, the songs, the vocabulary."

"Yes, of course."

And Shulamit was doing a good job. The children liked her. My secretary and I joked that more fathers seemed to be picking up their children than before. One father even asked me if Shulamit could offer a Hebrew class for parents.

After Shulamit had been teaching at my school for one month, she shocked me by telling me that she had just moved out of Judge Saltman's house.

"That's a surprise," I'd said.

"Why should you be surprised? He was much too old for me. Thirty years older. And you know, with the problems of most sixty year olds."

When I told Neal, I said, "She was just using him."

"So what else is new?" said Neal. "An older man is bewitched by a young and beautiful woman who has her own agenda."

Shulamit had given my secretary her new address. My secretary recognized the address as that of one of our fathers, a divorced doctor. "He's only forty five," said my secretary.

"You know him. Not too cute but has money. He's Jeffrey's father."

I spoke to Shulamit and tried to tell her, without being nosy, that it was important that she be discreet.

"It's really none of your business," she told me, "but I have only four and a half months to get settled before my visitor's visa runs out. I want to stay in America."

Two months later, she surprised us again by telling us that over the weekend she'd gotten married. Not to Jeffrey's father but to another divorced father, Mr. Schwartz, who did immigration law. He'd arranged everything and, as his wife, she was a U. S. citizen. He was a tall, bald man with a son and daughter enrolled in our school. Shulamit was now living in his large Paradise Valley home.

"She moves fast, you have to say that for her," said Orna. Shulamit was not too popular with the other teachers and she did not seem to care.

Now it was May and Orna was telling me to go on the Israel Mission. "Talk to Neal again," she said.

I did and Neal was vehement. This Mission was filled.

Maybe next year I could come along.

"So how is it that you have room for Shulamit?" I asked.

"Shulamit is a tour guide and she'll be a great help with the ministers and priests. And she called me in tears because she needs to go see her father in Tel Aviv. Her father is ill."

The next day, Orna approached me again. "You still should go. It would be good for your marriage."

And then I understood. Neal did not want me to go. "Orna, you have to tell me. What do you know?"

Orna was uncomfortable, looking down at her hands. "At the school Purim party, Neal came up to me and asked if I knew any nice women in Jerusalem. He'll have three free days when the ministers will be at that Minister's Conference and the priests are all going to Safed. He said he wants to spend the three days with a nice Israeli woman."

"And did you give him the names of women?"

"Of course not! I told him he was a shit."

I remembered three years ago on our Israeli trip. The Holocaust Museum, the Yad Vashem, asked me to come there and take a picture which would be displayed with the book I had edited, THOU SHALT NOT FORGET. Neal said he'd already been to the Yad Vashem and didn't want to go so I'd gone alone.

When I'd gotten back to the hotel, he was in the bar with a sultry, blonde Israeli woman, both laughing and flirting. They had given me the annoyed looks directed at someone who was interrupting them.

Neal did not want me to go to Israel.

Meanwhile, in the past week, Alex had said, "Why can't we go on a short trip together? Just for a weekend? Maybe to the Balboa house."

One wanted my company, with yearning, and the other did not.

THE DANCE RECITAL

Marisa and Talia had a dance recital to be held in a large auditorium. Alex had had the girls for the weekend and so we agreed that he would bring the girls and I would come to the auditorium at 2 pm.

"Neal, do you want to come to the girls' dance recital?"

"No, I'll stay home with Shoshana and Emmie. That recital takes two boring hours. The girls can show me their routines when they get home."

I got to the auditorium early and the seats were not filled yet. I spotted Alex in the third row, reading a magazine. I sat down beside him.

"The girls are putting on their costumes," he said. "It starts in about twenty minutes."

"Alex, may I ask you one question?"

"Sure."

"Alex, did you divorce Anita so we could be together?" I asked in a soft tone.

He answered quietly also. "Yes. We have to be together for some of the time. We've lost enough time. We have to be together, you and I."

"Are you two going to be talking during this whole performance? I came to see my daughter," said the woman behind us.

"Sorry," I said. I took my program and wrote, 'Neal will be in Israel for ten days starting June 19th.'

'Perfect' Alex wrote on the program. 'I have to be in San Francisco for a convention that week. Meet me there.'

"All right," I whispered.

"All right?"

"Will you two be courteous?" the woman behind me asked.

'SAN FRANCISCO!' Alex wrote on the program and then grabbed my hand and kissed it. Holding hands under Alex's magazine, we watched our daughters, and many other girls, dance. We applauded everyone with great enthusiasm.

We met our daughters in the lobby.

"The best, the very best dance recital I've ever been to." said Alex. "You two were great. And now, we're going to 31 Flavors.

You can get a milkshake or a banana split or a triple cone."

"Daddy never lets us get a triple cone," said Marisa. "Until now."

"That's because we danced well," said Talia.

A few days later, when Alex came to pick up the girls, he handed me an envelope. In it was a note in his loopy handwriting. 'Humor me. This trip will be a second honeymoon for us.

I'd like you to buy ALL new clothes, everything new. VILYA.' (Valerie, I Love You, Alex.) Folded in a sheet of paper were ten hundred dollar bills.

I started to get ready. First of all, I had to change the dates that Marisa and Talia were going to the JCC sleep away camp. I had signed them up for two weeks. I was able to change their dates to June 12th and they would be at camp during the five days that I'd be in San Francisco. Erica's twins, Beverly and Brianna who were nine years old, were signed up for the same weeks. Shoshana was going to day camp at the JCC and Emmie went to my preschool. Evalynne would stay at my house. Friends agreed to bring Shoshana and Emmie back and forth from camp. I said that I was going to see relatives in Los Angeles.

I went to three stores, including Fredrick's of Hollywood, and bought negligees, a nightgown and lovely underwear. I bought five new outfits and a warm coat and a raincoat. I had never before bought that amount of clothes or spent that amount of money in one week. It did seem amazing to have all these new things and I kept the tags on them so Alex could see that they were just purchased. I understood that symbolically I would be a virgin, as I had been with Alex before.

I dieted, no carbs, and lost the four pounds that brought me to 122 pounds. I went to exercise class every morning. And I called Dr. Jouzy in Houston.

"I don't know if you remember me. I'm Valerie and we spoke seven years ago. Concerning Alex Berk."

"Oh yes. The first wife."

"I'm a little embarrassed, Doctor. Alex and I have reconnected and are going away together. Does he have any um... restrictions? Something he shouldn't do—-that would hurt him?"

"He shouldn't forget his medications and his exercises. Oh, you mean sexually?"

"I wouldn't want him to get too tired or to have a relapse or anything."

"Valerie, this is fortunate for both of you. There are no restrictions sexually. No problems in that regard. He'll be fine. Of course he told me that he was nineteen when he married you. Now he's thirty four and he might not perform as a nineteen year old. But you should have a good time. I don't know you but I know Alex—-a hell of a nice guy—-and he deserves a good time. Especially after all he's been through in the, you know, second marriage."

WHAT HAS HE BEEN THROUGH? DETAILS, DOCTOR.

But I knew that the doctor wouldn't say anything more and Alex's code of ethics wouldn't permit any details either.

"Thank you, Doctor." THANK YOU A LOT!

My friend Erica and I stood in the JCC parking lot waving goodbye to our daughters. Her twins, Beverly and Brianna, were glad to be going with my girls for the same two weeks.

"Tomorrow, our second honeymoon! We've never been away from the girls for this long. We'll be touring England and Scotland and Steve will also be playing some golf."

"I'm happy for you," I said. I longed to tell my good friend that I too was having a second honeymoon but of course I said nothing.

Neal was also arranging his clothes for his trip and had bought some new clothing.

"I know you're disappointed that you're not coming so I promise you. Next year in Jerusalem! You'll come on our next mission. Meanwhile, what would like me to bring you? A painting, or a lovely menorah? Or jewelry?"

"Don't bother."

"Well. I'm going to bring you a gift so you might as well tell me what you want."

"Just make sure it wasn't selected by Shulamit."

"I'll surprise you. Shulamit is going to be with her sick father. Don't be so silly. Shulamit doesn't interest me. Bye, my dear. See you in twelve days." And Neal was gone.

The following week I packed for myself and prepared food for Shoshana and Emmie and Evalynne and also cleared up details at work so everything would go smoothly during my five day trip.

"I'll make all the arrangements," Alex had told me. "I'll take care of everything." I was scheduled to fly into San Francisco on Tuesday. Alex's symposium was over at 1 pm and he would pick me up at the airport. We were staying at the San Francisco Hyatt.

On Monday, I was making last minute arrangements at work when the phone rang.

"Valerie, it's Elliot Zimmerman. I'm so sorry to have to tell you this but there's been an outbreak of hepatitis at camp. Not in the cabins of either of your children but the doctor has said that we have to send everyone home. Your children may have been exposed, we don't know."

"Oh my God," I said. "I signed the paper that says they can receive a shot of gamma globulin."

"You want them to have the shot?" said the camp director.

"Yes. When will they be arriving?"

"About two."

I called the San Francisco Hyatt and asked them to contact Alex Berk. Within fifteen minutes, he called me back.

"What's wrong, darling?"

"Oh, Alex. I don't know how to tell you this. The girls are coming home in three hours because they have hepatitis at the camp. They're evacuating everyone."

"Are the girls all right?"

"Yes, and I had them give them gamma globulin."

"Good move."

"So is our trip off?"

"I've really been looking forward to it. So we'll change the plans a little. Bring them with you."

"But what about Shoshana and Emmie?"

"What the hell. Bring them, too. They have a wonderful concierge here and I'll have her find activities for them. And I'll hire an all night babysitter."

"Really, Alex?"

"Really, Nookums. Did you buy all new clothes?"

"Yes."

"Good. I'll call you back with the new arrangements."

An hour later, he called me back. The five of us could not fly in on Tuesday, the flights were filled, but he'd made reservations for us all at 11 am Wednesday. He'd reserved a room for us on the 5th floor and he was on the 6th floor. The nice concierge had booked them into activities including an art class at the Zoo and a chocolate making class at Ghirardelli Square and tickets for the Aquarium.

"You are absolutely wonderful," I told him.

"Resourceful anyway. And nothing solves problems like money."

"I'm sorry. This is going to cost so much."

"I'm kidding, darling. You'll make it up to me, in my room late at night."

"I will." We kissed on the phone and I felt that old excitement in my throat.

I was explaining to my secretary that I'd have to meet the camp bus at 2 when the phone rang again.

"Valerie, Elliot Zimmerman again. Listen, I hate to tell you this but the Singer twins' grandfather broke his hip yesterday and he's in the hospital."

"Oh no."

"And you're the backup emergency person with the parents in England."

"Oh dear. Have they had the gamma globulin shot?"

"Yes, they have. So all four girls will be on the bus."

"I'll be there to pick them up." I called Alex again.

"Alex, is the Universe conspiring against us?"

"Of course not. Just bring them along. You'll have six chaperones. DURING THE DAY. All of those little girls better be asleep by 10:30 because the babysitter comes at 11."

"At 11?"

"Yes, and then you come to my room and then you come." He wanted me to laugh and I did.

"I'll call you back."

"Darling, I got one seat on the plane. Can you hold Emmie on your lap?"

"No problem."

"And the twins are registered in the activities."

"I guess this will be a story that we tell our grandchildren." "I don't think so, Nookums. This is a story we tell no one. We'll have four nights together. No happening is going to spoil that for me. And DON'T CALL ME ABOUT ANY OTHER LITTLE GIRLS! SIX IS THE LIMIT!" We hung up, both of us laughing.

SAN FRANCISCO

The four girls got off the camp bus with no smiles. To cheer them up, I said, "We're having a mystery. There will be the first clue in an hour and every hour after that."

First Clue—-We'll wash our laundry because Second Clue—-we're going Third Clue—-on a trip.

Fourth Clue—-We each need two nice dresses and Beverly and Brianna can choose from Marisa's and Talia's.

"Where are we going?" the girls clamored.

"That will be told in another clue."

All the children were excited and helped me pack their things. In the morning, I said,

Fifth Clue—-We're going on a plane.

We all got into the car. As we arrived at the airport, I said Sixth Clue—-to San Francisco.

My girls had not been there but Beverly and Brianna had. All the girls cheered.

Alex was giving a presentation so he told me to get a cab, go to the hotel, get settled a little and then take the kids to the Zoo. He would meet us there and I was to be very surprised.

Their Art lesson was at 4.

My first mistake was not bringing Emmie's stroller. She wanted to walk. But the long walkways in both airports tired her and I had to carry her. A strange second honeymoon. At the hotel, we had a large room with long windows and six single beds and a crib for Emmie. It was done with many shades of green. The girls explored everything with excitement and then we went to the Zoo.

We were at the elephant exhibit watching a mother and baby elephant.

"That man walks like Daddy, "said Talia.

"No, he doesn't," I said.

"Yes," said Talia. Alex did have a distinctive walk.

"It's Daddy."

"No. Daddy is in Phoenix."

Talia ran up to him and he hugged her. "What are you doing here?" he said.

"We're on vacation."

"I'm here at an engineers conference. I thought you girls were at sleep away camp."

Alex and I greeted each other perfectly, happy actors in a drama and both of us amazed.

Brianna and Beverly hugged him, too. "Hi, Uncle Alex." Alex was one of Steve's closest friends and had known the twins since they'd been born.

"Do you mind if I walk with you?"

"Not at all, Alex."

We walked around the Zoo and Alex rented a stroller for Emmie. She said she wanted me to carry her but Alex looked at her very sternly and she got into it. "We don't want to tire your mother on her vacation."

We sat on chairs in the Art Room for the half hour art lesson.

"Are all those children yours?" asked a mother watching with us.

"Yes," said Alex "and we have two more at home."

"Eight children! Are you a Mormon family?"

"No, we just believe in big families."

"I get it," said the woman. "You're Orthodox Jews. They have a lot of children."

"If we were Orthodox Jews, I'd be wearing a kippah and she'd be wearing a wig."

"So what are you?"

"We're busy deciding where to have dinner." And he whispered silly things in my ear so I would burst with laughter.

There was a young lady from Phoenix Who liked sometimes kissing my penix.

I'll do it again

If you just tell me when

Because I think you are a genyix.

"You are a genyix."

"Now tell me a limerick."

"I can't think of what rhymes with Alex."

"Okay, I'll start you off."

There was a young man from John Marshall

Who said he had always been partial

"Now finish it off."

"To being on top. Until she said stop. But nothing else rhymes with John Marshall."

And there we were, giddy with our cleverness and happiness, a man and woman in their early thirties who were going to be together all night. Nothing had stopped them years ago and nothing would stop them now.

Alex drove us back to the hotel in a station wagon too large for a single man at a convention. Then the girls and I went swimming in the rooftop pool for an hour.

"Let me take you all to dinner," said Alex. "Do you like spaghetti?"

We had a delicious dinner at Tarantino's and went back to the hotel.

"Daddy, watch TV with us in our room," said Marisa.

"No, thanks. I'm meeting some engineers so we can work on our presentation for tomorrow." He kissed all the girls good night and waved at me. "Maybe we can go somewhere tomorrow."

One would have thought that the early morning plane ride, hours at the Zoo, a swim in the hotel pool and a fancy dinner at Tarantino's would have tired the girls. But no. At 9 pm they were still excited and raring to go, except for Emmie who slept. Alex had rented a Disney movie for them and I showered.

Finally I showed them a $20 bill. "I have one of these for each one of you and we're going to Chinatown in the morning. But any of you not asleep by 10:30 gets nothing and I mean nothing." I was not above bribery to get to room 608. By 11 they were all asleep and Mrs. Baum, the babysitter, arrived. She was a plump, kindly looking woman in her fifties.

"Your husband explained to me about your planned honeymoon and the kids coming home from camp. Don't you worry about a thing. Go have a good time with your husband." She had the number of Alex's room just in case. "Go. Go. I'll take care of them until you're back at 6."

I had on my new purple nightgown and over it I put my new long coat. I went to his room, a lovely room done in tones of blue with a king size bed. He offered me champagne. "Like on our wedding night," I said. He sat next to me on the couch and took me in his arms.

"Valerie, why are you trembling and your hands are so cold?"

"I feel very nervous."

"Nervous? With me? This is Alex, your Alex. How could you be nervous? But I see that you are. Remember the first day that we made love? You were nervous then, really scared and you looked up at me with large brown fearful eyes. And I said, "May I undress you?" and you said "Yes." You trusted me and you were such a brave, beautiful girl. I told you we would take it slow and we'll take it slow tonight, too. Remember I told you that if I loved you, you had nothing to be afraid of?

And I still love you and you have nothing to be afraid of."

"I do feel that you love me but there are so many women in Phoenix and in Israel, pretty women, that I can't figure out why you want me. Didn't you date women after we were no longer married?"

"Lynne for a few months."

"The children told me they met Lynne."

"She was nice but so pushy. And one night she decided to come to my place on a night that I had the girls. And she knew that. She brought them dolls, trying to win them over and she tried to hug them. So I asked her to leave and that was the end of Lynne."

"Didn't you date women in Israel?"

"I did. I dated two Israelis, for several months each. They were nice, young. One was a Yemenite woman, the other was from a kibbutz. And then Anita."

"And all of them liked vigorous outdoor sports, like you."

"They did. But I want to tell you. You are a cut above all women. There's something about you, your generosity of spirit, the tenacity of the way you love those you love, how you care for your family. Not only their physical needs but their emotional needs as well. You gave all of us the confidence to be creative. Your dedication is unwavering. Your encouragement got me through Caltech and helped me in the hospital. You follow what your grandmother told you to do, 'Have the courage to make your life a blessing.' Have some more champagne."

"Thank you." I smiled and held out my glass.

"Do you want to hear more about you?" he asked, smiling the I love you smile. I nodded.

"Whenever I have a new challenge, like at work, and I ask myself, 'Can I do it?' the voice in my head is not my mother's. 'Be careful, you'll hurt yourself.' It's yours, Valerie. 'Can I do it?' From Valerie, 'Yes, yes, yes.' Your love includes such faith in us. And I haven't mentioned your radiant smile. And how pretty you are. As I said, a cut above all women."

"Neal doesn't think so. He's in Israel right now looking for women he can date and probably more."

"Oh Neal. I wish I could offer you a real future, at least ten happy years. But——Dr. Jouzy told me you called him last week. So you know. So we're going to make the months we have into a lifetime of joy. Right?"

"Yes."

"And now Neal. Neal isn't a bad guy. After I came back I had a friend of mine do an investigation on him."

"You did?"

"He was living with my children and I had to know what sort of person he was."

"What did you find out?"

"First of all, he's very honest at work. Someone tried to bribe him handsomely when he worked for the state of Arizona. He threw the man out of his office. Also, a very bright man, completely dedicated to helping Israel and freeing Soviet Jewry. Other lawyers have told me that they respect him and like him."

"Okay. Good to know. Alex, let's not talk about Neal or Anita on this trip. In fact, Alex, let's not talk at all." I realized that I was no longer nervous and I put my arms around him.

At once he began to kiss me and love me.

By 1 am we were asleep in the way we had usually slept, with my head on his chest. Often he had held my tush and tonight he did, tightly and possessively. At 4 am I woke up again, looking at the glow of his travel clock. When my head moved, he awakened and, without pausing, lay over me and we made love again, what we'd called S and S, short and sweet.

"It's just like before," I said with wonder.

"Yes. And I'll tell you another reason why I have to have you. Did you have a Seder last April?"

"Yes."

"Last April I was in New York for Motorola and there was a Seder right in my hotel. So I went to it. And the Rabbi and the Cantor did all the usual Haggadah and songs. But also, in their talk about freedom, they told the story of *Over The Rainbow* from The Wizard of Oz. I always thought of it as a cheesy little song. But do you know who wrote it?"

"No."

"Yip Harburg and Harold Arlen. They were both the sons of Jewish immigrants who had escaped the pogroms of Eastern Europe to come to America. A land they only imagined in their dreams. You know this so well because you teach it, but Kristallnacht, the Night of Broken Glass, happened in November, 1938. They immediately wrote this song and several weeks later, "The Wizard of Oz" opened on New Year's Day, 1939. It's not a song about wizards and Oz but about Jewish survival. And I wanted to sing it to you, the woman who understands the Holocaust and fighting for freedom and survival. Do you want me to sing it?"

"I really do."

He sang softly because it was 5 am.

Somewhere over the rainbow, way up high There's a land that I heard of, once in a lullaby.

Somewhere, over the rainbow, skies are blue And the dreams that you dare to dream Really do come true.

Someday I'll wish upon a star

And wake up where the clouds are far behind me.

Where troubles melt like lemon drops Away above the chimney tops That's where you'll find me.

He stopped then. "Few other women would understand this song."

"Alex, so beautiful. About America, where a lot of dreams come true. And about us, how we want our troubles to melt like lemon drops."

"I knew you would get it. Because you're exceptional." And he held me tightly until I had to go at 5:30.

THURSDAY

So 5:30 am and I kissed Alex's mouth and put on my clothes and floated back to my room, filled with joy. Mrs. Baum greeted me and left and I was able to sleep for another two hours until Emmie woke everyone.

We had a lovely breakfast, then took the trolley car to Chinatown. We went to shops where the girls all spent their money. At about 1:30 Alex found us in an interesting shop. He told the girls that he would buy each of them a fan. As they bent over the display, he quickly showed me what was in his pocket. Ben-Wa balls. We smiled at one another. Fun tonight. We went to a museum showing early Chinese arrivals in Northern California. Then Alex took us to a fancy Chinese restaurant where he ordered a feast. Brianna was the twin who was a very fussy eater. She would only eat chicken soup with crispy crackers. Talia would only eat vegetarian dishes.

"I don't care what you eat and I don't care if you try something new," said Alex. The rest of us ate like emperors.

We returned to the hotel, had baths and showers and watched TV. Alex left to meet some engineers on his team.

Finally, all the girls slept and then it was 11 pm.

Tonight there was no awkwardness at all. We melted into one another and only came up for air around 12:30.

"You don't seem tired," said Alex. "Do you want to watch TV? Are you hungry or thirsty?"

"Do we have any juice in that mini bar? I'll turn on the TV."

As Alex looked for refreshments, I pushed several of the buttons on the large TV. Suddenly there was a picture of a woman with enormous breasts and approaching her was a bald naked man with a huge penis. Alex looked up, "Looks like you just purchased some porno," he said. "All right, here are your choices: men with men, women with men, women with women, Asian young women with older men (this really is San Francisco, isn't it?), Latina women with men, naughty women being trained or naughty men being trained."

"My God. Is that what porno is? I've never seen it. Have you?"

"Just once at someone's bachelor party. But you just spent $40 on my credit card so we have it for an hour."

I settled on the bed with Alex's arms around me and we switched from video to video. Both of us were fascinated, our eyes glued to the screen.

"His penis is really huge," said Alex.

"Yours is plenty big enough."

"You're so full of bullshit. Always the cheerleader."

"Do you want me to say a mean thing?"

"No, Valerie. Be you. The woman I love. The woman who brought six little girls to be with us on our first vacation in all these years."

"I'm sorry. I'm so sorry."

"I'm just kidding you. Having you here in my arms watching this artificial romance stuff is my idea of a good time." He laughed.

"This is all phony, isn't it? It's all pretend?"

"Well, that girl really is strung up on ropes. The slapping is probably sound effects. Neither the woman nor the man is a good actor. Is this exciting you or turning you on?"

"No and it's so repetitive. You could never call this a good story line."

"Do you want to turn it off?"

"Yes, let's just reenact it." I grabbed a small towel and started dusting with it.

"Is the room clean enough for you, Master?" I was rewarded with Alex's amused, broad smile.

"You missed a spot. Right here. Looks like you're going to need a good whipping to remember what a housemaid is supposed to do. I'm going to whip you with my tie here. Bend over the chair."

Wham, wham, wham. Both of us were laughing.

Alex turned off the TV, and threw me on the bed.

"Enough pornography for tonight, Vibila. Let's have Maid-Master sex and then cuddle up." We snuggled and kissed.

"Alex, are you going to spank me in this room?"

"Are you going to misbehave?"

"I might."

"Well, I might. Looking at your tush, that beautiful ass. It's crying out for a spanking."

"When will you do it?"

"When you least expect it."

FRIDAY

In the morning, at 5:30 am., I gave Alex a slight kiss before going to my room. But his eyes opened. "Good morning, darling."

"Alex, I've been thinking and I feel so badly about your spending so much money. And the $40 porn."

Alex laughed. "Don't worry about it. We had a problem and money solved it. I'm glad I have the money. I'm glad you're here, Vibila. I love you and I'll see you this afternoon at Ghirardelli Square."

"Alex, since tonight is Shabbat, could we have a Shabbat meal in the girls' room? I brought some travel candlesticks and candles."

"Sure," said Alex. "We can sing *Fiddler On The Roof* songs.'

Fiddler On The Roof had opened on Broadway in 1964. Since then, I had put on a modified version twice in my Temple Day Camp and once in my neighborhood Girl Scout Troop. Talia had played the part of Hodel and Shoshana had been one of the younger daughters. Marisa had chosen to be in the chorus. Alex had come to the Temple to see his daughters. perform. I had song sheets in my suitcase. Alex had seen the actual Broadway play with Zero Mostel on a trip to Philadelphia and New York. Alex's supervisor and the man's wife had gotten them tickets and Zero had spotted Alex sitting in the second row. Zero had invited the three of them to a restaurant after the show. Alex told me all about it saying, "Zero was Zero, irrepressible and funny, didn't seem tired after this long show. And the audience had adored him. Very different from when we met with Uncle Ted fifteen years ago and he was so depressed."

We had a room service breakfast and then swam in the pool. At noon we went to Ghiradelli Square and looked in many shops. At 1 all the girls had their chocolate candy lesson which they took very seriously. At 2, Alex appeared and we went to an expensive deli in Ghiradelli Square and bought two large cartons of matzoh ball soup, a challah and little cakes for dessert. We bought vegetable soup for Talia.

Then Alex drove us to The Aquarium. The girls flitted from exhibit to exhibit. Alex whispered in my ear," Last night there was this sexy, crazy lady in my room that made it worthwhile to be seeing all these fish."

"I hope so," I said.

We went back to the hotel and ordered some chicken dinners from Room Service. They set up a large table with a white tablecloth for the eight of us. The girls and I blessed the candles I'd brought and then Alex and I sang:

May the Lord protect and defend you.
May He always shield you from shame.

May you come to have, in Yisroel a shining name. May you be like Ruth and like Esther May you be deserving of praise.

Strengthen them, Oh Lord, and keep them from the stranger's ways.

May God bless you and make you good wives.

May He send you husbands who will care for you............

The beauty and irony of this moment had me holding back tears. Neal and I often sang this song to our girls on Shabbat. But Neal was in Israel with another woman and I had stepped back into time with my first love.

But it was Shabbat and a time of peace. So I couldn't cry.

The girls ate and chattered.

Alex left and we took bubble baths. I told the children that they had to sleep because we were all going sailing in Sausalito in the morning. Mrs. Baum arrived and I told her to eat all the remaining Shabbat food which she did. I went to Alex.

He was still in *Fiddler on the Roof* mode. *Wonder of wonders, miracle of miracles God took a Daniel once again.*

Stood by his side and miracle of miracles

Walked him through the lion's den.

When David slew Goliath (yes) that was a miracle.

When God gave us manna in the wilderness

That was a miracle, too,

But of all God's miracles large and small

The most miraculous one of all Is the one I thought would never be God has given you to me.

"For a while at least," he said.

Then we hugged and kissed and Alex held me on the bed.

"In all the seven years did you ever dream of me?" Alex asked.

"I did."

"What did you dream?"

"It was often the same dream. I was running and I could see you far in the distance. Sometimes I was running in a field or a deserted street. I was running so fast that I was out of breath. Sometimes I couldn't catch you but sometimes I did. You would hug me with your arms around me and I was so happy. Then when I woke up I was very sad that it was just a dream."

"I'm hugging you right now. This is not a dream."

"Did you dream of me, Alex?"

"Of course I did. I would dream about your face. Those first months we dated when you thought I was just another guy. Then your face changed when you began to care about me. After we made love you would look up at me with those long eyelashes and smile a satisfied, full of love smile. I dreamt about your face."

"You dreamt about making love?"

"No, about your face after. Having made you happy. Do you remember what you said to Sebastian when he was getting married?"

"Yes. I said 'I go to bed smiling and wake up singing.' And it was true."

Alex hugged me and arranged the blankets so I'd be warm enough. "Maybe the best thing in life is to hold a woman in your arms. And to hold the woman you love, that's the epitome of joy."

SATURDAY

And at 5:30, when the front office called, "Good morning, this is your wake up call," I was petulant.

"I don't want to go. I don't want to go."

"I know, darling, but you have to."

By 8 am we were all in beach clothes and got into Alex's car to drive to Sausalito. Beverly did not want to go. She said long car trips made her nauseous. I had little sympathy. I told her that she could stay at the hotel and I'd hire a babysitter. She decided to go and drove with a big bowl on her lap, in case.

Alex had to deliver papers to an engineer in Sausalito which took about fifteen minutes. He then rented a sailboat at the harbor and we all put on life jackets and boarded. It was a wonderful day for sailing, a little windy but also sunny.

"Daddy, could I drive the boat now?" Marisa asked. Alex was now using the motor.

"We'll drive together," he said and he put his arms around her and held the wheel with her. Their hair, the exact same wheat color, flew in the wind. It filled me with joy to see the close father and daughter. I smiled at them. Briefly, Talia, Shoshana and even Emmie wanted a turn to steer and Alex guided them. Beverly and Brianna were not interested. Then Marisa wanted another turn. After a while, he said, "Enough." because there was a large tourist boat near to us. All the girls were busy waving to the people on the boat.

"You made Marisa so happy," I said to him.

"She makes me so happy," he said. "She's so my child. Daring, risk taking. I am so ashamed that I cried when she was born because she wasn't a boy."

"You never told me that. You cried when we had a healthy child when it could have been a disaster?"

"I just said I'm ashamed. But I never told you I was disappointed and that I'd wanted a boy. And within weeks, I was thrilled with her. And I didn't realize that she'd be the best companion, better than any boy."

After an hour, the girls and I went downstairs to the galley to prepare lunch. Each girl had been allowed to choose one food item from the little store, so we had two brands of potato chips and two types of cookies. Only Talia had picked something healthy, celery. But I knew what Alex liked so I'd bought crab salad and shrimp cocktails and a variety of cheeses and fruits. I made turkey sandwiches for anyone who wanted them.

"I appreciate this lunch," said Alex. Then for a brief time, all the girls were downstairs. The boat had a shelf with board games and cards on it and the older girls played Yahtzee and rummy. Emmie slept in a large laundry basket, all curled up. I checked another time that every girl was occupied and then I grabbed Alex's shoulders and kissed him every place I could.

He turned and kissed me back and was very happy.

The girls wanted pizza for dinner so we got that. Then we watched TV and I counted the minutes until Mrs. Baum would come and I could go to Alex. Our last night! Our last night.

The sun and wind and the exertions of sailing had left both of us a little tired. We lay on the bed hugging, like a long married couple. Which we were. Which we weren't. A long married couple could skip a night. But this was our last night. Forever? Who knew?

Alex brought me hot spicy tea. "This is not our last night," he said, reading my mind. "We're going to plan another trip now. Then we'll have something to look forward to."

"I just don't see how that can be managed, Alex. You're so good looking and so highly respected. You could easily find a woman who would charm you, with lots of time to share with you. Without all the complications I bring."

"I could. I know it. Do you want to know the moment that I knew for sure that you were the girl for me, the only girl?"

"When?"

"We were already engaged and I was madly in love with you. So pretty, so sweet, so compliant in bed. And then in early October I drove from Caltech to UCLA to find you. It was a Friday and I'd had a test and failed it. I, who'd never had a bad grade, who'd sailed through all the math classes and the science classes and the literature and history classes also. I drove the two hours like a maniac, a failure, someone about to be kicked out of Caltech. I was always the director in our relationship but that night I could only think, I have to find her. I have to tell her. And I didn't want to tell you. I wanted to be the leader in your eyes. Please God, let me find her, I prayed. And there you were sitting at that bus stop, to go to your nanny job. You got into my car and I told you. I'm going to be kicked out of Caltech. And do you remember all the things you said?"

"I remember."

"You said, 'But you're a genius, how could they kick you out?' 'Every man is a genius,' I told you. 'It's not like high school.

Many of them catch on much more quickly than I. I'm in over my head, Valerie.' 'And you said 'Stop the car so we can talk. First of all, you're not getting kicked out, it's just one test. Nobody works harder than you do.'

"You should have seen the professor's face when he handed me the test. Loser! You don't belong here! They're kicking me out."

"And you said, 'Let's say they do ask you to leave. So what? We'll just go to Pomona, we both got in there and it's a great school.'"

"You'd go to Pomona with me?"

"'Of course I would. If it happens. And then I fully realized what a gem you were. Your absolute loyalty. How wisely I'd picked a great partner to stand by me. How lucky I was to have you."

I smiled. "I remember you said, 'To think I wanted you for your body.'"

"I know. You were exactly the woman a man dreams of having. By my side through thick and thin. "

And now Alex wasn't tired any more. He was on top of me and kissing me everywhere. Enjoy tonight, I thought to myself. Don't ruin our last night by thinking too much.

And Alex was even more passionate than he usually was and the second time, even more tender. And I was lost in feeling. We rested for a few minutes and then suddenly Alex flipped me over. He pulled my legs down the bed to the edge and said firmly.
FOR
Spank, Thrust
WHATEVER
Spank, Thrust
TIME——-,
Spank, Thrust
US, TOGETHER.
Spank, Thrust.
And I was off again in a dreamland.

After many minutes, he whispered to me, "Whatever spare time you have for me, I'll accept. And I won't drive you crazy with my demands."

And again we slept entwined.

SUNDAY

At 5:30, Alex was up and sat in a chair. "I want you to tell me before you go that we'll have another trip soon."

"I can't tell you that. I don't know."

"Darling, I'll take you anywhere you want to go. We could go to Paris or Italy or Israel. I could take you to Romania, to your father's town. Where have you been longing to go?"

"Alex, just last night you said you wouldn't drive me crazy."

"Asking you for a commitment is driving you crazy?"

"Alex, I just can't say right now."

"I told you years ago, not making a decision is a decision." He was angry or hurt or both. I tried to kiss him.

"Go. "he said. "Your kisses are meaningless."

I called his room at 7 to see if he wanted to eat breakfast with us.

"I'm going to sleep," he said. "Go ahead and eat breakfast." So I knew that he was very angry.

After breakfast, we packed and Alex drove us to the airport, not getting out of the car. We were both too sad. I didn't want to cry in front of the children.

The Singer twins were sweet. "Thank you for all the presents, Uncle Alex," they said. And my four girls all kissed him and thanked him also. He and I managed polite, perfunctory goodbyes.

We arrived back in Phoenix at 3 pm and a message on my message machine from Erica said that she and Steve would come to pick up their twins at 5.

I was feeling very saddened by Alex's coldness and distance. Evalynne was at my home. When I'd phoned her to tell her that she didn't need to babysit, that I was taking the girls with me, she'd asked to come to The Lakes anyway. "I can use a little vacation from Barbara Mae. That girl is not only mean to me but to Cletus also. It breaks your heart." Evalynne was there to take care of the dog, the cat and Talia's two ducks. She liked watching the sailboats from the back porch and watching her soap operas. She walked with a limp but had made almost a full recovery from her stroke.

"My daddy let me drive the boat two times," Marisa told Evalynne with excitement.

Evalynne came into my room. "You look tired. Let me help you get these clothes into the laundry. I don't mean to pry, Valerie. But remember what your Aunt Anna said when she came to visit? She said, 'Cream always rises to the top and love will always find a way.'"

"Thank you for understanding, Evalynne."

"I must say. The "Days Of Our Lives" soap opera has nothing on you. But Valerie, you know that I always loved Alex. And I was right there when he broke your heart. I just hope he don't break it again."

"I know, Evalynne. I know." And I hugged this woman, the best of friends, both wise and kind. Soon Cletus came to pick her up.

Erica had phoned her father from Scotland and found out from his housekeeper that he was in the hospital. She'd called me and Evalynne told her that I'd taken all the children to San Francisco. She and Steve came into the house and their twins jumped on them with hugs and kisses. Both girls spoke at the same time, telling their parents all the fun times they'd had.

"And we went to the Zoo and, guess what, Uncle Alex was there, too."

Erica's eyebrows went way up. "My, my, what a coincidence."

We sat in the living room and opened gifts. Steve and Erica had bought all of us Beatles T shirts, all different and all of us loved them. Even Emmie had a small Beatles T-shirt. The girls had ChinaTown souvenirs for their parents.

As Steve brought the girls' suitcases to his car, Erica whispered to me. "I'm so sorry that you had to bring my kids to your tryst."

"I'm sorry that I had to bring MY kids to my tryst."

"Don't forget, I'm always there for you. The Prescott cabin is usually available. I'll take your girls whenever you feel the need." We hugged, another dear friend who understood.

"Did Alex come back with you?"

"No, his convention goes for two more days, He'll be back Tuesday night."

"I'll invite him for dinner. And really, Valerie, thank you so much. When does Neal get home?'

"Tuesday morning."

MONDAY

All of us went back to our various camps. In the morning, Veda, Alex's secretary called. "Mr. Berk called and asked me to remind you that he is taking the girls overnight Wednesday." He wasn't even going to talk to me, that's how hurt he was. And in the afternoon, I received a phone call from Sister Mary Louise.

"I'm back from Flagstaff. And Mother Superior was so right. I took care of some adorable Navajo preschoolers and was able to show their mothers that their behavior wasn't wild, it was normal. And I went for some very long and lonely walks and I thought."

"So, Sister, did you come to any decision?"

"I did, Valerie. And you never judged me and you helped me."

"Good. What did you decide?"

"I thought, I'd been a nun for fifteen years and should be proud of that and some good things I'd done, for the Church and for a lot of girls."

"So?"

"So, Valerie, I've decided to renounce my vows and marry Jorge. We'll try to have a child and maybe we will but no matter what, we'll have Margarita's baby with us, to love. She's due in two weeks."

I started to cry. "I'm sorry to be emotional, Sister, but this is such surprising news."

"You thought I'd remain a nun?"

"I wasn't sure. Does Jorge know?"

"Yes, he's very glad. And so you shouldn't call me Sister any more. Jorge has started calling me Mary Lou."

"All right. Are you still at Good Shepherd?"

"No, Mother Superior helped me file all the many papers and then she asked me to leave. It's better that way, especially concerning the girls at the Home."

"So where are you?"

"I'm at Jorge's house in Maryvale. And I have experienced the joys of marital love, as you used to tell us about."

"Are you happy?"

"Very happy."

"What were the reactions of Sisters Cordelia and Agnes?"

"I'd have to say, mixed. Sad but understanding. After all, I've rejected their way of life, their purpose. But Sister Cordelia handed me an envelope and it was $300 in cash. There was a note,' For your new home' signed by Tessie Bamberger."

"Now that was lovely."

"And Mrs. O'Dell said that when the time comes, she wants to make food for my wedding."

'When could you marry?'

"It will be months before the permissions come through."

"And will you remain a Catholic?"

"Oh, definitely. I'll always be Catholic and I'll always bless all the people I've worked with. But I no longer feel shame. I feel that I'm still a good person, moving on in a new direction. And I feel that God understands. And my job now will be my new little family, Jorge and Margarita and the new little one. And if we're truly blessed, another little one."

"Sister, Mary Lou, I'm so very happy for you. What can I do to help?"

"Valerie, could you give me some cooking lessons? I don't know how to cook a thing. Jorge says he'll do it all but I want to help."

"Of course."

Cream rises to the top and love will always find a way.

TUESDAY

Neal came into the house Tuesday afternoon. "The trip was a great success. All the ministers and their wives and the priests loved it. Arthur's wife even took them on a special tour of the Knesset. And this is for you." He took a jewelry box from his suitcase. I unwrapped a very wide gold bracelet, I, who didn't like bracelets and never wore them.

"Thank you. Did Shulamit pick it out?"

"Shulamit! Shulamit! Get off that kick, will you? One of the lovely minister's wives, Joyce Jones, helped me choose it for you.' Your wife is a lucky woman,' she told me. And Shulamit spent a lot of time with her father in Tel Aviv but she did take us to some unusual tourist spots."

"And how did you spend your three days when the ministers' had their convention?"

"I hung around with the Baha'is and with Arthur in Haifa."

The girls rushed in at 3:30 to tell Neal all about their camp life and their trip to San Francisco. He listened to it all.

"You met Alex there?"

"Yes. He was busy with an engineer's convention but we went to a few places together."

"That was nice. It's good that I never have to worry about Alex, poor guy."

I had never filled Neal in on Alex's returned abilities, 'No problems in that regard', told to me by Dr. Jouzy. And Dr. Jouzy had been accurate.

Neal unpacked and the phone rang. It was Phyllis Auerbach, the president of a large Jewish women's group. Her Boston accent was very noticeable.

"Well, hello," said Neal. "Yes, I just got in. It was a great success. I'll tell you all the details at our meeting tomorrow. Well, I missed you too, my dear. How did the school calendar committee go? All right, we'll catch up on all the details tomorrow. See you, my dear."

"You call Phyllis Auerbach 'my dear'?"

"I call lots of women 'my dear.' It means nothing."

"You're meeting her tomorrow?"

"Look, if I had anything to hide, I'd have taken the call in my den. Tomorrow is the regular Community Relations meeting.

And there are ten women on that Board, some of them lovely."

"That is very reassuring, Neal."

"Sometimes you can be so annoying, Valerie. I don't know why you want to pick a fight when I've just gotten home."

"I don't want to pick a fight. I don't want to pick a fight." Flirt with all the women you want to. Call the women anything you want to. Instead of taking me in your arms, reassuring me that you cared. I couldn't keep the thought from my mind. As Alex would have done. Taking me in his arms and reassuring me.

That night, Neal was suffering from jet lag. I looked at him. "Look," he said. "I bought you a gold bracelet. It was the most expensive one in the shop." I said, "Thank you," as he turned over and was soon asleep.

WEDNESDAY

Every morning I woke up at 6:30, put on an exercise outfit and went to a nearby gym for their 6:45 class. I was home by 7:30, ready to grab my frying pan and make French toast or scrambled eggs, feed my kids and then brush their hair for school or camp.

This morning, I drove my car out of The Lakes gate and all by itself, without my conscious thought, the car turned left instead of right. Ten minutes later, I arrived at Alex's condo and rang his bell. He came to the door in his white karate gi.

"Valerie," he said in alarm. "What's wrong?"

"Nothing is wrong. I need to exercise. May I exercise with you?"

"You've come to the right place. But as every gym would ask you. Are you here for a trial lesson or for the series?"

"It depends on whether you're a good personal trainer."

"I am the best personal trainer."

"In that case, I would like the full series."

"Please come in." He smiled the joyous, victorious Alex smile. "Darling."

THE END BUT REALLY JUST THE BEGINNING

Study Guide For Book Club and You

1. What have you experienced, either for yourself or a friend, about a troubled pregnancy?

2. What is your opinion of Otis and Abigail and their marriage? Have you ever experienced abuse of this type?

3. Did you enjoy the story of how Isaiah became wealthy? What are your feelings about these affluent African Americans who are unsure if they can be served in a restaurant? (Or any minority persons?)

4. What would you do if you were a mother in Barta's situation? Were you inspired by her cleverness in outwitting the Nazis for a long time?

5. Would you participate in an all day Sit In?

6. What was your opinion of the Claudia/Saul love story?

7. What did you think about Sister Mary Louise who fell in love?

8. What were your thoughts about Valerie and Alex's San Francisco trip?

9. Did the ending surprise you?

10. Are you ready for more Valerie and Alex love?

About the Author

Natalie is the editor of the book, TO SECURE THESE RIGHTS, an exposure of discrimination in 1950's and 1960's Arizona. She also edited THOU SHALT NOT FORGET, the memoirs of four women who survived the Holocaust. She co-authored, with Rabbi Gerald Kane, the play ALL BUT MY LIFE, a story of Holocaust survival.

Also by Natalie Freedman

The Family Saga Series

The Family Saga/Romance series LOVE SONGS OF A MARRIAGE tells about the explosive love of Valerie and Alex, who refuse to be separated but must deal with a horrendous problem. Book One, PURSUIT was awarded Number One on Amazon in 2022 in the categories Family Saga and Woman's Literary and Jewish American Literature. Book Two, WHOSE HEART? contains the story "Flying Saucer Convention In The Desert" which was chosen to be performed at The Horton Theater in San Diego in 2017. The third book, PERMIT ME REFUGE, has received many enthusiastic comments from fellow authors. EACH OTHER'S ARMS is Book Four. All books contain the popular and musical comedy songs of their era. All contain an authentic Holocaust story, and all contain stories of historical events; the civil rights movement, the Viet Nam War, Nazis attempting to take over the movie industry in 1930's Hollywood, the St. Louis ship not allowed to land in America, the Bielski brothers, partisans who saved 1100 Jews in the forests of Belarus during WW2, the Kastner train, the Warsaw Ghetto, the Six Day War in Israel.

www.ingramcontent.com/pod-product-compliance
Ingram Content Group UK Ltd.
Pitfield, Milton Keynes, MK11 3LW, UK
UKHW020746280225
455691UK00012B/462